LIGHT

OF

EVANORA

BOOK ONE

THE LEGENDS OF LIMORIA

LIGHT

OF

EVANORA

T R NICKEL

LIGHT OF EVANORA
Copyright © 2021 by T R Nickel

ISBN: 978-1-7324643-4-6

Represent Publishing

Cover Design by Lidia Puccetti

Edited and Formatted by Chelsea Lauren

For my sister, Shawna.
Thank you for always being the best parts of me.
It helps me notice them in myself.

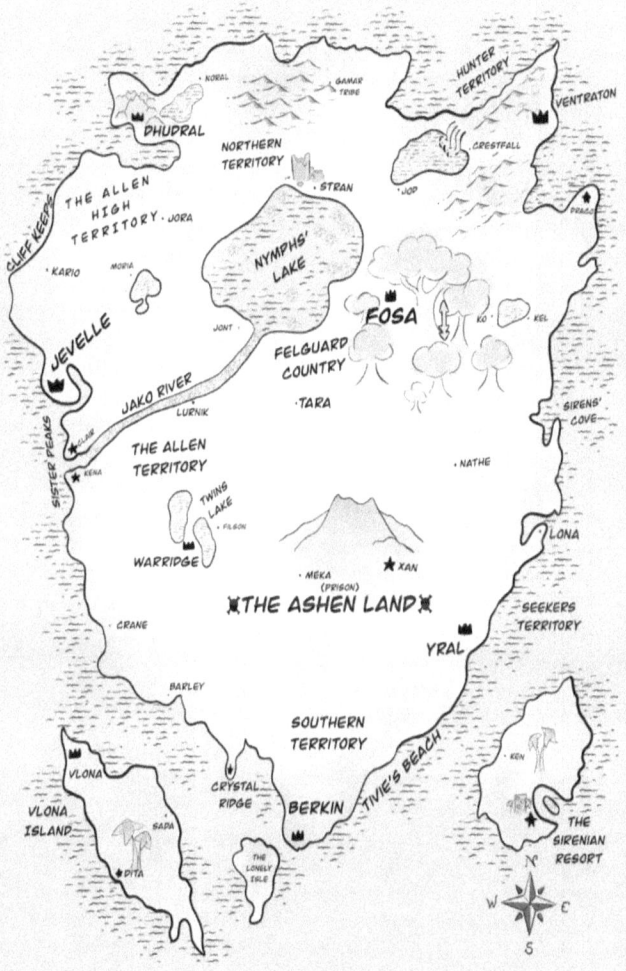

AUTHOR'S NOTE

As long as I can remember I had a pen and notepad at the ready, scribbling poorly spelled words with no grammar in sight. Despite being horrendously mocked, I continued writing because my life has always been filled with the imaginary. I fought off giant spiders, crossed plains and deserts, captured fairies, controlled the wind, moved oceans, and built mountains. The world of magic was something I saw around me.

I wrote this book, and am writing more, to bring that magic to life for those who may have lost sight of the imaginary.

Anyone can be Xylia. Anyone can be the hero. Anyone can be a legend.

Imagine, write, sing, dance, paint, create. See the magic that is right there in front of you.

I hope you enjoy the world I created, and the chaos that I've put inside of it.

At the end of the book, you'll find an index that helps explain the unexplained and brings you closer to understanding the Legends of Limoria.

CHAPTER ONE

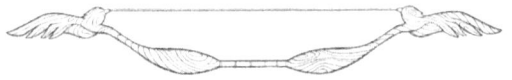

THE COOL MORNING wind sends a chill down my spine, making my toes sink into the damp earth. My leather boots, which I just let slip from my grasp, disappear into the knee-high grass. I stretch upwards towards the canopy, where the yellow, orange, and red leaves dance around in the rays of light making their way through the mesh. I inhale the **Vermilion Forest**, smelling the dust and sap that the trees produce.

Crisp mornings like this give me a reprieve from the responsibilities awaiting me a few kilometers south of this paradise. Spinning around, I let my hands brush the tall grass taking in the incredible view of the ever-expanding tree trunks that crowd the space around me and create a perfect place for the **Adamina Clan**, my home, to flourish.

The twisting limbs stretch out across every which way, going a far cry above my head. As my mind begins to wander, staring at the marvel that is the largest forest in the realm, a voice familiar yet foreign begins ringing in my ears. My heart starts to race as the voice's hum sinks deep into my bones.

Closing my eyes, in a pathetic attempt to capture and

remember where in my memory this very voice resides, a burning feeling begins to spread across my chest. It only takes a few moments to pass before I'm enveloped in a blinding light that I know all too well. A mixture of fear and longing begins to build up, and I cannot even begin to describe how torturous this is.

The heat melts the chill that was once in the air, and as the temperature rises, the voice seems to grow in volume. I can hear it calling my name, almost like it's begging for me to listen closer. I steel myself and reach forwards towards the voice, but my attention is torn away as I hear the clashing of metal.

My eyes burst open, and I see a mop of blonde hair inches from my face. I take an unsteady breath as I realize I am now lying in the sweaty morning grass. Vasile smiles at me with that goofy grin of his.

"Hey there, Xylia, stay up too late? You should really tell Codrin to sleep in the parlor if he is gonna be too tempted with sharing your bed," Vasile says. His confidence almost challenges his smart-aleck mouth, standing there with his swords drawn.

"Is that jealousy I hear or just self-pity since you haven't anyone to share your bed with?" I shove his face away.

The smile fades, and his eyes focus. He takes a few steps back as I climb to my feet and adjust the crimson armor I adorn. Glad he still takes me seriously.

"I see that we are as fiery as ever, my Lady! Just waking up too, very impressive." His smile reappears and he tosses me a sword. I spoke too soon.

"Well, if you were ever on time, maybe I wouldn't have the time to snooze." I wink before turning my back to him.

I nearly miss the shuffle of his hasty footsteps drawing near as I attempt to bring myself back from the daze I was just in. I twirl around quickly, our blades connecting, our faces beaming with excitement. I push off and slash towards him. He quickly slides his feet and hips backwards—the blade gently kissing the leather chest piece. His footwork has improved considerably, but not quite where I want it to be.

This is going on the fifth **sidereal year** of my mentorship, so I can only honestly blame myself for his laxity. He turns his hips and thrusts forwards. I smile and aim my sword up knocking the steel from its path.

Pathetic attempt, really.

I can see his frustration and feel him pick up the pace as he stands and slashes towards me. He slowly begins to push me back with the sheer strength he is putting into his onslaught. I continue to let him wear himself out until I see his fatigue begin to eat at him. I lean forwards, twisting downwards, so the blade just misses my face, leaving a moment open for me to grab his wrist and put my back to his chest. I shift his weight onto my back and use his forwards motion to flip him over my shoulder and onto his back. He slams onto the ground, and he gasps for air. Vasile tries to recover, but my blade is already pressed tightly against his neck.

"Have I ever said how impressive you are, my Lady?" he says breathlessly.

"Only every morning." I flash him a cheeky smile as I pull my blade back.

Vasile slowly scrambles to his feet, taking a few deep breaths to steady himself before looking back into my eyes with more fire than the last time.

We clash swords for a few more **sunshifts**, not noticing the even higher rising sun. I pin him down, his face buried in the grass and my body weight sitting on top of his back.

"Your horrendous swordplay distracted me, and now I'm late." I stand and straighten myself out. I'd rather run the length of this forest than face the wrath of Rose.

"I'm sure our First Lady will understand the importance of training the less talented folk of the Adamina Clan," Vasile says.

I bite my lip, knowing that our First Lady doesn't actually approve of him being my mentee. Though I'll keep that between Rose and me.

Vasile stands and looks down at his grass-stained garments and chuckles. I shake my head in a mocking disappointed way, garnering a pitiful whine from my protege. I give in and smile, patting his shoulder as we turn towards our home.

We march our way south, following the chant markings carved into the trees. Vasile talks about his heroic tale of how he rescued a **Floaress** from being eaten by a youngin, definitely trying to spin it into a far more entertaining story than it actually is.

Just as his head is about to explode from his narcissism, we hear someone approaching. I quickly adorn my hood and unfurl my cloak to hide my armor. Vasile takes a few steps ahead, putting himself up front, with that brilliantly goofy grin resting on his face. We wait and watch as a familiar figure appears from behind a tree.

Codrin, his handsome smile and dark complexion fills my view, and I jog up to him as he opens his arms. His dark curly hair, free from its normally-bunned form, gently frames his face. I grab his hands, him gripping them tightly as he pulls me in. He lets go as I wrap my arms around his neck before he leans in, kissing me like we have been apart for eons. Codrin pulls my hood back and twirls one of my braids in his hands while he runs the fingers from his other hand over one of my pointed ears.

I instinctively shy away, causing our lips to part. As I withdraw, Codrin follows my lips, not wanting to separate, but

Vasile's gagging noise pulls him back out of our bubble. Codrin smiles a bit at me before looking up at his best mate.

Sandalwood and leather fill my senses as Codrin leans in, his green tanned leather chest piece pressing against me to slap hands with Vasile. Codrin's armor fits his strong frame nicely, but I can see a few nicks here and there from where branches and creatures have caught on.

"You had Crina in quite the tizzy this morning, Angel," Codrin says with an amused look, knowing my natural dislike of the **Passerinnet**.

Her featheredness is not what bothers me. It's her own bigotry towards someone like me. Of course, she would be the first to notice I'm not where I should be and make the most noise about it.

"Well, thank you for being such a gentleman. I'm sure you've had to scour these woods tirelessly searching for your second Lady in command," I fondly commend Codrin.

Codrin laughs, and a small scoff sneaks out from Vasile. I turn back to glance at the mop-headed boy whose arms are crossed with a look of disbelief nicely etched on his face.

"What makes you think he came out here just for you? It's like you are implying that this handsome hunk of a guy, meaning I, isn't worth the interest of our heroic Codrin here," Vasile complains, causing me to quickly slap my hand over my face, desperately trying to maintain my composure. "I take great offense to that." He throws his chin into the air tilting his face to the sky and away from me.

Codrin chuckles, gaining Vasile's attention. I step to the side as Vasile quickly runs up on us to wrap his arms around Codrin's neck. Vasile lovingly ends his little scene with his tongue sticking out towards me. I give him a devilish smile and grab his tongue.

Immediate regret is apparent as he looks into my unwavering eyes. "Wight, swowwy, wy Wady."

I release him and a shock of relief washes over him. "It's my fault really, I guess I didn't wear you out enough with this morning's session. I won't make the same mistake twice." My comment sends a shiver through Vasile.

Codrin bursts out laughing and returns his friend's embrace.

"You are definitely worth saving Vas, but our dear Lady is right. I came out here for her sake. You were an afterthought this time around."

Once our little rendition of **Mystique in the Promise Land** ends, Vasile, Codrin, and I make our way towards the Clan about a kilometer south of where we were in the Vermilion Forest. The forest itself is nearly 1300 kilometers wide; even parts of the Felguard Countries capital, Fosa, are inside the forest. They once tried chopping parts of the forest down, but by the next day, it appeared as if the tree line had proceeded even further into the Capital's territory. The only hole that's ever remained without the forest healing itself, was the one I had made.

I clench my fists, not really wanting to think about why I had to make that hole.

The trees themselves are large enough to support miles of docks on top of the canopy, where the Adamina Clan resides. The climb up is long, rough, and dangerous for those who don't know what they are doing. The red dust from the trees rubs off, staining our hands and our sweaty faces. If any of us were none the wiser, we might mistake it for blood at first glance.

As we reach the foliage that hides the Clan from the prying eyes of any passersby, the leaves begin to tickle our faces and allow us to slow our pace now that we have coverage. With the cross support beams and bottom of the deck coming closer into view, Codrin begins to call out in wounded bird cries, notifying the **gatekeeper** of our imminent arrival. A rope finds its way over the edge where little chuckles can be heard and little faces are peering over, excited to see who is approaching.

"Lady **Maresal**! Here, let me assist you," Engel says as he is staring over the edge.

He extends his hands out towards me, and I take them willingly before he pulls me up onto the dock. Vasile and Codrin are close behind me, having to climb over the edge of the dock themselves.

"I see. We are just chopped liver then?" Vasile, half-kidding, comments as he is now on his back, breathing heavily.

Engel raises his eyebrow before sticking out his rosy-colored tongue to mock Vasile. "Our Lady is always first, Blondie."

I laugh at the two of them bickering like youngins.

"Careful now, the Maresal herself has the same golden-colored locks as this young idiot," Codrin says, placing a hand on Engel's back before pushing him a bit.

Engel widens his eyes while looking at Codrin before moving back over to the edge to pull up the dangling rope. A nervousness washes over him as he fumbles with the rope.

"No worries, Engel. I'll just make a permanent mental note that you are prejudiced against the color of my hair," I tease.

Engel nearly drops the rope all together, hearing my words, but relaxes as he spots the mischievous smile I'm putting on.

I hear the pitter-patter of footsteps and look over my shoulder to see into the hustle and bustle of everyday Adamina life. Small livestock are being carted across the way into the agriculture district. Youngins are running and screaming as they chase one another through their parent's legs, who are currently trying to bargain for a row of eggs and a fresh bottle of milk.

7

You wouldn't believe that such normalcy could live on the top of trees, but the Adamina Clan is here, where outcasts, runaways, and those who dream of a place without a tyrant King come to rest. Even though we are still a part of the King's land, we are separate from his ruling. The protection that the Adamina Clan provides the Felguard Country has fit the bill, in the people's eyes at least. The King often charges us with a new tax every year, his way of maintaining some sort of power over the Clan. We fend off the demons and ancient creatures that inhabit this forest, even capturing them on occasion to sell to the Capitol for their entertainment.

A shiver rushes over me. Thinking of the King rattles my bones. Codrin, now at my side, rubs my back, seeing that I am not all there. I snap back and look up into his eyes.

"You ready?" he whispers in my ear.

I nod, seemingly confident.

Codrin is the only one who ever sees *me*. It's almost infuriating not being able to hide my emotions from him. No matter the face I put on, he can tell when I'm not *me*. As the Maresal, I was trained and taught how to care for the Clan, protect the Clan, and ensure the Clan's survival. My mothers, Rose and Rye, were the ones who named me Maresal and the ones who have trained me since I could walk. They also showed me that real love exists, even if you cannot always show it. They loved each other so deeply ... I bite my tongue pushing the thought of Rye from my mind.

I can't show the same emotions everyone else does. I must remain calm in all situations and face death with a smile because I should know I will escape it. Even with the abilities I am born with, there are demons not even I can overcome—but am expected to—when the time comes.

Codrin makes that part of my job hard, but every other part

easy. He is my solace, my home, and where even the worst of things melt away.

"Whispering sweet nothings in her ear again there, lover boy?" Vasile calls out in our direction.

I roll my eyes. I will never get used to the cheeky smile he wears so proudly. "Sorry to disappoint your degenerate-self, but us adults have actual work to do." I take the sword that has been sitting at my side since after our training this morning and toss it over to him. "Sharpen and polish. I want it to glisten."

Vasile takes my command and bows sarcastically low before we all turn away, Codrin following closely by my side.

"Do you think he will ever be ready to take over as Mare-sal?" Codrin asks with genuine concern in his voice.

I give Codrin a side glance, trying to hide my surprise in his question. "If you plan to doubt him, your dearest friend, then you doubt me as well."

Codrin furrows his brow and takes my hand softly. "My question was not to doubt your choice, Xylia. I simply desire the future we see for ourselves. The quicker we can obtain that dream ..." He uses his free hand to gently rub his thumb against my cheek.

That dream seems so far away that it feels like it is unattainable. I smile up at him though, hoping he might miss the doubt in my eyes. I kiss his cheek quickly and untangle my hand from his.

Codrin and I part ways as I head to the **Command Deck**, where our central **Command Post** dwells.

I have a mountain of work to do and many things I still need to mull over, while I'm sure he is off messing with his **Forged Magicae** studies, or perhaps his newest carving project. I can't blame him for feeling ready to move on and begin settling into our life, but there is more to do. We have had missing member reports coming up by the dozens, which is very uncommon. Meaning the talk I need to have with Rose about my future is going to be delayed once again.

I had to instate a curfew as a way to protect those who still travel from our Northern Deck to **Ko**, the neighboring city. From the safety of our **crow's nests**, I've stationed more **Birdsmen** than usual to monitor the forest's movements. I've even pushed some of our crow's nests further south towards our farming lands to try and cover more distance.

So far, no one has seen such a beast that matches the basic description we received from **Ko's Forest Border Headquarters**.

I need to start thinking about the western side of the forest as a possible weakness. Most beasts come from the eastern side, where there is a lot less foot traffic, but this beast seems intelligent and wants to make this a game of sorts to entertain itself for a while.

"Oh dear, I'm sorry."

I jump back a bit instinctively but look to the older woman with long greying hair that just bumped into me. Her woven basket full of herbs now spilled across the wooden planks.

"Pardon me," she says, looking into my deep blue eyes. She pauses a moment before bowing towards me and placing her shaky hand onto the right side of her chest, her left knee slightly bending towards me. A way most Adaminians greet my mother and me.

"I beg your pardon, Maresal. I did not notice it was you," her shriveled voice matching the texture of her leather-tanned skin.

I acknowledge her bow with a simple nod and wave.

She stands to meet my gaze, but her eyes do not; they focus on the embroidery of my red leather armor. "I pray for your safety, Maresal, and thank you for your protection," her voice holds genuine gratitude, but I see her look up under the curls of her bangs to peer at my elvish ears.

The woman and I both bend down, silently gathering up her belongings. A brief smile stretches across her face again before she slowly stands. I give her a small smile and nod in her direction once more.

As she walks away from me, into the small intersection, another woman around her age waddles over to her in a hurry, apparently intrigued by our little interaction. They both glance over their shoulders to see my eyes intent on them. They turn their faces forward and move on quickly.

My title as Maresal makes some of the Adaminians nervous because of the power I wield, but most say they are comforted since they can depend on me to keep them safe; but really, it is my race, these ears, that make my people terrified of me. They are always a little nervous to look me in my eyes.

I take a deep breath and look up into the cloudless sky, the blue and green colors swirling together in an endless dance above me. A soft humming tickles my ears as I concentrate fully on the emptiness that is the sky. A large clatter breaks my trance. The humming disappears.

I take a look around and see that two carts have slightly merged together from the lack of attention their owners had. No one seems to be injured, so I smile and continue walking on.

The wood planks that form the decks on the Vermilion Forest trees' tips creak under the weight of my heavy footfall as I near the Command Post. It was the first building built, on the first deck ever built. The beginning of the Adamina Clan started from this singular point before expanding for kilometers on our North, Eastern, and Western sides. History shows itself clearly in the wood here, patch-worked and stained from prolonged exposure to the sun and red dust carried up from the base of the trees.

This deck is the same one I learned how to crawl on, walk on, and eventually fight on. As my feet carry me forwards, I look up and focus on the heavy studded doors ahead of me. The Adamina symbol burned into each door, an upside-down tree with an arrow pointing towards the sky as its trunk. The same symbol I adorn on my chest and the symbol placed behind my right ear.

I stroke the scarred flesh in memory of the day I became an official asset to this Clan, to my mother who claims the title of the First Lady. The founders of the Adamina Clan all wear this scar to show the pain and aspiration we have for the future of our people.

The wind picks up, blowing my hair into my face. I sigh in irritation, as it seems one of my braids has loosened enough for a few stands to have freed themselves. As I make my way to the Command Post entrance, I put my hair back into the three long braids. A complex weaving for those who don't practice as I do every day.

I flip the braids over my shoulder and push the doors open, not quite ready to face the terrifying wrath that most likely awaits me.

Inside, the round table in the center, has a map of Limoria spread across it. Little flags dotting its surface, each one signifying its own purpose.

Conflict, trading posts, allies, enemies, anything that could ever pertain to the Clan and its survival.

The few commanders here are having a hearty laugh in the corner around one of our bounty boards, which lists different people and creatures on the **Fel Watch's** wanted list. It's an easy way for the Adamina Clan to make money and keep our patrols on alert since we share some of the reward with whoever turns in or kills them.

I greet Betty, who is sitting at our information desk, and walk into my office just left of the entrance.

There is no stopping my sigh as the sight of fiery red hair, being illuminated by the sun pouring in from the window, comes into focus. She whips around in my chair to face me, her curls bouncing around her shoulders, her bright green eyes shining like malicious stars, and her darker almond skin riddled with small scars.

Her beauty is equal to that of her talent for fighting, a woman most men wouldn't want to mess with but desire nonetheless. At least, that's what my keen ears have been subject to hear from a very early age and on.

"There she is, my Maresal," she says with a not-so-convincing smile.

I return her smile and bow in her direction. "First Lady, good morning to you as well."

She stands up briskly and walks around, gesturing for me to sit in my own chair. I oblige and take my place as she now sits on the stool facing me.

"Where are we at with these missing member reports? I'm sure since you came in late that you've already worked your rounds?" she asks, flipping through a few papers that were left on my desk.

I raise my eyebrows in a way to make myself look more nonchalant than ambushed, knowing my answers are not going to please her.

"Those being attacked are generally far outside our regular perimeter. The Clan itself is safe. Even still, I've been gathering intel on this creature, but gathering the information takes time, which sadly means more bodies will be found. It's not giving me anything to go off of."

I look up to see the expected displeased look cross her face —one for not telling her what she wants to hear and second for avoiding the second question.

"Xylia, do we have any leads at all as to what this creature is?" she asks.

I shift through a few papers and find an old bounty ad we removed months ago.

"This is the only creature that even closely resembles the intelligence we are facing," I answer, handing the parchment over to her.

She nods and looks up over the paper, meeting my eyes. "This is a start. With all the intel you've gathered over the last few weeks, I think it's safe to say we can release a description to our men."

"I think it's a little premature. I understand the urgency, but if we push out incorrect information, then we could be closing our minds to other possibilities," I admit.

She looks up, her brow raised, unsure as to what I'm getting at.

"Continue," she says, extending her hand forwards and setting the parchment down.

"The number of attacks this creature has been able to sneak in between our Clan's patrols, we could be looking at a **Werecreature**. Perhaps even a beast that is tamed and trained by someone playing a sick sort of hunting game."

Rose's eyes widen but quickly refocus on what I'm saying. She fidgets on the stool for a moment.

"Rye died to make sure those beasts were taken care of. You're saying she failed?" she snaps at me, sudden anger begins to rise in her throat, and I can't blame her for it.

I don't take my eyes off of hers, as she stares me down. "I'm saying that sometimes when you think something is extinct, they have a way of turning up again." I point to my ears, proving my point.

Five hundred sidereal years have passed since the Elves were forced into extinction, but here I am—the only elf. Of course, if the King heard even a whisper of where I am now.

I shiver again at the thought.

"I understand. I'll trust your intuition on this. I've been receiving some pressure from our people, so slowing down is not an option. We can still send—" the door opens, and a worried and out of breath gatekeeper comes rushing in.

"There, there is a survivor."

Rose and I freeze as we turn to two Birdsmen carrying a dying man. His torso is shredded to bits, and it's clear he had been strangled with the heavy bruising and deforming skin around his neck. They gently lay him on the ground in front of us. Rose strokes his nearly bald head covered in sunspots as I carefully try to move pieces of his semi-fresh blood-soaked clothes out of my way to find his wound.

"He's one of our farmers, was coming back from his morning shift." The slightly taller Birdsman mentions.

The red dust from the trees has created a paste on his body from mixing with the blood, making it harder to pinpoint the exact spot the blood is coming from. The farmer lifts his hand slowly to point to where he is hurt, and I quickly place my hand over it.

I close my eyes and pull forwards as much of that familiar light that resides within me as I can without losing control. I steady my breath and focus solely on the man that lays dying in front of me. Utilizing the healing effect of the light, the bleeding slows down just enough for some of the color to return to his face, his eyes blinking slowly. They are bloodshot and full of fear. I can feel him shaking in my arms as he knows these will be his last words. He opens his mouth hesitantly before mouthing something.

There is so much pain holding him back. I close my eyes and reach for the light even deeper, so he finally can take a gasp of air that is not riddled with so much pain.

After taking a moment to relax, his voice finally arises.

"**Feserpentline.**"

CHAPTER TWO

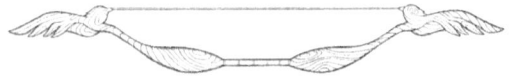

THE TWO BIRDSMEN LEAVE SILENTLY, carrying his limp body with them. Rose ordered them to the **Healers Ward**, where they will tend to the farmer's body. Rose quickly steps out of the room to notify one of the commanders to investigate the scene where the farmer was attacked.

I go to rub my face but notice the blood that is painted onto my palms. The ringing in my ears begins to encompass me as Rye's cold and empty stare returns to the forefront of my mind. The warmth of the light I produced is now entirely gone, and a chill runs through my body.

The door slams waking me from a nightmare I was beginning to replay in my head like I used to do—often—all those years ago. Rose walks in, the normal angry look has returned to her face. She reaches into her trousers and pulls out a handkerchief. I take it from her and begin wiping the crimson from my hands.

"I'm sorry, Xylia, but after this, people are going to really be pushing us to take action. Half the commanders are roaring out there."

I hadn't even noticed the shouts and hollers coming from just outside the door. They are angry just like I am angry, just like Rose is angry, but that doesn't mean we can move blindly.

"It's not their decision. They have their own roles they should be worried about. If we jump without a platform to land on, we could just end up worsening our position."

Rose sighs, rubbing her eyes in frustration. There is something else she's holding back. I stand from my kneeling position and walk towards her.

"I know you're right, Xylia." She looks at me with that very something screaming in her eyes. "But our hand is going to be forced in one way or another. A hunt is our best option."

"You're going to ask me to send our men out there looking for a creature that may not even exist? The Feserpentline has only been ever recorded in that book youngins read to scare themselves." I want to ask her a very different question, but I know she won't be giving me an honest answer if I do.

What are you not telling me?

"Xylia, these woods are filled with unimaginable things. You've seen some of them for yourself, and the creature he spoke of would be capable of the wounds inflicted." I toss the stained handkerchief onto the desk, knowing that my words will no longer sway her, but I have to try just once more to make her see reason.

"If we go in ill-prepared, our men will die."

"And if we sit here and do nothing, the same will happen. Except that our people may lose faith in their leadership, which means *you* and *me*."

She's right. At the end of the day, the people we are here to serve need us to make a decision that will comfort them as well as protect them.

"Then please, send me, and send me alone." The words I

chose were purposeful, as I just relived one of the most horrifying nights in this Clan's history.

I remembered Rye was the person to use them in the exact way I just did. Only that she said them the night she died. Rose didn't send her alone though, she couldn't knowingly send the love of her life out there with no protection. So Rose sent twelve **Hunters** and me to accompany her. I was only twelve sidereal years grown at that time. It was my first actual hunt where there was more than just the goal to feed empty stomachs to accomplish. Werecreatures had been rampaging Fosa, Ko, and the Adamina Clan quite devastatingly. They were intelligent and fast and could blend in with their surroundings within seconds. They were cruel and terrible things that were only after monetary gain. I was the only survivor that night. I couldn't save Rye, and my attempt in doing so killed the rest of the hunters.

Rose looks at me with wide eyes knowing the seriousness of my request, and most likely, reliving the same scene only it was eleven sidereal years prior. She faces her back to me, looking out the window and onto the small kingdom she has created. Rose shakes her head and scoffs, but it seems like she's already made up her mind about what she wants.

"No, you will go at least with your crew to support you. You will go out tonight. As your First Lady, this is my command."

I close my eyes and take a deep breath. I'm praying history won't repeat itself here tonight, not for my sake, but for hers.

"If there is no debating this any further, I'll go gather my crew." I turn to leave, but Rose gently grabs my shoulders.

"I have faith you will make the right choice, Xylia. Just remember that you are not untouchable. Strong and capable, yes, but you are still vulnerable. Keep the voice quiet. This power belongs to you," Rose says as she rests her forehead in between my shoulder blades.

My lip quivers slightly as I breathe in at how gentle she is being. I hear a nearly silent sob escape her, and it takes everything in me to walk away without looking back.

I leave the Command Post knowing very well that I blatantly stabbed Rose with her weakness to try to sway her decision, and failed, but that tells me that she truly thinks this is best. As her Maresal, I will follow her orders and do her bidding. I need to trust that whatever she is holding back will not affect her judgment.

I make my way home in a hurry, hoping that Codrin is there. As I approach the residential district, I can see it, the dark cherry wooden exterior with the painted yellow trimming we did last summer. The open porch with a set of chairs perfectly placed to watch the sun as it sets through a small hole in the canopy. I open the yellow-painted front door to hear the crackling of the fireplace, making the interior warm, shaking the cold from me. Codrin is sitting in his whittling chair, throwing his extra shavings into the fire as he goes. The kitchen to my immediate left has something cooking inside the wood-burning oven, currently tantalizing my appetite.

As my footsteps creak on the wood flooring, he turns to me slightly and smiles. "Home already?"

He is focused on his project at hand, and my heart flinches, knowing I have to pull him away from this peace he is in. I look to the slightly cracked door that leads into our bedroom. I'll have to go in there and open the wardrobe I've left shut for nearly a sidereal year.

"No, I'm actually here to recruit."

The sounds of wood being scraped stops. I look up and see him placing his project into the chest that sits to the right of him. I hold my breath as he looks up with sadness in his sapphire eyes.

"When?"

"Tonight."

"I thought you were still investigating?"

"I am, but there's a warranted need for us to act now. So you, Vasile, and I are going on a hunt."

"And the First Lady is expecting us to be ready in ..." he looks out the window, "six sunshifts?"

"We will be ready. I have full faith in our abilities, and this should tell you, so does our First Lady."

Codrin slowly walks over to me, trying not to look so bothered by the sentence I just said, but he is just as unable to hide his true feelings from me as I am from him.

"Angel, you honestly believe that this is what we need to do?"

"Would you decline my request if I said no?"

Codrin's shoulders drop.

"You're right."

He wraps his arms tightly around me, placing his chin on top of my head. I bring up my hand and caress his arm.

I know this is his least favorite activity we do together. He wishes I would just step away so we can have our dream, but this job demands so much of me, both physically and mentally, that I can't focus on more than just that. I wish Rye were here so I could ask her how she did it while raising me. It's because of her that I cannot just stop, why I desire to succeed in the role I've been given, why I try so hard to become better with every breath. I don't want to fail her again.

"You really got me wrapped around your finger, don't you?" Codrin kids.

I smile slightly, hearing his soft chuckle. "Perhaps."

As Codrin runs out to fetch our missing link, Vasile, I walk into the bedroom and head for the wardrobe. I quickly disrobe out of my everyday wear and stand in front of it, my hands resting on its handles. The distant memories of Codrin and I fighting over some of the items inside call out from a deep part of my mind, knowing that our last fight is why I haven't touched these doors since.

I open the large doors to look inside. Despite all the things that fill the space, my eyes immediately dart to the withered satchel hiding under an old tunic. My skin grows warm from the light inside me just being close to it. I hesitantly reach over, listening to make sure Codrin is absent from our home, and pull the satchel out. Sitting on the bed, I run my hands over the cracks that have taken over the once smooth texture.

I bend down and I swear I can smell the grass stains that were on every pair of trousers I ever wore as a youngin, the sap of the trees from when I was still learning to climb, and the lavender; something Codrin wore quite often when he was growing up. I smile softly, remembering just how in love with me he was then, always there waiting for me to give him the smallest ounce of attention. My worries back then were training and learning the proper etiquette of being the daughter of The Ladies of the Adamina Clan.

I open the satchel up, revealing an even older, tattered blue leathered book. The gold lining traces the edges of the book forming into leaves in the corners. Each page is solid as a rock, and pictures are drawn as if they are stained glass windows. There are also gold markings that go around the pictures, nearly as beautiful as the drawing themselves. I let my fingers run over the pages when I finally notice Codrin standing in front of me. I jump for a moment and close the book. He kneels down, placing his hand over mine while holding his other out.

The only other dream I ever had. The life this book had me

so desperately craving for, but one that took me away from here and him.

I place the book back into the satchel, and he lets his hand fall. We both stand, and he watches me put the satchel back into the wardrobe.

"You're lucky I shut the door after I walked in. Vasile was right on my heels with all the excitement he has. Can't have him seeing our Lady in the state she's in."

I look down to my less than clothed form and smile, thinking about Vasile's crude reaction to seeing me like this. "Thank you for that."

I guess we are dropping the conversation where we talk about the book. It's probably best, with us needing to be focused.

I look back into the wardrobe and smile as I see the traditional hunting uniform that all the previous Maresal's have worn. Leather carefully weaved together to create textured patterns resembling an older time. Despite the Torrin Family ruling, most of the Felguard Country outside of the Capital still holds onto some of the old Countries traditions. Even the ancient language, though it has been dead for hundreds of years. There are certain phrases and words we still say in the ancient language to this day. To think there was a time where we all spoke as one, and there was peace.

Codrin walks up behind me, lightly moving my braided hair to the side before kissing the base of my neck. My shoulders relax, and the crease that had been forming on my forehead smooths out, like the stress of today and tonight is already far behind me.

"I'll be out there if you need me."

I nod.

I take down the vermilion colored armor and matching epaulet to begin getting dressed. I view myself in a long mirror attached to the door to make sure I have every belt fastened, and there are no current damages.

Just as I turn for the door, a rowdy young man bursts through my bedroom door. Vasile's face is full of excitement and determination. He already has on his leather armor, matching the color of mine but with a different design.

Vas strides up to me and places his arm over my shoulder, looking at both of us in the mirror. "Well, don't we look good." Vasile gives me the dopey smile before looking at a not as enthused Codrin, who is leaning against the door frame.

"I told you she was getting ready," Codrin nearly growls.

"She is ready! See!" Vasile says innocently, splaying his arms to show me off.

"What if she wasn't!" Codrin lunges at Vasile, who quickly jumps on the bed to avoid his mate.

"But she was!" Vasile shouts as Codrin grabs Vas's ankles and pulls them towards Codrin, causing Vasile to fall straight on his back. Codrin climbs on top, pinning him onto the bed.

"Apologize."

Vasile shakes his head with a smug smile before Codrin slaps him on the face."That hurt!"

"Apologize!"

"Never!"

I bite my lip and walk over to the two boys fighting on my bed and grab them by the ears.

"You both are going to apologize for messing up my bed."

They holler as I tug, and they both quickly get off the bed and each other.

"Sorry."

"Sorry."

I smile and release. "There, now that we have that figured out. I think Codrin had something cooking."

We all migrate over to the kitchen, where the late lunch

Codrin had been prepping is nearly finished. As we wait, I quickly discuss the few things we know about the creature. It's a cat/snake-like creature that stands 213 cm tall and at least 304 cm long. Yellow piercing orbs with dagger-like pupils for eyes, fur black as night, and a tail similar to a snake's body that can constrict its prey. Besides that, we are in the dark.

Vasile seems unnerved by hearing its description and retells his first read-through of **Fiends, Demons, Monsters, and Creatures alike.** The book is very old, not to mention that some of the creatures are not even real. Regardless, that book was something we all use to cherish together, pretending to defeat them as a team. Though, I guess all that make-believe is what led us to this.

I begin setting out the bowls when Vasile quickly kneels before me, his fist pounds onto his chest and then onto the floor.

"I will follow my lady into the dark and slay the beasts that threaten our clan." I can't help but laugh hearing him recite the hunt's acceptance ritual so abruptly. "I almost forgot!"

Codrin follows suit and kneels in front of me, pounding his fist to his chest and then to the floor. "I will follow my lady into the dark and slay the beasts that threaten our clan." Codrin stands and kisses me deeply.

Hearing him say those words both eases and tightens my heart. I am asking him to risk his life, but I know that he will be there by my side.

"It's so gross when you two do that," Vasile chimes in as we separate.

I glare at him as Codrin kisses my cheek with a smile. Codrin leaves us as he heads to our bedroom while Vasile and I are locked onto one another.

"You really are quite jealous. Who can blame you when you so desperately are wishing to do the very same thing but only to Madi's lips," I mock, knowing quite well about his constant failed attempts to win her over.

Madi's a woman even I would fall for if she ever had the desire to settle down with a partner. She's a first-class fighter we send out to protect the large caravans we use for trade. She definitely is not someone you would want to make your enemy. Though, I'm sure Vasile is getting to that point with her by continuing this suicidal crusade of his.

"Well, if it was her with anyone I don't think it would be gross," he says, looking off as if daydreaming.

I shove him a bit and shake my head.

"Madi and I have trained with each other for far longer than I have with you, Vas. I don't think she will ever take your attempts seriously."

Codrin rejoins us, his hands behind his back. I give him an inquisitive look, and he smiles back. He pulls out a rosewood longbow, with vines twisting around its grip, leading into carefully crafted Nightingales on both ends. Codrin hands it to me and sits beside me, leaning back on his arms to watch me examine his work. I turn the bow over a couple of times, testing the balance, then tugging the string to make sure it is taut. I smile as I trace my fingers over one of the bird's heads.

"I was waiting for the right moment to give this to you, but now seems like as good a time as any," he says, kissing my forehead.

I suddenly feel an excitement I have yet to feel in a long time, as well as a confidence, knowing that whatever this beast throws at us, we will be able to handle it. I kiss him again and again until I feel Vasile will faint from watching such a display of affection.

Codrin holds me tight for a moment before pulling away to see my face entrapped between his hands.

"It's beautiful, Codrin. Thank you."

He nods in satisfaction, enjoying the excitement I am openly expressing.

Codrin, Vasile, and I collect ourselves and sit around the table to enjoy our meal together.

"We need to keep in mind that we have no idea what this beast is actually capable of. The things we do know are its claws, its intelligence, and that it tends to stalk its prey."

"Some beasts have natural cloaking abilities, and due to its nocturnal nature and dark fur, it could be that it just blends in with the shadows." Vasile nods, understanding Codrin's explanation.

It's a reasonable assumption. I'm just worried because anything we assume may come back to haunt us later.

I chime in, "We also need to keep in mind that the canopy may offer the Clan protection and a way for us to keep hidden. But, it also blocks out our only natural light source when we are down below. So our ears are what we will need to rely on as always."

We all stare at each other as our light-hearted conversation turns into a serious one. We have a sunshift before it officially gives way to the moon.

As we make our way to the north side of the Clan, the decks are now empty due to the curfew we have in place. Lights begin to flicker on, filling homes with the warmth to break this frigid evening air. I hear Vasile giggle behind me as a unique and loud drunken laughter erupts from the tavern just ahead of us. I smile, happy to hear someone enjoying their evening.

Codrin keeps up with the fast pace I have set, practically jogging our way over to the dropping point. As we arrive, both the Gatekeeper and **Screamer** are chatting, waiting for us. The Screamer on duty bows, placing his hand on his chest to greet me. I nod in his direction acknowledging his respect. The

Gatekeeper, quite a few years younger, watches the Screamers' greeting before showing a moment's panic and copying his counterparts' same greeting.

"Vasile, you two could be best friends! Catching on right at the last minute." He laughs at my comment, and like a puppet, bows towards me—the Gatekeeper now red with embarrassment.

Codrin pats the young boy's shoulders, trying to alleviate some of the stress we are putting him under.

I glance down and see below the start of the tree's canopy. I turn to my team with a fire in my eyes that I imagine matches my mother's. They both face me, noticing my eagerness, and as they ready themselves, I place my right hand onto my chest.

"It's time for a hunt."

It's a quicker descent than it is a climb. We swiftly make our way down to the canopy and gather ourselves before rushing off towards the east. The leaves brush across our faces as we rush through the trees. Jumping from branch to branch is beyond freeing. It's what I guess birds feel when they are flying. The excitement rings in my soul once more as we pick up the pace and begin to drop ourselves a bit lower. Codrin sticks close to my right as we continue forwards, and Vasile covers our rear. Normally, a hunting party would be made up of at least six or seven to cover all angles, but due to my power and uncertainty of control, it's safer to keep our numbers small.

We communicate through a series of chirps and clicks, notifying each other of broken tree limbs or a possible lead on where our beast might be. I jump to a lower branch than my crew to investigate for any usual tracks, but I come back up empty-handed. We all ready ourselves again before leaping forwards once more. Codrin jumps ahead, notifying us that he sees an opening in the canopy. As we reach it, the moon shines brightly down for just a moment, making our eyes readjust to the darkness we find ourselves in.

Codrin, a few leaps ahead, signals for us to halt. Knowing I cannot just halt my momentum, I leap off my branch, reaching out to grab the branch next to him. As my hands wrap around its rough surface, it snaps. In a split second, I begin to fall. Codrin reaches out, but his hands slip through mine. I immediately look down, trying to find anything to grip onto. I spread my arms wide, grabbing at everything that rushes past me as I plummet. Dark orange and red leaves swoosh past me while smaller branches scrape and cut my hands and face. I can't focus on the **magicae** to stop my falling with such panic rushing through my veins.

Suddenly a branch finds my chest, knocking the air out of my lungs. Gasping, I cling to it with every ounce of my strength, wrapping my body around the branch. I swing onto the top of it and look up at the hole I left in the trees' foliage.

Codrin and Vasile swing down after me, leaves and twigs falling with their hurried movements, all while I am still trying to regain my breath. As Codrin's eyes meet mine, I can see the worry melt from his face. He lands next to me and wipes a bit of blood off my cheek. I pull away from him instinctively as the adrenaline is still coursing through me, his touch setting off every nerve in my body. I give Codrin an apologetic stare.

"That was a close one, even for you," Vasile says as he pokes his head in front of mine.

"Yeah, not my finest moment," I say with a self-scorning laugh.

Codrin shakes his head in utter disbelief but cracks a smile nonetheless. We gather ourselves there for a moment before I hear rolling thunder in the distance. I furrow my brow. It'll be even harder to find the beast in a storm.

"Aw man, I hope it doesn't rain," Vasile whines just as the thunder dies out.

I immediately put a finger to my lips, which are still trembling in pain, as we hear a twig snap below us.

Every bone in our bodies locks into place as we realize we are vulnerable. I shoo the boys to run to help disperse the noise we just made. As they quickly jump away, I lean up close to the trunk of the tree, gathering myself from what just transpired. I can feel Codrin's eyes focusing on me even in this darkness, trying to read into what I am about to do.

I slowly turn my head to find a better vantage point, noticing a branch lower to the ground I can jump to. Steadying my breath, I swallow my pain as my hand begins to gingerly make its way to my bow. Codrin quickly swings back over, seeing this, and grabs my wrist, putting us both in danger. I flash him half of a smile as I jump out of his grasp. I flip backwards off of the branch I had just fought so desperately to find only moments before.

As gravity begins to pull me back to the ground, I notch an arrow. My eyes dart every which way to find movement in the darkest of night. I see a brief shadow pass by one of the trunks of a nearby tree. My arrow is released just before I land on a branch. I quickly extend my hand, pushing the force inside of me to attach a ray of light onto the tail of the arrow. A bright glow now illuminating a path to our target. I push the voice far away, needing to stay focused on what is ahead of me. It's persistent, though, and feels as if it is screaming, warning me, but it doesn't matter. Not now. I have a job, no matter the danger.

I can't slow down, not while I have its location pinned. I take a steadying breath before quickly descending and notching another arrow as I follow the faint trail. There's a whimpering cry in the near foliage and the faint smell of crimson. I keep to the shadows and slowly maneuver around the trees as I hold my arrow, waiting for the beast to rear its ugly head from the bush. Bird chirps and cries call out to me, and I reply, notifying them of my location. The soft ruffling of leaves lets me know Codrin and Vasile are rushing towards me now. Just as my beacon begins to fade, the bush begins to shake and the creature crawls out from its thick cover.

As I take a step forwards, completely ready to finish this monster off, I see him.

CHAPTER THREE

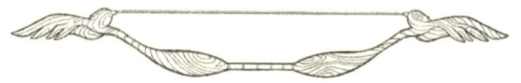

A LOUD RUMBLE comes from the black sky. A few drops of rain hit my face that freeze as they make contact with my skin. I can see my labored breaths in the night air. I tighten my grip on the bow and hold the notched arrow steady. My heartbeat pumps in my ears as I stare down at this strange man.

His black mane covers his face. I can only see bits and pieces of his features through it. He quickly extends his hand out towards me, still whimpering. I notice my arrow lodged into his left leg, a steady stream of blood flowing from it.

"Name and place of residency," I bark.

It takes him a couple of tries, but he finally gets his words out. "P-p-please, I find myself lost, I-I didn't mean to trespass or transgress-s," his voice shakes as he speaks.

The pain must be overwhelming to him. His skin looks very pale, sweaty, and tired. I take a quick glance around to make sure we are alone. My arrow's gaze never leaving its target. He finishes his crawl out from the bushes and attempts to stand before collapsing back onto the ground. He looks up to meet my gaze, and for a moment, I'm trapped in his emerald eyes. They seem to shimmer even in the dark of night.

I look him over once more and notice his sword at his side, decorated with sapphire and amethyst gems with gold trimming around them. Not really combat material, but it could cut something and would be worth a pretty penny. It also means he doesn't really belong out here.

He pushes himself up against the nearest tree and begins to apply pressure to his wounded leg. As he whimpers to himself quietly, I reluctantly lower my bow and crouch beside him. He flinches as I draw closer, but he doesn't move away. His gaze is intently on me, watching not my movements but my ears. I put up my hood and break our eye contact. He relaxes a bit and lets me move in a bit closer, hopefully convincing himself that he just imagined seeing long pointed ears.

"Please, help me. I do not know what comes after this, but I do not wish to die just yet," he begs. His voice breaking at the end, but a pleading smile still appears under his messy locks.

"Then, tell me your name."

He's silent for a moment, nervously looking away. He looks back to me, again with an intense gaze.

"Kage."

My heart skips for a moment, hearing his name. I swallow hard and lean in closer to examine him. As our breaths touch each other, I hear a couple of twigs snap behind us. Codrin and Vasile approach with their bow and swords drawn.

Kage tenses up and reaches for his sword. I grab his wrist and shake my head. Even in his state, he still has courage. I can admire that.

"They are friends of mine," I explain.

He relaxes back into the tree and drops his hand.

"He is wounded and not an immediate threat," I yell out

over my shoulder as Codrin and Vasile pause somewhere near behind me.

"I would say I'm not a threat at all," Kage claims with a small scoff.

Probably some shame or embarrassment adding to his tone. Codrin approaches Kage and looks at his wounded leg.

"We are going to have to get the arrow out. Otherwise, he won't even be able to limp his way anywhere."

Kage inhales sharply at my words, his eyes darting from the arrow to us. Kage pushes himself harder against the trunk. He hastily bites his navy blue jacket collar as I wrap my fingers around the shaft of the arrow. Codrin kneels down and grabs Kage's shaking leg to steady it. Codrin then looks up at Kage to meet his eyes before turning to me and nods his head.

"This may hurt," I admit to him.

I snap the shaft of the arrow where it entered his leg. I then pull the arrowhead and the remaining shaft through the bottom half of his leg.

He yells out in pain for a moment. Codrin quickly covers his mouth and shushes him.

"I said it may hurt. Now quiet before you attract something."

I begin wrapping his leg with some extra cloth I packed. He begins to pant, grabbing a hold of my wrist. I look down at his blood-covered hands before turning my head back up to meet his eyes, now filled with an emotion I'm not entirely sure how to describe.

"Thank you, Xylia," he says, gritted through his teeth, almost breathlessly.

My breath catches.

Is it really him?

It can't be.

I turn to Codrin, who noticed my reaction, before looking

back down, making sure I wrap the cloth enough to help stop the bleeding.

Once Codrin sees me finish, he pulls Kage off from the cool earth floor and wraps one of his arms around the stranger's waist. I step in front of him, stopping him in his tracks. He looks into me as anger and sadness are stirring inside of him.

"Not the time to get hot and heavy, guys. Maresal, what should we do?" Vasile says, trying to break up the tension and get our minds focused on the dangers of being out here.

I grab Kage's face, making him inhale sharply. I need to look him over just once more. His skin feels moisturized and has a small amount of stubble on his chin, but it is clear he shaves quite frequently.

I take a step back and look at his clothes. They are well-made and have the royal insignia on a torn sleeve. I assume he is from the capital. I grow nervous, thinking it could be him.

"You two take him back to the Clan. I'll continue the hunt myself."

"I am not going to leave you out here," Codrin argues.

"Cod-man, this is not the time to argue. I'll escort you back and hurry back out to cover Xy," Vasile interjects.

Codrin shakes his head. "Well, Xylia, you were the one who shot him. So you should be the one to take him back. Vasile and I will continue the hunt."

His voice begins to deepen, and his shoulders broaden. Codrin clenches his jaw as he takes a step forwards, now attempting to hand our wounded tag-along over to me.

"The storm is almost here. We need to wrap this up, guys," Vasile says, his face turned up to the sky.

I look up to feel the cool drops on my face. My hood falling off my head as a bright stream of light shoots across the sky. Another echoing roar following behind, but this one is coming from the ground.

I quickly spin around to look and lock eyes with it. A chill shoots down my spine. There is not even a moment to warn them before it lurches, baring its teeth and its claws reaching out towards me. I try to grab my bow, but the creature reaches me first, knocking me down. It's hot breath pressed against my face as its claws slowly dig into my chest.

I cry out as red fills my vision.

I try to focus on my breathing as the beast rests there on my chest. Its eyes are focused solely on me at this moment, the reflection of a terrified and screaming face residing inside the yellow-daggered eyes. I can hear Codrin yelling, but the roar of this beast makes it impossible to make out what he is saying. The thing whines as Vasile stabs its side with his curved blade.

It quickly jumps off of me to refocus its effort, noticing our numbers. Vasile takes another swing, this time as the beast reaches out towards him. I'm able to get a good look at the Feserpentline as Vasile occupies its attention. It's a tad smaller than what was depicted but far quicker than I could have imagined. Four long legs, each with razor sharp claws. Its tail seems to have its own mind as it twists and curls, striking out in every direction. Through its matted fur, green and yellow scales seem to riddle its body like freckles, growing more obvious near its rear leading into the fully scaled tail. As quickly as I can, I try to stand up and gather my thoughts as blood begins to drip from my chest.

Now, it's my turn to even the score.

I immediately notch an arrow, pull the string back, and fire. Time slows for a moment as I extend my hand out. Pushing and pulling the space around me, manipulating an object instead. As the arrow finds purchase in its target, I shove the arrow deeper into the beast, causing it to recoil back in pain.

"Geez Xy, take it easy on the little guy! Two stellar powers over its pathetic claws!" Vas chuckles while ducking under its tail.

"Not the time to joke, Vas!" I shout back, unamused.

"Pretty sure it could eat you in one bite!" Codrin chimes in.

Codrin drops Kage behind him and pulls out his bow. Vasile steadies himself and his swords. I fire again.

The beast swiftly moves, the arrow missing its target, but I flick my finger rerouting the arrow's destination. The arrow stabs into the beast and its hisses. Its large yellow burrowed eyes begin to count each of us as we start to circle it.

It lashes out at me again, but this time I read its movements and dive to the side, rolling back up onto my feet. My body screams at me, but I can't stop moving. Vasile runs forwards, striking the ugly creature once more while its back is still turned towards him.

Vasile shouts with excitement as the thing cries out in pain again.

Codrin and I take our shot with its legs up, exposing its belly. It whips its tail around, but all three of us duck as it approaches us. I take a steady breath and extend my open hand, focused on the arrows resting in my quiver. Closing my eyes, I control the chaotic fluid of matter that swirls inside of me to grip a dozen. With a flash of light within me, I twist my hand slightly and send the arrows flying—each one burrowing into its scaled fur.

Overpowering the beast with the last of our efforts, it tries to flee from the onslaught of arrows and slashes. The beast backs itself into a tree as we surround it.

I'm about to give a signal when Vasile quickly moves towards the beast. My heart lurches for a moment, watching him dive forwards.

"Vasile, wait!" I scream.

The creature's eyes focus, seeing an opening in Vasile's

reckless action. Vasile is too slow to notice as the beast swings its tail, smacking into Vasile and sending him off his feet, and slamming into a tree a few meters away.

I yell in frustration and anger, clenching my fists tightly. Codrin fires again and again with the same frustration, slowly circling around the small opening of trees we have found ourselves fighting in.

I turn and begin to climb up a nearby tree, jumping from branch to branch until I am right above the creature. Slowly, I unsheathe my dagger as the beast begins to stalk towards Codrin, taking each arrow that he fires. Kage is now backing up in terror, attempting to stand, but his leg is failing him.

Just before the beast can extend its claws towards them, I jump from the tree, dagger in hand, and land on the beast's bony back. My dagger tears into it. It screams out in surprise and anger, quickly rearing its backend, trying to buck me off.

I look to Codrin, who focuses on me with such intensity waiting for my signal that he is clear to approach. "Codrin now!"

The words barely escape my mouth before its long snake-like tail wraps around my throat tightly. It slowly picks me off its back and hangs me there, suffocating me. My legs flail as my eyes dart, trying to find a solution. It's squeezing the life out of me. The only thing I can hear is the beat of my heart piercing my eardrums. My vision begins to blur, and the noise of gasping fades away as no air can reach me.

My hands frantically rip at its tail, trying to pry my throat free. As I struggle to release myself, I feel myself fall out of its grasp, my body slamming onto the wet earth. I blink out of shock and confusion, the rain pouring down on me now as I gasp for air. The tail relaxes and limply lays next to me. The creature cries out once again, sounding desperate.

It's heavy footsteps landing and pouncing around nearby,

the ground shaking slightly as it does. My eyes dart, waiting to see the beast's ugly face in front of mine, but I can't move to see what's happening. A hand grasps my arm and pulls me to my feet suddenly. Codrin is pinned underneath the beast. Kage is standing, barely, in front of me with a bloody sword in hand. Kage yells something to me, but I can't even process it. The only thing I can focus on is the blood coming from Codrin's left arm as the beast bites into him.

I quickly grab the elegant sword from Kage and run towards the beast. Its mouth wide open prepared to finish off Codrin with a second bite.

I throw the sword, extending my hand to guide it, pleading for it to listen to my desire. It plunges into the mouth of the beast, down its throat, through its body, and out its back. The creature's body freezes for a moment before it goes limp.

I don't give myself a moment to rest, knowing both of my men are down. I do a quick scan to find that bushy blonde hair and am immediately relieved to see him picking himself back up.

I rush over to Codrin, who is still trapped under the weight of the Feserpentline. As I reach him, blood is filling his mouth. I immediately grab under his arms and pull him out from underneath. He moans in discomfort as I move his battered body. I notice that the lower part of his left arm is now gone, and blood is gushing from it.

His normal ebony color is turning grayer by the second. I take a shaky breath in, tears promptly blurring my vision. I force a smile even though I know he can see right through it. He tries to muster the same smile for me but winces as a surge of pain rings through his body. He begins coughing up more blood.

Codrin can barely keep his eyes open.

I need to do something.

Anything.

"Vasile, grab Kage and get out of here now!"

My command comes out a panicked scream. Vasile, who is already on his way over, nearly stumbles seeing Codrin.

"Codrin ..." Vasile freezes, his face contorting into a mesh of emotions.

I snap my fingers at him, his eyes peeling off of Codrin to look at me. "Please! I can't worry about you too," I cry out. Vasile bites his lips, freezing in place. "Go!"

Vasile shuts his eyes tightly, turning around and dashing off towards Kage. He throws Kage over his shoulders and begins making his way to the Clan as hastily as I'm sure he can muster.

I look back to Codrin and place both my hands on his arm, putting pressure on it. I close my eyes and begin to call the light from inside forwards, allowing the voice in.

"Xy, I'm going to be with you no matter what," his voice is quiet and weak. He reaches up slowly with his only hand and places it on my heart. "Don't do this to yourself," Codrin pleads.

My heart shatters as I scream out and bury my head into his chest.

"I can't just watch you d—" I shake the thought from my mind. "I need to try."

I ignore his wish and begin to transfer my light into him. I can't let him die—I won't lose him. The voice calls to me desperately, trying to steal my attention away, but I won't allow it to. I continue to focus, the light getting bigger and brighter. My body begins to feel the burn from the light like my body is about to combust in flames if I continue to push further, dive deeper into the magicae that is spilling out of me. The fatigue is quickly catching up, the cuts on my chest dripping with blood. As my hands begin to shake, I scream again, my body trembling in pain, fear, and exhaustion. Losing him would mean losing a part of myself. He's everything that is good. I'm not losing him. I'm going to save him.

I am going to save him.

"Please, let me save him!" I whimper as my voice gives out, along with whatever strength I had left.

I begin to lose sight of Codrin as the light grows even brighter. I quickly lean down and touch our lips. I can't hear but feel his words on my lips.

"I love you, Angel."

CHAPTER FOUR

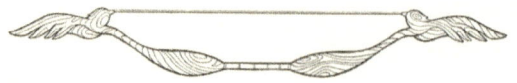

I WAKE up with the cool rain evaporating the moment it touches my skin. I gasp for air as thick smoke fills the space around me. Sitting up, I see flames surrounding Codrin and me, the trees that had been nearest are now burned to ash. My heart is pounding as I see no escape from the ring of fire approaching us. I look up, my eyes widening as I see the moon shining down onto us. A massive hole in the canopy allows the rays to find us.

The rips in my chest feel like they will split even further open as I make another move, protesting that I am even conscious. I turn to see Codrin's wound is no longer bleeding and nearly completely healed.

Taking in a shaky breath, I sigh in relief and happiness.

I did it.

I reach up and brush my fingertips across his face but he does not look my way. He's unconscious. My vision blurs as I look closer. The color hasn't returned to his face.

He is just asleep. He's just sleeping.

I trained for years, learned how to reach and turn off the

voice. I learned how to master the two different magicaes I contain within me so I could control them.

I thought I was ready.

I was confident that I'd be able to save the ones I love. I shake my head no, I *did* save him.

I poured my soul into him.

I felt his heart beating.

He just needs to wake up.

"Please get up," I say in a whisper, as that is the only volume I can muster. "Codrin. Open your eyes."

Tears begin to stream from my eyes as a silent sob builds up in my throat. Despite the bodily pain, I push myself to sit upright. My lip quivers as I shake his stiff form.

"Open, open your eyes. Wake up, please. Wake up. Please, please, please, please, please."

Even the tears sliding down my cheeks are evaporating because of the heat. I lay my head down on his chest to feel the gentle rise and fall that brings me so much comfort and ease, but it's solid and unmoving.

Resting there for a moment, an emptiness washes over me. My heart is shattering into a million pieces all over again.

A horrifying scream erupts; it's deafening and unnerving. My lungs burn as I gasp for air, realizing now, that the scream is mine.

"Xylia!"

I hear a voice in the distance calling out. It takes everything I have left just to lift my head. The flames have grown even taller, closer, hotter. I squint my eyes, trying to see the person calling my name, but all I see is white. I break into a fit of coughing, sweat now dripping from my brow as both the smoke and heat overtake me.

I lay my head back down onto Codrin's chest.

This is it.

I failed again.

I failed to save a man who cared for me—loved me. Now I have put every single one of the clan members in jeopardy. If the fire continues to spread, I don't know if our **Ignis Troopers** can even stop it. Maybe the Capitol and the King will burn along with it.

I smile at the thought of someone so cruel being taken from this world. He should have been the one to die, not Codrin. I raise my hand up in front of my face. If there was a way for my powers to trade a life, that's the switch I would make.

"Xylia! Answer me!" I don't raise my head this time.

There is no point.

I no longer have the strength nor the will to continue. Everything I have done for the Clan means nothing if there is no Clan. They should leave me here and focus on the fire. They should leave me to die.

I no longer deserve my position, both in the Clan or in life.

My eyelids feel heavy, and my chest rings with pain. The heat is excruciating as flames start to lick my armor. Staring into the fire, it looks like flames are dancing, enjoying themselves as they begin to eat away at the burning carcass of the Feser-pentline.

I close my eyes, ready to accept my punishment.

I can feel the heat, but it's no longer scalding, it's comforting. I open my eyes and see myself once again surrounded in bright light, my light. The voice is humming something that sounds like a lullaby. It circles me as it fades in and out.

"Xylia."

The voice sounds gentle and sweet. Like it's calling me home. I want to reach out my hand. I don't want to feel this pain.

"Xylia."

The voice is sad, desperate, almost as if it's begging me.

Much more familiar and so much closer. I can feel their breath on my face.

"Xylia!"

I jolt awake, sitting straight up, breathing in smokeless air, the flames and the light replaced with a cool wind and darkness. I turn and see a relieved Vasile's face. He quickly cups my cheeks and kisses my forehead. His lips are cold and wet.

Vasile whispers a thank you to a deity I do not catch the name of. I push his hands away and look around. A mile or so away, smoke is rising, no flames, though. I look back to Vasile, confused. His face and hands are covered in black soot.

"Where's Codrin?" I ask as I stand up, my body shaking from both exhaustion and tender wounds.

Vasile is quick to grab my arm and assist me. Kage is sitting at the base of a tree across from the one I had just been resting against.

I shuffle my way over to him, Vasile still attached.

"I'm glad to see your eyes open again," Kage says with a brief smile.

I fall to my knees in front of him and grab his collar. His eyes widen, but he doesn't pull away.

"It's your fault. We announced a hunt! Why the hell were you out here? Why did you have to be out here."

I found my voice, talking in the loudest volume I think I've ever used. I shake him roughly, his hands quickly grabbing my wrists and Vasile grabbing my shoulders. I yelp at the pain that radiates through my wrist. Kage quickly drops the one that is swollen and changing color.

"I am sorry, truly sorry," he whispers, still maintaining eye contact.

My eyes fill with tears again as I look at him. It's not his fault, I know that, but I want it to be. I want there to be a better reason than I failed. That I lost another person, and I am still here.

"Xy, we can deal with him later. Lay back down for a second," Vasile says tenderly.

I collapse back into Vas, sobbing, screaming, feeling everything I know I cannot feel, cannot show when I climb these trees back to the Adamina Clan. I bring my knees to my tattered chest. Vasile gently wraps his arms around my shoulders and buries his head in my neck. I hear his sobs along with mine. Kage lets go of my wrist and places them on my knee.

They allow me to stay like that, broken.

Vasile, my pupil, is watching his mentor unravel into a pile of frayed rope. I don't want him to see me as weak, as hurt. I'm supposed to be a pillar, someone who can support and help him, but he's here, holding me.

Once my breathing is steady. I slowly lift my head once more, meeting Kage's gaze, who seems to have been watching me intently. He raises his eyebrows, almost surprised at my composure. Vasile's grip is still tight on me, my neck and hair soaked not just from the rain but his desperate longing for his friend. His twin flame. I reach up and run my fingers through his hair, ruffling it. He looks up and presses his nose against my cheek as he sniffles. His breath is hot, but we are all shaking. I kiss his cheek lightly, and he looks into my eyes. His normally clear brown eyes are now dark and teary.

I need to get us home, out of danger, but I need to know first.

I straighten my shoulders against Vasile's protest and wipe my tear-soaked face. "Tell me."

He wipes his face a few times, but tears are still streaming down his face. Vasile's shoulders are slouched and his voice low, "When you told us to run, I thought you might level the forest trying to save him. So I kept running along with Kage until the sky lit up, and a single beam of light struck where you both were. Everything in me told me to turn back, so I immediately left Kage here and went back to find you two. There was fire everywhere. The Ignis Troopers were already there calling for you to come to them because the flames were too large for them to pass through."

"Tell me, Vasile." Urging him to get to the point.

He swallows hard, his breath shaky and hands trembling. "Eventually, the rain started winning the battle against the flames along with the help of the troopers. I was able to climb high enough to jump past the flames and get to you. If I had waited any longer, you would have been ash, Xy. I'm so sorry, Xy ..."

I throw my hand up to make him stop. His lip quivering. Codrin was gone, not just his soul but now his body as well. I nod in thanks for his explanation and slowly stand. Vasile grabs my arm again and helps me stand.

"We need to head back to the Clan. I'm sure Rose is in an uproar, and I should be there to calm her down," I mutter.

"Xylia, I'm sure—"

I throw my hand up again, pleading him to stop. "I can walk. Take him." I just need to keep moving. I don't want to think anymore.

Vasile nods and quickly picks up Kage, allowing him to lean on his shoulder. Unable to hide in the canopy, we stick close together and walk slowly towards our destination. Vasile assisting Kage nearly the entire way. We take a few breaks, gathering ourselves from the pain of our undressed wounds, but we continue on, knowing that if we stop for too long, it'll put us more at risk.

As we grow closer to the Adamina Clan, I use a cloth to cover Kage's eyes and plug his ears. We walk a little longer before Vasile hands the stranger off to me while he climbs high above to alert them that we are here and with a wounded guest.

Kage rests on me and shivers. The freezing autumn rain chilling our bones. I feel him nestle closer to me, trying to keep what heat we have between us.

"Thank you," Kage whispers into my ear.

His head is leaning against mine now, his breath warm against my skin, his wet hair dripping water onto my cheek. Something about him is definitely familiar, his voice soothing as if I had fallen asleep to it many nights before.

Maybe it could be him.

I shake my head, startling Kage, before refocusing myself as a creak slightly echos. I look up to see a pulley slowly lowering a raft to carry us up. I lower Kage onto the wooden planks gently. I sit beside him, tugging on the rope, and we begin to ascend.

I look out at the dark landscape in front of me. The gigantic trunks and the tall canopy are being lit up by a small spark of light as it strikes across the sky. The rain drips from the leaves above us onto the damp wood we rest on. Kage's teeth chatter as we sit here motionless. I don't feel the cold anymore.

I assist Kage up again and hand him off to Vasile while the Gatekeeper ties the raft back to the deck.

"Vasile, take Kage to the Healer's Ward. I want both of you stitched up by the time I arrive."

Vasile nods, taking my order and leaves without further questions. I steady myself, and march forwards towards the Command Post.

Both my body and soul are battered. The rain is the only thing keeping me awake as each drop splashes across my face.

Stepping through the doors, I am greeted with a room filled with commanders and generals. Rose standing in the center of it all, bickering orders regarding the forest damage. Some of our training grounds have been scorched, and some of our crow's nests were taken out along with the trees I had burned to ash.

"Maresal," Brig's, an orcish man standing a few inches away from me, voice rings out louder than what he should in such a compact room.

Everyone's head snaps towards me. All of their faces are horrified seeing me in the state I'm in. They have never seen me so weak. My normally golden hair is now covered in dark black and red ash, my armor is in shreds, and blood is dripping from my face and chest. Not exactly what I was hoping for, but I should have expected Rose wouldn't be sitting here handling this mess alone or quietly. This is something that will have very negative effects on the Clan, and I'm at fault.

"Lady Maresal, glad to see you were able to survive the lightning strike," Rose says with a face harder than stone. "Let's talk in my office for a bit, so I can hear what all happened."

She quickly turns and heads for the stairs without hearing a response.

As I make my way through the crowd of my underlings, they say graces that I was able to return to them safely. I tighten my fists.

They all think I'm weak.

Rose's office takes up the entire second floor. After climbing the stairs, I enter to see her sitting at her large desk in the center of the room. Bookcases and cabinets line all four walls. She gestures for me to sit on a stool in front of her desk. I take my place, my head spinning a bit as I do. I wince, placing a firm hand on my chest to try to stop any more blood from dripping out, and wait for her to speak.

"What of the beast," she says more than posing a question.

"It's dead."

"Explain the damages."

Another command, but I pause. I build the courage to admit to her my failings.

"Codrin, he, he suffered a f-fatal wound." The words taste

bitter, causing my mouth to run dry. "In my-attempt-to save him; I lost control."

Rose's face drops. I can see the pain written on it as she looks down at the desk. I hear a shaky breath escape her, but her face hardens. Her posture straightens, and her eyes look up and lock with mine. Her fire-filled gaze meeting my tear-filled one. She stands up slowly and walks over to me. I look up at her just before her hand slaps across my face.

I let my head hang there for a moment as a single tear drops from my eye. Not because it hurt, but because it stung of disappointment, and I know I deserve much worse.

"Twelve sidereal years. That's how long I've been training you. So you could control it. I broke protocol to give you a small crew so you wouldn't harm them. I gave you every chance to make things better for yourself, but you still haven't learned from your mistakes. You still allow that voice to control the power instead of you."

"You think I don't know how many shifts I spent expending myself? Day in and day out of being whipped and beaten to tame the power I hardly feel is mine. I feel like a monster!" I shout, quickly covering my mouth.

I have no right to be angry because all I have done is fail. The number of victories won means nothing when you have a few failures that amount to lives lost. I shut my eyes tightly, knowing very well that I did everything I could to keep control, to keep him alive, and I couldn't do either in the end. I put countless lives in danger and risked the Clan's security.

"Go get yourself cleaned up. I'll be there once I finish cleaning this mess up. We will be lucky if the King lets this mistake slide like he did the last."

She walks back to her seat and sighs, her hands shaking. I thought I could do as she asked before leaving my office today, but I made all the wrong choices. I jumped in when my team wasn't ready. I let my guard down and got myself trapped by the beast's tail. My mind was distracted. I let my team down, and the most important person in my life is gone because of it. Now, I'll do the only thing I can—do as I am commanded.

The intense smell of alcohol immediately fills my nostrils and stings my eyes as I arrive at the Healer's Ward. The red walls surround me, containing the sounds of coughs, screams, and cries. White sheets hang on thin wires running from every direction, and there are a few private rooms to the left of me.

As Lani, a young healer here, notices me, I'm informed that Vasile and Kage are just finishing up with their treatments. I nod in gratitude that neither of them had any serious injuries.

Just as I take a seat on one of the benches, Seb, my regular healer, comes around the corner. His bent glasses rest on the bridge of his long nose that try to hide the dark circles underneath his baby blue eyes. He smiles weakly at me, glancing at the front of my blood-soaked apparel. He takes me into his operating room to stitch my chest and fix up my wrist. Seb tells me I'm lucky my esophagus wasn't crushed when the beast had me by the throat. I made it out with just some heavy bruising. It doesn't take him long to finish before he sends me on my way.

"Which rooms are Vasile and our guest, Kage, residing in?" I ask the front desk woman.

She smells of heavy lilac perfume, and her hair is tied back a little too tightly. She smiles at me, though, bowing slightly, before pointing me towards the two rooms at the end of the hall.

I poke my head into the first room where I see Vasile laying on his side, back towards me. His shoulders rise slowly, letting me know he is breathing, but a soft sob follows suit as his body shakes.

I'm so sorry ...

I close the door quietly and poke my head into the next room to see Kage looking at his sword. Hearing the door open, his attention is drawn to me. He smiles, inviting me in as if he really had a choice to keep me out.

The room is small but much more private than the cubes most of our members use when being treated. The walls are red, a few tables lining the left wall, tools scattered across them —his temporary bed sitting on the right side.

"You look lovely, Xylia," he says with a fake happy tone.

I sit down on the stool next to his cot, not willing to return his smile or greeting. "This is a very rare exception we are making here, Kage," I inform him.

He looks away from me, nodding his head in understanding. "I am very grateful for your kindness," he starts, "I had been out here for far longer than one should."

I just stare at him.

"Given the location and talk of participating in a hunt, I take it I am in the Adamina Clan's base. A group segregated from the crown yet still under its protection. A group that is not known for its warm welcome to strangers." He adds a soft laugh trying to ease the tension in the room. I can see him rubbing his thumb over the blade as if it were a nervous habit.

"You know your stuff. So tell me, why were you in the forest?" I ask.

He smooths his long dark hair back, which I realize I am seeing dry for the first time. It's more curly and has a silky shine to it. I also notice his more prominent features, like the small blemish next to his left eye.

I can't believe it.

"I was running," he says simply. He doesn't offer anything more, but I've already answered my own question.

I stand up from my seat to lean in closer to him. Grabbing his chin, just as I did in the forest, I look him over once more. He furrows his brow before widening his eyes, seeing the anger in my eyes.

"Do you mind if I guess your real name?"

He pulls out of my grasp and turns his face away from me. "If you know it, then there is no need for you to say it aloud, my Lady." He looks back to me, his eyes empty.

I stand once more and grab his hair, pulling back his head. He winces as I probably pull a few strands out.

He's nothing but a disgusting piece of garbage that Codrin died for. I wouldn't have been distracted if he hadn't used the name Kage. I would have been fine. He would be alive.

I hate this man.

I hate his life.

I hate his family.

I want to kill him.

"Second Prince of Fosa, Bren Torrin," I hiss into his ear.

CHAPTER FIVE

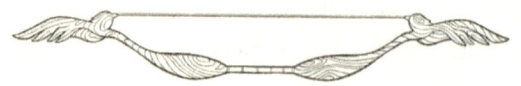

I THROW Kage's head forwards, letting go of his hair. He tries to back away but falls off the cot and hits the ground with a thud. He lets a curse slip from his lips as he hits his leg. I put my hands out to try to facilitate peace and control the anger that is beginning to overwhelm me. Everything in me wants to wring his neck, but I can't do that.

I shouldn't do that.

I came in here to get some answers, but I wasn't really expecting this.

What's the protocol for this?

Horror washes over me as I reach up, and my hood is gone. He can see my ears clear as day. I step towards him, moving the cot out of my way.

"Xylia, I can understand your frustration," he says, holding both his hands out. "I am who you say I am, but I am also who I claim to be."

He knew my name earlier. He said my name before anyone else did.

"Get up," I command.

This is dangerous, he knows too much, seen too much, but he is the prince, the son of our tyrant King.

Bren scoots his way over to the wall to help himself stand. "I implore you to listen to the reason, my Lady. I was telling you I was running." He backs himself into the corner, hands still up out in front of him.

"I'm sure there are a lot of people who you would need to run from because of who your family is and what they have done, but you cannot run from us, Second Prince."

I'm petty, but I don't care. I'm an empty shell, but that doesn't mean I can just stop going. I am still the Maresal. He can rot in **infernum** for all I care, but he will not stop me from doing what I need to.

Vasile opens the door to the room, his tired eyes surveying what is going on; Kage in the corner and me in a fighting stance.

"Xy, what's happening?" Vasile instinctively stands in front of me.

"He's the Second Prince."

Vasile lets out a low growl, looking at Bren. He jumps forwards and grabs the prince's wrists without hesitation. Bren doesn't resist but shakes his head, almost like he is in disbelief.

"You saw the state I was in, am in. My Lady, I am asking you to reconsider. To at least lend me an ear to elucidate the situation."

Vasile, now pinning Bren's arms behind his back, jerks him to shut him up. "She's not your lady."

I gesture with my head for Vasile to escort him out. I was hoping I wouldn't have to see Rose until the morning, but this information needs to be shared.

We take the Second Prince to our Detention Center, placing him in a cell separated from our regular, just overly drunk inmates. We don't have much crime, but we do have too much alcohol. Sometimes we need to put them in a time-out.

Bren, now silent, sits there in the dark cell, avoiding our eyes. Vasile and I step back outside, both exhausted—both unsure of the protocol. Vasile slams his foot against the wall of the Center, letting out a few curses as his entire body shakes with rage.

I don't blame him.

I walk up behind him and put my hands on his shoulders. He looks up to the sky, the storm clouds have passed, and the stars are shining brightly above us.

"Why Xy?" His voice breaks as he yells out.

"I wish I knew," I whisper. If he looked over at me, he would see me struggling to keep my composure.

Vasile reaches up, placing his hands on top of mine.

"How are you doing it?" he asks, his voice so quiet it was almost stolen away by the breeze.

I sigh and look up towards the night sky, the same moon I looked at as I laid on Codrin's dead chest only a few moonshifts ago.

How could I move knowing half of me is now gone, knowing I destroyed so much of what I love, risked the lives of people I care about?

"Because I have to. There's no how, just the requirement to put one foot in front of the other."

I turn my head from the sky and look towards him, and for the first time, I see him cry with no shaking, or guttural noises, just tears streaming down his face. Slowly, he turns around, my hands still in his. He cups his face with my hands. He bends forwards and leans his forehead against my shoulder.

"I know you think I'm brainless, but I know why you spend every morning with me out in those fields. Why you correct me, why you constantly berate me on the traditions of the Clan. I know that one day you will need to step down from being Maresal, but if ripping your heart out for the sake of others is what it takes to do the job, I am not the right person to do it." He gasps for air finishing his statement.

I figured he'd catch on eventually as to my future plans. He's right though, you can feel when it's appropriate, but there can be no tears in front of other Clan members. There are a few things I can publicly feel. Anger, if it's for the good of the Clan. Happiness, because it'll make the Clan feel more uplifted. Love, because that's what we should always feel for our people and country. Pain, sadness, grief, turmoil, anything someone could see as more of a weakness than strength is for your personal abode where no eyes can see you. It's the lesson that took me the longest to learn, and I'm still working on it.

"You saw my heart out there in the woods, Vasile. There are even times when Rose shows hers. It's not about ripping your heart out but controlling it. If you think you cannot master that, that's okay. I still struggle. I wouldn't be a living being if I could just turn it off."

Vasile nods. I'm not sure if it is out of understanding or just taking it all in. He takes a few deep breaths as I wipe his tears away.

"Why don't you go get Rose. She needs to be notified. I didn't fill her in on the details, so do what you do best."

As Vasile walks away, I can feel my own tears welling up. I take a few unsteady breaths before heading back inside. Bren stands hearing the door open but pauses as he sees it's me. I grab a chair from the corner of the room and set it down in front of the cell. I sit there watching him, him watching me until the door opens once more. Rose and Vasile step into the dimly lit room.

Rose walks over to the cell, looking at him. Her breath catches for a second as she confirms for herself that he is one of the Princes of Fosa. She looks between Vasile and me, knowing that the night's events are still not over. She sighs heavily, shaking her head, gesturing for me to move from my seat.

I do so, and she takes my place.

"Second Prince Torrin, I've heard my Hunter's side of tonight's encounter. I am interested in hearing yours," she says with her eyebrows raised.

Bren clears his throat and nods.

"I honestly mean no harm to the Adamina Clan nor its people," he starts, "I am here in the woods as I have given up my title as Second Prince. Many years ago, I made a promise that when I was ready, I would leave Fosa behind." His eyes are now on me. Rose snaps her fingers, drawing our attention back to her.

"Good for you, handsome, but dropping a title means nothing. If anything, you've put a spotlight on us, like the King looking for his rogue son. Not to mention the strict laws you broke. You were trespassing on Adamina Clan soil, interfering with a hunt, and partook in the killing of an Adamina Clan's target. All three of those things are good enough to send you to **Meka Prison**. Give me a reason why I shouldn't," she says, slowly standing.

We can all see him gulp and shiver, just thinking of ever going near that land. **The Ashen Land Territory**, where Meka Prison is located, is exactly that, ashen. Nothing grows, nothing survives, it's a land where things go to die.

"I saved your daughter's life."

Rose furrows her brow while my breath catches.

"Right. The beast was strangling her, and you used your sword to get her down."

"With all respect, that was not the moment I was referencing."

No. Kage was a servant boy who lived in the castle. He was the one who freed me. He is the one who likely died for his actions.

"Please allude to the moment you are referencing then."

His eyes turn to me once more—a light smile on his lips.

"We were five years alive at the time. My father found a treasure," Bren gestures to me, the last elf, "wandering on her own. I would sneak away from my guards to talk with her. Tell her about my abusive father and sick mother."

My heart skips for a moment, hearing him say this. It throbs as if it is already wounded and barely beating to begin with.

"Xylia, those were not lies. I am Kage. I was afraid that you wouldn't talk to me if I told you my real name. Those miserable nights."

All of our faces are riddled with surprise.

That's impossible.

How did I not notice Kage was the second Prince?

"I recognized you the moment I saw you tonight," Bren admits.

The feeling of confusion and wonderment wash over me. I put my hand on Rose's shoulder and excuse myself. I won't be of any use here if he is using me as a linking point. Rose is better off if I'm gone so he can focus on her instead of me.

Before I pull my hand away, I feel hers gently rest on mine. "We will talk in the morning, Maresal." She releases my hand hastily after that.

Vasile gives me a weak version of his signature smile. I push through the door and walk, then jog, then sprint. I sprint until I see the home I once shared, a home once filled with love, the place I should have gone right after Seb released me. I should have left it as is, not pushed myself as I did.

Standing on the porch for a moment, I ready myself to walk in, knowing that he will never be waiting for me inside. I grit my teeth and open the door. Instead of looking around, I dash for the bedroom, where I slam the door shut. I grab a pillow from my side of the bed, wrap it around my face, and scream.

⇩

Soft green light fills the room as the sun begins to rise. I hug the pillow even tighter to my chest and wipe the last few tears from my eyes. My face is sticky from the salt water, and my hair is tangled from the amount of tossing and turning I did during the remaining moonshifts.

I give myself the solidity to sit up and toss the pillow to the side. I stretch upward, sigh, and begin my day. My mind, body, and soul are rattled and overstimulated. I can barely keep up with myself.

It almost doesn't feel real.

I splash some water onto my face and braid my hair back into its usual three braids. I turn to the large closet that now feels like it's looming in my room and open the doors, ignoring the clothes that will never be worn again, and will never smell like him again. I put on a black tunic, the Adamina Clan's symbol stitched in red on the back, paired with some tan trousers and red leather boots.

My eyes rest on the wardrobe I opened before we left last night. I reach for the handles and open the doors, looking for the tattered satchel. I smile a bit, seeing that Codrin must have tried to hide it, as a couple of blankets were folded and placed on top of it. I pull it out, feeling the book inside of it. I never shared this part with him, only fought about it.

I figured one day I'd let him read it—I should have let him read it.

I throw the satchel over my shoulder and head out the door, grabbing my cloak as I go. I know what's waiting for me at the

Command Post, but I need to do something more important first.

I breathe in the smell of freshly baked bread and squashed berries for jam and listen to a few birds chirping in the trees surrounding this dock. A few clan members wave and smile good morning as they pass me. With my hood now hiding my ears, I straighten my shoulders and wave back with a smirk on my face, allowing the allure of my statice and personality shine through on this dark day. Their smiles of joy will soon be replaced by tears and howls of sorrow for a lost member as kind, involved, and loving as Codrin was.

Some Adaminians whisper about the fire they saw from their windows last night and how they prayed it would end before reaching the docks.

I continue to pass through until I reach the morning shift Gatekeeper. He lets me through without issue, so I slip under the canopy and start to make my way to the blackened spot I created out there in the forest.

My legs begin to shake as my heart pounds in my chest with each step I take closer. My mind replays scenes I wish to never visualize again. If Codrin were here, he would mention the heroics and bravery that could have been seen. He would try to make me forget about the pain and panic.

He would be with me.

I never realized just how much I depended on him to be my strength.

From the moment I saw him pinned under that beast, I could feel the desperation, the weakness inside me. Like I was a twelve-year-old girl all over again. I grip my satchel tight and continue my journey.

I can tell I'm close as I see the sun beating down into one spot ahead of me. I muster the courage to continue forwards, pulling out the blue book as I do. I can see the scorch marks from where the fire started and ended.

I've never created so much damage.

My eyes flicker from the trees to the ground to the hole in the canopy. I was trying to save him, and I burned away everything around us. This is now the second hole. Another piece of me is gone, just as I have taken a piece of the forest. Maybe it's the loss, my agony that keeps these spots from healing. Maybe that's just wishful thinking, that someone—something is just as damaged as me.

I make my way to the center of it all, wanting to be close to him.

"I wanted to share this with you. You constantly asked me to open this one piece of me to give to you, but I was too afraid. Terrified, actually. I realize now that I'll always be a coward because I'll never have the courage to be brave enough to do as you wish. So, if you're still here, please, please listen." I take a deep breath. If anyone from the living is watching, they will, for sure, think I'm losing it.

I bend the leather binding once more as I open it, brushing my finger across my name so delicately written on the bottom left-hand corner. I flip to the first illustration, the stained glass images are lined with leaf and vine engravings in the same pure gold paint as the cover. Symbols I cannot read running through the picture. There is an Elvish couple holding a small child surrounded by a crowd of smiling faces.

I imagine Codrin would wrap his arms around me and place me in his lap, looking over my shoulder, excited to hear a story I had read to myself more times than I could count. The tears are already welling up as I clear my suddenly dry throat.

"In a place, I do not know, and at a time, I do not know, a little elvish girl was born into a family who had nothing but love for her."

I turn to the next page, the father and mother smiling happily as they do daily chores and the child sleeps in a bassinet.

"An ordinary life was all they led, but happy nonetheless."

The next page shows three different panes. The first, the family's attention is drawn outside. The second, the scene turns to terror as images of villages burning and what looks to be the small family fleeing. The third, the man and woman grab the child and begin to run. I choke back my tears.

"Just as their future had once looked peaceful and full of happiness, tragedy struck. The world around them began to burn, and they ran for their lives."

Turning the page, the illustration becomes darker as the family gets separated by the masses running.

"Being pulled away from one another, hope seems to dwindle."

The following few panes on the next page show the woman traveling with the child until she finds herself in a large forest.

"Desperate to find shelter from the chaos she was trying to flee from, she wandered further away from her love. With her heart being carried in her arms, she felt vulnerable and terrified."

I turn the page again, the woman now praying over the child, when suddenly a light begins raining down on the young child's form.

"She prayed for her heart to be protected, to be safe from any harm."

Turning to the next page, it is full of several panes showing the woman leaving the child trekking through harsh environments. The woman ends up getting captured by a group of dark figures who take her and throw her somewhere dark and cold.

"Knowing her heart, her child, was safe, she went on a search for the piece of her she had lost—her other half." The words come out as a whisper. I close my eyes tightly, hugging the book close to my chest. Tears drip onto my lap. I let out a few shaky breaths before taking in a deep breath to steady myself.

I need to finish this.

"She never found him, though. They would be forever separated."

The next page shows images split into three columns, the first one of the child growing into a young elvish woman as she wanders the forest as if looking for something.

The page mirroring the last one is also split into three columns, a young human male sneaking through a stone building. The male eventually finds himself holding a very ornate silver ring that emanates light and has engravings similar to that of the books binding and borders.

"Two lives destined to intertwine, grow up on their own. Unknowing of their tethered strings and what fate awaits them."

Turning the page, the father, the lost love, is in the center of it. His face filled with agony, loss, and hatred. Behind him is a familiar village that shows a slow progression to a large city that frames his face.

"Him, having lost his other half, along with his heart, became a cold and spiteful man, who took back the very village that was once destroyed and made it into a lavish city."

The next few pages show the elvish woman and the human man both lost and eventually meeting. As they find their way, they stumble upon a city that is enslaved by its tyrant ruler.

"Not knowing the last of the very family she had been searching for resided on the throne, she swore to free the people she saw crippled by her father's ruling."

The very last page shows the grown daughter and the young human male figure walking together into the castle. The very last pane shows the human man impaling her father and the girl wearing the ring. She is raising it above her head, rays of light covering the people, healing them. The father is shown reaching towards his heart, smiling.

"Only the father knew that his heart would continue to beat as the steel penetrated his flesh. The world grew brighter, happier, and both the elvish woman and human boy lived the ordinary life her parents had once hoped and dreamed for."

I close the book gently and store it safely back into my satchel before I begin to sob, gripping my stomach tightly knowing our dream would never come true. The house we always imagined, somewhere far from everything else. Just us and the family we would have created.

"I'm so sorry, my love."

I whimper there alone.

ONCE FEELING returns to my body, I slowly stand and make my way back to the Clan. Their Maresal cannot be gone much longer. Climbing up, the gatekeeper quickly pulls me up.

"Lady Maresal. The First Lady is searching for you. She has men running through the forest."

My eyes widen, and I take off running towards the Command Post

Something is wrong.

I burst through the front doors, the post is completely empty. I don't stop to catch my breath as I run up the stairs to see Rose sitting at her desk, a letter crumpled in her fist.

"Rose ..."

I enter her office but jump back when I see Bren standing in the corner of the room. My breathing causes my chest to rise and fall heavily. I look between Rose and Bren, waiting for one of them to look towards me.

"I should have known. My lady ..."

Rose slams her hands on her desk, silencing Bren.

"This day was coming, Xylia. Don't let this fool convince you that it's all on him."

I look at the letter in her hand, an ominous air swirling around it.

"Rose."

She hands me the letter, and I quickly read it over.

THE SECOND PRINCE, BREN TORRIN, IS NOW STRIPPED OF HIS TITLE AND CONSIDERED A TRAITOR TO THE CROWN. ANY WHO HARBOR HIM WITHOUT NOTIFYING OUR KING WILL THEN BE VIEWED AS TRAITORS THEMSELVES. AS BY HIS ROYAL POWER, THE FEL WATCH HAS BEEN DISPATCHED AND WILL BE ARRIVING SHORTLY TO MONITOR FOR THE TRAITOR. THEY WILL BE EXPECTING ACCEPTABLE ACCOMMODATIONS.

LETTER APPROVED AND DISTRIBUTED PER HIS MAJESTY'S REQUEST

8TH KING OF FOSA, HENRY TORRIN

"Xylia," Rose says as I look up into her eyes. I can see an actual sadness I've only seen once before. "The Adamina Clan is no longer safe for you."

CHAPTER SIX

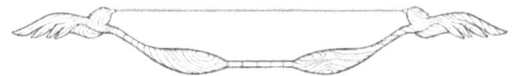

WHY?

My legs feel weak, my stomach turning. He's coming. He's sending people here. I don't want to go back there. I'm barely breathing as my eyes dart around the room, praying that something stands out, something that will give me strength and support because I know I won't survive this.

I drop the letter and back away, clutching my chest. Rose runs around the desk and wraps me in her arms. I breathe in shakily.

Everything is crumbling.

"I already have supplies and gear being packed for you. We have to move quickly." Her voice is soft, and she's shaking, too. Pulling away, she wipes her face quickly. I've only ever seen her sad once.

"Are you going somewhere?" Vasile's voice cuts through the room like a knife.

We all turn to see him standing there, looking between all three of us. My eyes begin to well.

"Vasile, this is a private meeting. You will wait outside until I ask for your presence."

He walks into the room. Rose's eyes widen as he disobeys her. She is going to have to tell him. *Tell them all how I will be leaving and never coming back. It's funny that Vasile asked* me *how I do it, but here is Rose, having to exile her own child.*

"I'm conflicted. My Maresal ordered me to stay by her side as a way to learn first-hand how she protects, serves, and cares for the Adamina Clan. Now, I'm ordered to not do that." A cocky smile resonates off his pretty-boy face making complete eye contact with Rose.

"As of tomorrow morning, Xylia will no longer be the Maresal of the Adamina Clan. Her order is void, so you may leave. Now."

Vasile's face drops in terror. He swiftly moves forwards and latches onto me. Though my heart is feeling the same terror, I pry his hand away. Biting my lip, I try to stop the tears that threaten to fall.

"Is this because of last night? We were all there, First Lady. I won't allow Xylia to take the fall for this!" His normally-charming self is replaced with a scared little boy. He clings to me tighter as I almost slip away.

"She will be leaving. Bren is to accompany her to the city of Stran, where from there she can do as she pleases, but her presence anywhere near here is a danger to the Clan."

"It will be a lot safer with us traveling together," Bren comments.

"Safer?" Vasile shouts.

What am I supposed to do?

I deserve this. I know that much, but my heart is being crushed, it's bleeding, and it's all my fault.

"Bren knows and is familiar with the kingdom," Rose says.

I can't control it anymore. I can't control the ground crumbling underneath me. My world is shattering.

Vasile drops his grasp on me and runs straight for Bren, who's eyes widen, seeing Vas's rapid approach. Vasile slams him against the bookshelf. I'm sure the bruising and still freshly dressed wounds are roaring in protest, but that doesn't seem to be stopping his rampage.

Bren grabs Vasile's shoulders and squeezes them tight to brace himself, letting go of the cane I did not realize he was holding.

"Why the hell did you come here! Just answer the question!" Vasile yells, spitting in the Prince's face.

Bren opens his mouth, no sound coming out.

"Answer it!" Vasile screams.

Bren begins to try and push off the bookshelf to gain dominance, but Vasile just slams him against it again. Bren lets out a low-pitched grunt as his eyes narrow and his brow furrows. The fear slowly turning to anger. Vasile leans in closer, their noses firmly pressed against each other. A growl escapes Vasile's lips, this time a fear washing over me.

"Vasile stop," I plead. I do not wish for him to lose his home too.

"Say it, you bastard! You owe us this. My mate died out there, and I am choosing to blame you. So say it!" Vasile's voice sends a chill down my spine.

It was blind of me to think he wasn't just in as much pain as me. Just as I am losing my home. He is losing me.

"For her! For her!" Bren barks, his head slowly turning towards me, "I came for you ..."

Vasile drops him.

Bren stumbles a bit with his leg still recovering. Vasile reaches down slowly and grabs the cane from the floor, shoving it into Bren's chest before taking a few shaky steps back. Vasile's blood is still boiling.

"My Lady, I've waited years to come find you. Waited until I could fulfill the promise I made to you back when we were youngins," Bren says in nearly a whisper.

"He told me the same story you told me all those years ago, Xylia. He is the servant boy, Kage, who saved you all those years ago when the King abducted you," Rose confirms, wrapping her arm around my shoulder.

I shake my head. Impossible. Kage is a popular name. He guessed the name. The boy I saw was skinny, sickly, and dirty. There's no way the Prince who stands before me today is the boy I met all those years ago.

"You're lying."

"I told you about the time I snuck into the Vermilion Forest and was nearly killed by a beast. I told you that story as I broke you out of your cell underneath the castle and showed you the path, the same path I used in the memory I shared," Kage explained, taking a step closer towards me. "I told you stories about the castle and my family. Stories I made up in the spot to help calm you down. You really liked the one about the birds and their kingdom they all fly away to when it gets cold."

My eyes begin to water, but I stifle the tears. He is not wrong. These are the same stories I had once heard, and fallen asleep to, when I was alone and terrified in a castle ruled by a Tyrant King. Kage was the one to help me escape.

Could it be him?

"You can trust me, Xylia."

Vasile quickly jumps in, stepping in between us, breaking the eye contact between Kage and me—Bren and me.

Vasile grabs me by my shoulders and looks me in the eyes as his eyes begin to water. "I can't lose you too. I'm not ready." He grabs my hand and places it over his heart, making my eyes well up.

"When we first met, Codrin and I swore that we would cherish what the other cherished, to love what the other loved, even hate what the other hated, so we would always be on the same page. When he took an oath to love you and protect you, I made that same oath, Xylia. I refuse to just let you slip away. I refuse to let anyone take you away."

Bren grips Vasile's wrist and begins to try and loosen his grip on me. Rose places her hands on my shoulders, pulling me backwards and away from Vasile.

I want to say, 'I understand Vas, I can feel the love Codrin shared for both of us.' Say that 'separating feels like we are losing him for good, that there will be nothing left of him.' Though that would just make this all the more challenging. I don't want—I can't have this be any harder.

Vasile shoves Bren back as Rose starts pushing me backwards towards the door. My time is up. If I don't leave now, I may never even have a chance of surviving. Whether Bren is Kage or not, Rose is right. I don't have to trust him, but I do need him. At least for now. Vasile and I remain in eye contact as I am forced to take each step.

"Vasile. You are ready," I say as I stop the two from pushing me back any further. I hear Rose scoff slightly under her breath, but I can't care about that now. "Tell Engel and Madi that I'm sorry that I had to leave, that I failed them. Please let them know that I am entrusting the future to the three of you." I turn and face the doorway, about to pass the threshold, before I look back over to a mess of a boy struggling to stand. "Oh, and Vas? Take care of the house, it's yours."

He nods, now kneeling on the ground. I face forwards, knowing he is going to have to watch me walk away.

"He is always going to be with us." I pound my hand to my chest before I descend the staircase, leaving him behind.

⇓

A part of me knows that this is what Rose and I had always planned for. One day the King and his men would show up, and I would have to leave the Clan behind. I just thought it would be Codrin that would be going with me, not a stranger I currently blame for taking everyone I love away from me. Not even a full day's cycle since the hunt, and I am having to say goodbye to everything I've ever known.

Brigs is already at the raft as Rose, Bren, and I arrive. Two horses, saddled and loaded up with packs and gear.

"The horses and supplies you requested, First Lady." Rose nods as Brigs hands the reins over to her.

He steps away, only briefly glancing over his shoulder with widened eyes, a look of curiosity towards Bren, but knows his place and continues to walk away.

"The supplies should last you a few days, so I'd recommend stopping in Ko before heading any farther. It will probably be your most dangerous stop, but let's hope the crowds keep you well enough hidden."

Bren and I nod, understanding. Rose quickly brings me into a hug before separating again now that we are in public. Showing affection to a soon-to-be-reject Clan member would not look too good on the First Lady.

"Maybe we will get to see each other again in another life, kiddo."

She pinches my cheek, something she used to do when I was young. Her way of saying I love you. It's comforting knowing that this is not what she wants to do. It's something she has to do, something *I* have to do.

72

"I don't think I can handle another life filled with your wrath."

She laughs and looks out at the top of the canopy. "Right."

She steps off the raft and walks over to the pulley system. She begins lowering us down and looks to Bren before she leaves our view.

"I'm leaving the rest to you."

It's a silent descent, neither of us really knowing what to say. I kick the wood planks with my boot, watching the forest trees in this view for the last time. The raft connects with the ground, and I guide our horses off from it, tugging on the rope to signal that it is safe to pull it back up.

"Are you going to be okay to ride with that?" I ask, pointing to his leg.

He shrugs his shoulders. I'm sure he's never had to put his body through this much stress all at once. I see a lot of breaks coming up in our future and sigh in anticipation.

I quickly look over what supplies and gear Rose provided. My heart soars seeing the Nightingale bow hanging from the other side of the horse. I quickly unhook it and swing it over my shoulder, immediately finding my quiver. Having this bow makes me feel a little more sure and confident.

We mount our steads and begin our long trek through the Vermilion Forest. It will take us at least a full day cycle and a half to reach Ko, and that's if we survive the one night we will have to spend in this forest unprotected. With Bren's leg and the horses, there is no chance of sleeping in the trees, and even worse, we are at a much slower pace. We will have to sleep on the ground, no fire to keep us warm through the night. Already, there is a soft cloud that appears every time I breathe out.

I lead Bren, keeping us closer to the roots of the trees to hide our hoof-prints. Bren tries to start conversations every so often, but his attempts are thwarted almost immediately. It baffles me how he got as far as he did all on his own without getting himself killed. The Capitol is nearly two weeks of travel if you are not stopping to rest.

We travel long enough to watch the sunshifts turn to moonshifts. I figure we could probably continue on for a few more shifts before I turn and see Bren nodding off atop his horse. I make a wounded bird cry to get his attention, signaling my hand for us to stop. I set up camp, laying us, so our backs are right up against the trees.

We begin our meal in silence. I light a small cooking fire for the meantime, but it'll die out soon enough, which will let the cold sink into our bones. I begin to think about our travels to another city. Now that I am leaving the Clan, hiding myself will become even harder.

I'm not supposed to exist.

No matter where I am, my ears will always give me away, not to mention the whole magicae powers and not being able to control them thing.

Though, what if I'm not the problem?

I can do my best to hide, but the Felguard Country is not looking for me. They are looking for him. His face is plastered on every statue and portrait of the eighth royal family. I unsheathe my dagger and hold it into the fire.

"Bren, how exactly are you planning to hide your face?"

His eyes perk up, thinking about it. "I figured growing out my facial hair would do it, likely cut my hair to fit in with the common folk."

I shake my head, knowing how quickly I could recognize him despite his roughed-up state. I point to the blemish by his left eye and wave the hot metal in my hand, hoping he gets what I am trying to suggest.

"You intend to mutilate me?"

"No, just put a scar on your face. The hair thing is a good idea too."

He shakes his head no, but it doesn't matter if he wants it to happen or not. If I have to lose everything, he can give up that pretty boy hair and face. A look of dread and fear flash across his face knowing it's going to happen anyway.

I grab his bedroll and stick a corner of it in his mouth to bite down on. Lowering the dagger close to his face, his eyes weld shut, and his body jarring. I line it up so the scar will heal alongside his cheekbone and less towards his actual eye. As I press the metal to his skin for a few seconds, I hear him scream against the cloth. Moving the fabric, his scream dulls into a breathless whimper. I grab my waterskin and pour some water onto it before placing a cloth over his wound, applying pressure until Bren is capable of doing it himself.

I won't lie and say I didn't get pleasure out of that. It takes him a couple of minutes, but he eventually sits up so I can cut his hair, leaving the top a little longer and his back cut short. It frames his face well, making him look less regal and more rakish, dashing. I bend down in front of him, brushing the long bits of hair away from his face.

"Go ahead and sleep. I'll keep an eye on things for a while. I'll wake you up when I need a break."

Bren looks up with his emerald eyes piercing through me. I'm sure it's anger that is running through them. He grabs my wrist as I back away. He opens his mouth to say something but shuts it. Letting go of me, he lays back, continuing to hold the cloth to his face.

Having the bedroll underneath is helping me generate some more heat which I am thankful for. The cold helps keep you cool on hunts, but just sitting here, the chill just settles. I fight the urge to close my eyes, but the dark and lack of adrenaline makes that easier said than done.

I allow my mind to wander for a bit, thinking of Codrin, Vasile, and Rose.

What craziness is going to happen when Rose announces my banishment to the Clan? What she will say and how she will say it? How will the Clan feel knowing Codrin is ... gone?

I try to imagine Vasile in all the Maresal apparel he will be given to wear daily. He'll no longer have to make those terrible fashion choices he normally makes with all the brown he likes to wear. The voice reaches out, but I push it away, not ready to acknowledge it after the chaos we caused.

I slap myself out of the guilt. Now is not the time to wallow in self-pity. Not with Bren depending on me to get him to safety, at least that's what I'm going to continue to tell myself.

As the night gets later and darker, I'm too tired to think until I hear what sounds like a horse approaching. I equip my bow slowly, notch an arrow, and wait. If it's wild, it won't mind us, but if it's a person, I better be ready in case they try to rob us. I can finally feel my heart pumping and my energy returning. As the horse comes into view, there is a cloaked figure bouncing up and down on the horse, traveling through the forest. They slow as they pass us. I take a deep breath, waiting to see what they intend to do. They make a complete stop as they notice me sitting there. I see their hood flip back, and I draw my arrow.

Vasile's hands swing up with a smile spread across his face. "Whoa there, I'm just a fella trying to find his friend."

My heart flutters hearing his voice, seeing his face. The sound of a voice wakes Bren up. He quickly recognizes the person in front of us to be Vasile, and his face expresses the same amount of surprise as my own.

Jumping up, I drop my bow as Vasile hops off his stead. I punch him in the shoulder, causing him to mouth the word 'ow.'

"What the infernum, Vas," I say in a hushed tone.

Vasile shrugs and walks over to get a closer look at Bren, who is still holding the now probably frozen cloth to his face. "Man, she got to you already, huh?"

"Is she always this controlling?" Bren asks.

"Oh, much worse. I shouldn't even mention that time where she had Codrin and I ..."

"I am not controlling. He needed to be unrecognizable," I say, trying to put it simply.

"We might want him to get a tattoo or something then. Like a skull for his face! You really wouldn't be able to tell then," Vasile exclaims excitedly.

"Do not give her ideas, I beg of you," Bren whines.

"Why are you even here? You are supposed to be protecting the Clan, not out here."

"I told you, I wasn't ready. To lose you or to take something like being the Maresal on. So, you have room for one more?" Vasile's explanation sounds more like an excuse.

"You are giving up everything, Vasile. Rose won't forgive you for abandoning the Clan," I say, trying to reason.

"It was my parent's choice to join the Clan. It is my choice to follow you wherever you may go." My heart swells as he gives me his signature smile. Vasile kneels down in front of me and pounds his hand to his chest and then to the ground. "I will follow my lady into the dark and slay the creatures, men, and beasts that may ever threaten her."

We both let out a whisper of a laugh. I gesture my hands towards the small little cove we are huddled in. Bren watches us confused.

Vasile lays out his bedroll and settles in. "It's my turn. A Lady needs her beauty sleep."

CHAPTER SEVEN

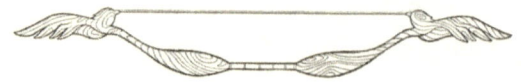

We arrive in the outlands of Ko late into the evening. The trees are now behind us, patches of farmland rest ahead. The last leg of this torturous journey with these boys has made me feel weak and more annoyed than I have ever been before. Between Vasile complaining every few minutes, Bren nearly stepping into every beast trap, and their constant bickering, I thought we may never make it.

Approaching the city's border, we hear the sound of carts and slamming doors, people shouting left and right about selling their wares, or to step off their feet. I pull up my hood and fasten it, so it doesn't fall down as easily. Luckily there are enough people around with their hoods up, so it doesn't make me look out of place.

We dismount when we get to the stable at the entrance of the city. There's a small elderly man hammering, looking like he is adding an expansion onto the current standing structure. From the looks of it, it is not the first one they have done.

As I watch the elder slowly climb down his ladder, a much younger but similar-looking man walks up to us. He chews on a small piece of straw, hanging from his mouth, spitting it out right before he reaches us.

"What can I do for ye?"

Bren steps forwards, a few coins already in hand. "Just wanting our beasts boarded for the night."

The man takes the coins and twirls them in his fingers. I look back to the elderly man who is slowly making his way over.

"Heh, don't worry, little lady. He may look old, but he be young here." He slaps his chest a few times where his heart is.

"With all the newcomers, we have been seeing a lot more visitors. Needing some more room!" The old man pipes in, a large smile on his face.

I smile back lightly, trying to ignore the fact he openly called me a 'little' lady.

They tell us to pick the horses up by the same time tomorrow or come back to pay for another night.

I glance over to Vasile, who is already peeking around the corner and into the city. Bren and I join him, and a goofy grin appears on Vasile's face. We begin walking through the streets, all keeping an eye out for someplace for us to rest for the night.

My breath catches as Bren pulls me closer to him. I look up at him and he pulls my cloak over my eyes. Irritation surging from within me, I throw my elbow back into his stomach. He crumples into himself a bit but doesn't let go. I try to see under the rim of the fabric. I don't see what got him so twisted. I wiggle a bit, fighting against his grip.

"Be still," Bren hisses.

"Piss off," I hiss back.

Vasile shoves Bren off of me, a few people around us giving us looks.

Vasile takes Bren's place, keeping a tight arm around me, both of them noticing something I have not.

"Sorry Xy, but he's right. Let's walk like this for a bit," Vasile whispers.

I relax and agree to keep from causing a scene.

Moving further in and tired of tripping over strangers' feet, I shift my hood back to its original resting place. Just enough to cover my ears. I begin to see splashes of color everywhere, banners waving the colors of the various cities and settlements over the Felguard country. Stalls with knick knacks and various foods. I start to notice eyes looking my way every so often, ugly smiles greeting me. A man reaches out with a knock-off-looking necklace praising its worth and claiming he dreamed of me wearing it last night. Bren steps in between us saying, 'not interested,' and we keep moving forwards. I pull the hood of my cloak tight to my head, now understanding the boy's reason to do it in the first place.

Killer beasts and demons in the night seem like better company than the people in this place. Adrenaline sparks through my nerves. We continue to push through the crowd before stumbling into a tavern or inn, I'm not sure which. I can't even see the name on the sign with so many people pushing in and out.

An older-looking woman with graying hair tied haphazardly up into a bun greets us unenthusiastically, barely looking us in the eyes. I move over to the bar, where there are a few seats left open.

"Kage, Vasile. Let's sit," I say, already taking my seat in the middle and ready to get away from the constant shoving. "Did either of you even look to see if this place has rooms?"

They follow suit to their seats. I grab a barmaid's attention, whose tired and panicked expressions are blatantly painted on her face, and order us all a drink.

Glancing around the place, I can see the majority of the furniture and seating arrangements seem to match but, due to the massive surge in population, there are multiple pieces that seem to stick out. A blue chair, in particular, stands out in a room full of dark oak wood furnishings. There are worn yellow tables in the back that don't seem to match either. Though the vermilion colored benches, the ones lining the walls, those are all too familiar.

Rose, this is the place, isn't it?

"I'll work on finding us a place to sleep. I do have the superior people skills anyway," Vasile says leaning in, interrupting my recall of memories.

"Sure, let's go with that," I say, pushing his face back.

The barmaid returns and throws us some steins filled to the brim with some dark mystery liquid that smells a lot worse than it tastes.

Reminds me of the first time I tasted alcohol. I thought I was gonna puke from the bitterness. Now my taste buds have grown quite immune to its bite.

Vasile makes a disgusted face, which warranted him a glare from the lady who served it. He smiles back as he tries to recover with those people skills. I look over to Bren, who is sipping his drink casually, observing the rest of the patrons here as he is turned around on his seat.

"I'm surprised a noble tongue such as yours can swallow this," I whisper, leaning in so only he can hear me.

He gives me a half-smile, charming, of course, and sets it down. "As a Prince, you get very used to doing things you don't want to," He whispers back, a sadness in his eyes.

The little hairs on my arms stand up. I hate that I find myself starting to trust Bren despite him being difficult to read. It's unusual for me to be unable to read someone. I've been watching everything he does, waiting for him to prove that I am right to have my guard up, that he truly is just the Second Prince of Fosa, and nothing more.

A small band begins to play, and the sounds of tables scraping across the floor fill my ears. I look to Vasile, whose face begins to light up. People of all shapes, sizes, and races jump onto the impromptu dance floor—they twirl and shake, beckoning their friends and partners to join them.

Bren glances over his shoulder before returning to focus on his cup.

My smile starts to emerge, watching the colorful array in front of me, but fades into a frown as my thoughts wander. Codrin would have loved this place. He loved to dance at the parties the Clan would throw. Closing my eyes tight, I imagine him standing in front of me like he used to, a sad face occupying his charming one until I would take his hand. He would twirl me around and hum along to the tune playing. We would smile and laugh until we felt our legs giving out on us.

I open my eyes to see Vasile with his hand outstretched towards me, offering a dance. His face is serious, with no smile or comment to make because I am certain he just imagined a similar scene. I take his hand slowly; he is not offering a dance with him but for Codrin instead.

As I stand, he twirls me around, forcing a laugh to appear. He smiles slightly and pulls me close to him, his arm around my waist and his head resting against my ear to make sure my hood doesn't fall. I wrap one arm around his neck, making me stand on my tiptoes. Our free hands intertwine together. He begins to hum terribly off tune but trying to do just like Codrin used to. He leads our steps. Vasile is surprisingly good at dancing. I hold onto him tighter, tears in my eyes.

"He would be so jealous. It always took him at least a moonshift to get me onto the dance floor."

Vasile laughs, knowing all too well just how upset Codrin would get if I denied his invitation. He would often convince

Vasile to talk me into the idea that having fun was a normal thing.

"Thank you, Vasile."

"This is for both of us, My Lady. This is for Codrin."

We continue to dance and dance until I feel myself grow exhausted, even more than I already was. Vasile walks us back to our stools, where Bren appears to have watched us, a small smile on his lips. Feeling parched, I promptly finish my drink.

"I should warn you to slow down. I am finding out for myself that this beverage is far stronger than it seems."

I roll my eyes and look at Vasile, who has been drawn over by a very pretty-looking couple sitting at a table a little aways from us. Turning back to Bren, he's also looking at Vasile.

"Does that make you jealous?" Bren asks with a raised brow as he leans back, looking towards the overworked barmaid, and orders us another round. It takes her only a moment before she slams the next round down.

I cock my head to the side curious why he would ask something like that, but remember that he doesn't know us. Bren's attention turns back towards me. His eyes sparkling for a moment.

"He is," I pause, knowing what I said was a lie. "He ... was ... my partner's closest friend. Though Vas and I have always had a sibling type of rivalry fighting for Codrin's attention." I smile into my cup, remembering the constant play bickering.

Bren's shoulders relax a bit. I clear my throat, realizing what I just said out loud.

We sit silently for a while, watching Vasile flirt and the patrons either dance, laugh, or argue. I didn't realize how tense my shoulders were until I feel them drop. Nor did I notice that my seat is uneven. I begin to shift my weight from one side to the other, causing the chair to lean with it.

Kage—Bren—looks at me with an amused smile.

"Have you been to Ko before?" I question. "You seem to know your way around the city. It seems a lot more crowded than I ever imagined it could be. The stories I was told about the number of people here now feel undersold."

Bren shakes his head, eyes on the dance floor.

I stare at my drink until it's gone, jumping at the sudden screams, my eyes darting to women's skirt being lifted by the men they are keeping in their company.

My patience is tested when more than two drunks spill a bit of their drinks on me. Bren orders us another round. For how busy it seems, the service is impeccable, almost immediately waiting for us.

I look around for Vasile as I just am noticing that his spirited personality has been missing. It takes me a moment to find it, but the mop of blonde hair is there in the corner talking to a new guy whose smile takes up his entire face. I let out a laugh seeing Vasile swoon him so easily.

"What's so funny?" Bren asks, breaking his focus and arching one eyebrow.

I smile into my cup and point over to Vasile. Bren looks in the direction and blurts out with the same laugh I just had.

"That definitely settles that. I don't care about the cost. We are all getting separate rooms."

"Here, I thought we were going to try to be conservative. Either way, Vasile is the one who has the money for the rooms. It'll be up to him to decide your fate for the night."

Kage lets out a sigh before taking a long drink.

I start to feel a warmth spread across my body. It's been a long time since I've drunk anything this strong. I can't even taste it anymore.

"This place reminds me of the stories my mothers used to tell me, from before the Clan existed," I admit with a small smile on my face.

He tilts his head as I point to a couple who are drunkenly dancing and singing. I remember the many stories Rye would tell me of the olden days of her and Rose. I could hardly believe them since I never even witnessed Rose tapping her foot. She hasn't left since the accords were signed, but she's never forgotten this place and the memories she's had.

I take another big drink as Bren happily watches the couple.

"I can't imagine Lady Rose being so relaxed," he says with a laugh under his breath.

Well, I doubt she could be at this point, but from what the stories say, she used to be quite the firecracker. She never let anyone tell her she was wrong or what to do—danced on tables and sang out of tune—type of woman. I mean, she went out and started her own sanctuary for those looking for a place with no stigmatisms and where they can live in semi-peace. Not having to live under the fist of some crown, who only sees people as gold.

Though, I'll keep that thought to myself since I'm sitting with said crown now.

I feel a breath blow against my neck. I jump, spinning around to see goofy-grinned Vasile now chuckling.

"Sorry, couldn't help myself." A short hiccup follows Vasile's excuse.

He hands Bren and me both a key, a room for him and Bren, and a room for me. Bren is wide-eyed, knowing very well what Vasile will be doing in there in a few short moments.

We notice a familiar guy with his arms wrapped around Vasile's waist and his lips on Vas's neck. "The rooms were incredibly hard to get, so I better be receiving some praise!"

I pat Vasile's head, which seems to have covered for the praise, as he places his hands on my knees and lowers his head into my palm.

"Behave yourself, you people person."

Vasile leans in close, kissing my cheek goodnight before wrapping his arms around the guy, both of them disappearing into the crowd. The old Maresal in me would want to stop him from running around, but we are all on the run now. I'll let him live his life as long as it doesn't get any of us killed.

"So looks like you'll be keeping me entertained while I have to wait for those two to finish their business," Bren says with a smile.

"Scared to be left alone?"

"More like I enjoy your company."

I roll my eyes. I think it's him who has had too much to drink. I don't think I'm great company in the slightest right now.

This is okay, though. He seems less of a Prince, more like the Kage I met as a youngin.

Bren orders us another round as I catch sight of a few guys at the bar, looking over at me. I try to focus on the people still dancing, but the guys start to approach. I shift in my seat, feeling pinned down with their attention.

"Hey gorgeous, why are you hiding that pretty face?" One of the guys asks.

He grabs my hood with his massive hand, but I grip his wrist and twist it, forcing him to let go. As the man is hollering in pain, I glare up at him.

A familiar arm quickly wraps around me as a fist grabs hold of the man's shirt.

"Do not touch her," Bren growls at him. He quickly throws his only hand up to ward off any problems, and both of the men wander away, grumbling to themselves.

"I could have taken them."

The problem was already being handled. Since leaving the

Vermilion Forest, these two boys seem to think I am at some disadvantage. It is infuriating.

"Not the point."

"What is the point?"

"That we want to avoid attention."

"I'm not stupid. I meant the point to living, like they do."

Bren pauses and stares at me, maybe waiting for me to continue a thought, but I forgot what I was saying. He looks away, handing the drink he ordered, and takes a sip.

"Where did you run off to the other day?"

I don't answer, confused by the question.

"Rose had everyone out looking for you. Where did you go?"

Oh.

"To show Codrin something I should have shown him a long time ago." That's not what I wanted to say, but I guess I said it.

Bren leans down and looks directly into my eyes. "He's the one that passed, right? The partner you refer to?"

I grab his ear, and he winces. "What about him?" My voice is raspy and nearly breaks away at the end. Like I need to be reminded that he is gone.

"I just want to better understand."

"He was my everything." I drop his ear and look away, not in the mood to cry, be upset—be anything.

He leans back and takes a heavier drink from his cup. "Right, that's what I thought. I wanted to make sure your heart was taken."

I turn to him with a bewildered look.

"Didn't want you falling for my handsome face and gentlemanly charms."

I burst out laughing, louder than intended.

Bren grabs my drink with an amused smile on his face,

setting both of our drinks on the bar. He asks the Barmaid where the lodging area is, and next thing I know, I'm being corralled like an animal up the stairs.

A rush of paranoia washes over me as we near one of the bedroom doors. Slamming my foot onto Bren's makes him yelp. I grab his hair and pull his head back, forcing him to drop to his knees. I almost fall over myself with how much the room seems to be spinning, but I keep my composure.

"Just because Codrin isn't with us anymore doesn't mean he is gone. Take your witless charms and go to sleep!" I say before trying to unlock my door.

Bren climbs to his feet behind me before bursting out laughing. I turn around, and in my frustration, throw the keys at his head. He catches them before hitting their target, making him laugh even harder.

"Whoa there, my Lady, I was escorting you to your chambers. Just because I am without a castle does not mean I live without my manners."

He dangles the key in front of me before opening the door and pushing it open. He gestures for me to enter while holding out the key for me.

A little embarrassed, I grab the key and walk into the low-lit room. Though I am still brewing over him laughing at Codrin's missingness. His goneness. That he's gone.

"Good, because I'd hate to have to kick your royal ass," I say with a devilish smirk.

Bren puts a finger to my lips, trying to quiet me. He begins pushing me into the room and eventually down onto the bed. He pulls off my hood before kneeling down. I try kicking him away, but he catches my foot and unlaces my boots. Bren moves up and begins to unbuckle my chest armor, but I grab his wrist. Smiling up at me, he breaks free of my weak grasp and pins them to my sides.

"Remember, gentlemanly."

He finishes unbuckling and orders my hands up before pulling it off of me, leaving me in my tunic and trousers. Shoving my shoulders down, he swings my legs onto the bed, turning me completely. He pulls the blanket out from under me and throws it on top of me.

"There. All tucked in."

I groan with irritation. My head is spinning worse than it was before. I feel for my satchel and panic as it is not on my person. I sit up, an upsetting feeling stirs in my stomach as I do, and see it's all piled up against the wall next to the door. He must have had my things in his hands.

I didn't even notice.

"My stuff," I mumble as I try to get up, though Bren places his hand on my shoulder and smiles.

He walks across the room, picking up my satchel and weapons, bringing them to the side of the bed. I take the bow from his hands and lie down. I place the bow down in bed next to me, where Codrin should be, and run my fingers over one of the carved nightingales.

"Leave now," I whisper, tears beginning to prick my eyes.

I don't want him to see me weak ever again.

He smirks and makes his way over to the door. I don't even hear him close it before my eyelids become as heavy as stone.

Just as I begin to drift off, I hear a tap on my door. I quickly reach for my knife and half-drunkenly stumble my way to the door. I try to listen for claws of an animal or the rustle of weapons but I only hear heavy breathing. I open the door quickly, knife forwards just in case. My jaw drops as I see him standing there with a bag packed, a smile that melts me to my core, and tiny beads of sweat dripping down his beautiful face.

"I'm sorry it took me so long to get here. I ran as fast as I could."

I wrap my arms around Codrin and kiss him deeply. He pulls me close, spinning me around, matching my glee. It kills me to pull away, but I need to see his face again.

"How are you here right now?" I ask breathlessly.

He leans in for another kiss, one far more gentle and sweet. "I've always been right here."

I pull away once more, a smile I felt I'd never wear again returning to my face. As I look into his eyes, there is nothing but darkness. I step back as flames engulf him and his screams begin shaking the room. I go to reach out, but he turns to ash in my hands.

I wake trembling, my hair sticking to my face as tears stream down my cheeks. Making my way over to the side table, there is a pitcher with water and a bowl. I pour the water into the bowl and splash the water on my face. Steadying myself on the table, I try to control my breathing.

"What the hell is happening?"

I slap myself a few times, trying to get the horrifying images out of my head.

I don't think I'll be drinking again.

Turning around, the blue book is open on the floor. Climbing into bed, I grip the book tight. It now feels more like Codrin than the fantasy I once lived in when reading it. I hold it close to my chest along with the bow, hoping they both might bring me some solace.

There really isn't anything extraordinary about me, is there?

A hero, *ha.* What did my birth parents think when they left me with it? Was it so they would make me feel special or any more wanted by them? All they did was curse me with the magicae that runs through my blood instead of being around to teach me how to use it. I'm no less of a monster than the ones I've spent my life hunting.

There's another knock at my door. Setting the book down

on the bedside table and resting the bow on the floor, I brush my hands through my hair a few times. I freeze as I begin to take a step towards the door. An uneasy, almost terrifying feeling that the nightmare I just experienced is a never-ending cycle.

"Xy, open up. It's me," Vasile hisses through the door.

I shake off the horror on my face and open the door with a fake groggy expression.

"I know, I know it's late."

I gesture for him to come inside. "What's up?" I ask, crossing my arms and leaning against the wall. Relieved to not be in the room alone after seeing *that*.

"I know we had our hearts set on heading to Stran from here, but there is a huge caravan headed to Jod. It's right on the border, and we'd be blending in with others," he says excitedly.

His cheeks are rosy as a hiccup comes out of his mouth.

"You hear this from that guy?" I ask, skeptical.

He shakes his head and sits down on the bed, taking his boots off.

"There were these guys talking downstairs. Some rich merchant hired them to transport some goods or something. That cute guy, though, was the one who introduced me to the caravan leader. The couple I talked to introduced me to the hottie. They were nice."

Another hiccup.

He lays down with an exhausted sigh, and before I can even protest, I hear his heavy snores. I sigh as I push the curly hair out of his face before throwing the blankets over him. I take a seat at the chair in the corner of the room and wait for daylight.

I wonder what Vasile thinks of Kage-Bren.

SITTING in the chair all night made my back impossibly stiff. I don't even think I can stand. My moans and groans stir Vasile awake. He sits up slowly, rubbing his eyes, and stretches out as if he just experienced the best sleep of his life. I clear my throat, startling him, as he has yet to recognize he is not in his room.

"Holy Awemother, Xy! Why are you just watching me?" he swears. Rubbing his eyes once more, he takes a look around the room. Realization crosses his face.

He hops off the bed and bows towards me.

"I was watching a drunken boy climb into my bed and fall asleep when I got lost in thought. I was thinking about all the terrible things I could do to him," I say with a wicked grin on my face.

Vasile looks up guilty but tries to play it off as nonchalant. "You know, I am just so comforted by your presence, my Lady."

I nod slowly as I listen to him try and work his way out of this.

"My drunken state must have just been so desperate to see someone so beautiful that I came up here without a second thought! Yeah, that's it."

He stands up and walks out of the room backwards. As he reaches the doorway with only his head sticking in, he cowardly throws in, "I just need to go, freshen up. I'll make sure they have breakfast waiting for you. Also, flowers, maybe a necklace. I'll just go buy whatever I think you'd like."

I definitely needed that after the night I had. I'm thankful Vasile came though. I can't imagine my night being any better having been alone.

My bones creak as I move over to the bed, wanting to shut my eyes for a few minutes. Except, Bren comes walking through the door. He glances back at the door, his brows furrowing. Apparently, Vasile didn't lock the door on the way out.

I don't bother to sit up. I just look at him from under the covers.

Bren points to the door, his eyes remaining on me. Breaking eye contact, I roll over.

"Restless night, My Lady?"

I simply shake my head no, hoping that will be the end of it.

"Oh well, I was hoping to go over something with you that Vasile mentioned to me last night."

Now, I sit up.

"Did you send him in here?" I ask, but the words come out more as a guttural growl.

Bren's eyes enlarge as he hears my unsatisfied words. "No, but I see this is not the appropriate time to discuss things."

He backs out of the room in a similar fashion to Vasile. As the door shuts, I throw my face into the pillow and let out a loud groan.

I WAKE MORE rested and no nightmares to remember. Before leaving the room, I pull my hood up tight, then make my way downstairs, ready to find the boys and give them hell. I take a peek around the common area and see a larger group of men laughing boisterously—Vasile among them.

Instead of joining, I sit at a table within earshot as I order my breakfast. A group of attention-seeking men is not what I should be jumping into right now. I lean back in my chair with a gentle smile as the same woman who served us last night delivers my meal with that ever-loving frown. I don't blame her though, working a sun and moon shift back to back like that seems terrible.

I watch the bar's patrons come in and out, some already passed out from the ale, their cups laying sideways and empty. I try to suppress my laughter and judgment but fail in brief moments of unfortunate spills, mistaken fondlings, and pure idiocy. Sitting alone in a place that, even during sun hours is busy, allows me to relax a bit. No one seems to be minding me or the mysterious ambiance, I am probably giving off.

My curiosity is piqued as I hear a large grey Orc with a few Dwarves sitting at one of the round tables mention King Torrin and the Capital.

"Another tax raise. This Magicae army he keeps blabbing about is driving me crazy. By the time that tyrant is satisfied, there will be no people to protect."

"Where is he even getting these wizard folk? He's had to of collected every last one in the Felguard country at this point."

"More and more people are fleeing the Capital as we speak due to the restrictions he's putting on the kingdom. Ko and Kel aren't meant to be holding this many people."

"Of course not. Even being a major city, it can't take in the mass of another large city without notice. Let's just say we are lucky Kel is taking some of the overflow." They all nod and grunt in agreement to the Orc who made the last statement of that topic before moving on to a more grotesque subject.

I know of the King's obsession with Magicae. I was the start of it.

"Xy!" I jump hearing Vasile shout. He excitedly gestures for me to join him and his newfound friends.

I sigh and stand, making my way across the floor.

"These are the guys I was telling you about, the caravan."

"I'm surprised you remember anything from last night from the way you handled your drinks. I thought you would have forgotten your name," I say with an arched brow.

A couple of the guys laugh. Vasile squints his eyes into a scowl but takes it.

"Yeah, yeah. Anyway, they said they wouldn't mind if we

tagged along since we pretty much would be handling ourselves. Just safer in numbers."

"You mentioned that a merchant was the one paying for this caravan to travel to Jod?" I ask.

They nod in agreement.

"What are you transporting exactly?"

"Some materials for a Forged Magicae user that lives in the Hunter Territory. We are only passing through Jod."

"So if something were to happen, and the caravan was attacked, would we too be compensated for our heroic acts?" I hope they can see where I am going with this.

They all look at each other for a moment before a large green orc steps forwards.

My hood nearly falls from tilting my head as I look him directly in the eye, unintimidated by his size.

"We are offering a favor, little girl. I wouldn't push your luck."

I let a chuckle slip from my lips as he stares down at me.

"You are saying we can walk behind you while you move in a direction. It's us who are doing you a favor, offering extra hands if something tragic were to happen. I'm not saying we need a cut just for making it there, but if I have to save you from a **snapper** or bandit. Then, there's something to be owed." I cross my arms.

We stand there looking at each other for a minute before a smile breaks across his face. He pats my shoulder and laughs.

"Nice to see such a woman in charge. I'll agree to those terms, not like it's money coming out of my pocket. Now I'm almost hoping there's a fight. Would love to see ya work." He winks at me and pushes Vasile lightly, almost putting him in his place for me.

"Heh, I'll keep that in mind. When are you heading out?"

"At the beginning of this next cycle. It'll be a few days till then. Let me know if your crew will be joining us."

I nod in agreement. Vasile drops his shoulders a bit and we head back to the table I was eating at.

"I keep coming up short," Vasile mumbles.

I slap the back of his head while shaking my own. "No. You just are not seeing the whole picture yet. There is always more to a deal than a simple trade-off. As Maresal, you'll have to," I pause, realizing that he isn't my mentee anymore, "you did fine, Vas. We need to think this through first. Let's go out and train for a bit. It'll help us clear our heads."

A big smile appears on his face, like a little boy ready to take on the **vitaterrium**.

We get changed into some more durable wear and head out to the fields, making sure to leave Bren a note since he wasn't in his room. The large hill that divides the Felguard Country in half seems like the perfect place to spar just outside the city. No peering eyes to watch too closely and notice something I don't want them to.

Vasile whines, knowing he will be climbing right back up the hill every time he tumbles down. I raise my dagger to his short sword.

"You aren't taking it easy on me, are you?" he says, sizing up my chosen weapon.

He is clearly excited, bouncing from one foot to the other, to take whatever advantage I give him.

He swings at me, but I take a step back, hearing it ring through the air. I slash my blade towards him, making him swing his sword arm away from me, leaving an open space to his chest. I kick him hard, taking advantage of the uneven hill. He quickly loses his footing. He falls to a knee, catching himself from tumbling down the hill.

I chuckle a bit, watching him dust off his chest. I raise a

brow as he looks up, slightly panting from me kicking the air out of his lungs.

"Definitely not taking it easy, Xy."

"Never."

He smirks and stands, readying himself.

We continue to swipe at each other, Vasile getting dirtier with every false swipe he makes and every victory I tally.

"Okay, I think I've gotten shown up more times than I can handle," he says, sheathing his sword.

As he heads down the hill, I put my foot out. Vasile trips over it, tumbling down the hill. I join him though, rolling myself down, and we meet at the end laughing.

When we get back to the tavern, I can finally read the sign: **The Slattern**.

Very fitting indeed.

The streets are less crowded in the early afternoon, which I am very thankful for. Heading in, Bren is sitting at a table with a few maps and pieces of parchment sprawled out.

"Are you trying to find some buried treasure?" Vasile asks, joining him at the table.

I walk around and peek over Bren's shoulder, seeing a bunch of scribbles that I'm sure make sense to him. Vasile sits down at the table with Bren and starts picking up some of the papers.

Bren sighs and stops what he is doing. He looks up at me with his brows crossed, eyes narrowed.

"I'm trying to work, and your pet dog is getting into my things," Bren says, pointing to a taken aback Vasile.

"I'm a dog? You're the one whining," Vasile comes back, crinkling the papers in his hands.

"Such a clever fellow." Bren gives Vasile a smirk and looks back at me, his smile fading quickly.

"I think we should move this conversation into my room." I

grab Bren's arm, but he pulls away to collect his belongings.

Vasile jumps up right away and begins to help him. I must have had inferum fire burning in my eyes to get such a reaction.

We all head up the stairs and funnel into my tiny room. The three of us barely fit. I shove Bren and Vasile down onto the bed as I stand over them.

"I am not going to listen to you two bicker, nor am I the one taking orders," I growl at both the boys. I point my attention to Vasile. "Vas, I'm thankful you were able to show some of that leadership potential, but out here, we all need to be on the same page."

Vasile leans back, his eyes darting to the ground.

I quickly turn to Bren, whose eyes are already telling me he is prepped with some princely talk, but I'm not going to give him the time. "And you, newbie. You might be used to getting your way, not sharing your room, but you are here now. You agreed to go on the run, so stop acting like a prince and start acting like a man who has to survive."

Both of them are quiet, neither meeting my gaze.

I'm taking my hurt out on them, but they are acting like children.

"Vasile came up with going to Jod?" Bren asks.

"Yeah, I did. Henry was telling me about the old magicae training grounds they had there," Vasile says, looking at me. "Xy, I don't want *that* night to ever happen again."

"**Lunamatrem**, please give me strength," I whisper to myself, pressing the bridge of my nose with my index and thumb finger.

Does he think I'm wanting something like that to happen?

"Well, I know that Jod is not going to be impacted by the immigration like Ko and Kel currently are. It is also where Felguard keeps most of its magicae history, with the Countries largest Library residing there," Bren mentions.

"Rose planned for us to arrive at Stran. She gave us a list of contacts that are all expecting our arrival. A library is not a good enough reason to take a detour."

"Xylia, I saw what you could do out in those woods. I've studied magicae my whole life, and it is not something many people possess. You have more of it than I think this country has ever seen, maybe even the realm." I throw my hand up, cutting Bren off.

Vasile begins nodding his head in agreement.

They won't be able to understand.

"I'm going to have to split the both of you up if you are going to team up against me," I say, furrowing my brows.

"Imagine if I was given a sword but never taught how to properly use it. Bren is telling you he can help you learn how to wield it. This was something he mentioned the night of the hunt, and when Henry started telling me about the history of Jod, I knew it's where we needed to go," Vasile says, standing up and grabbing my arms gently. "Let us help you for once."

He is always so easily swayed by the romantics of things.

I sigh. "You both cannot comprehend how chaotic Magicae is. A few days of learning how it works has nothing to do with what's actually happening to me on the inside."

Bren stands this time.

The thought of hearing the voice without losing my mind or pouring everything I have into something—Bren's eyes lock onto something, pulling me from my thoughts.

I turn around and see my book sitting on the bedside table. He gets up and goes to grab it, but I grip his wrist instead.

"It's a book," I say.

He is persistent, as if in a trance, reaching with his other hand, tugging it towards him.

I let go as he begins to flip through the pages. My heart races seeing someone other than me even holding it.

I'm curious to know what is going through his head, though.

"Why does he get to touch your book?" Vasile whines.

My foot begins to tap as I impatiently wait for him to set it down. Instead, his page flipping slows.

"Xylia, are you aware of what this is?" he asks, turning to me with it open. "It's an oracle book. It's meant to show you, metaphorically, a path or journey you take in your life. Do you see these runes?"

My heart is racing now as I look at the page he's on.

Is this real?

He points to a symbol on one of the structures in the book.

"I wanna see!" Vasile jumps up, yanking the book from Bren, whose eyes are now fixated on me.

Bren holds up his hand that is adorning a silver ring. It has the similar symbols engraved on it and a faint glow, just like on the page.

I take his hand to get a closer look at the ring.

How did I not notice this?

"That's kinda freaky," Vasile whispers.

"When I first put this ring on, I saw quick bright flashes of a blue leathered book and golden blonde hair. I thought it was my imagination, but when I saw it just sitting there and you standing next to it ..." his voice trails off into the same disbelief I am feeling right now.

"So, you're saying, this is us?" The words barely escape my lips.

All those years, constantly daydreaming of being the hero in the book I always thought was for me—it's all real. I want this to be real.

Vasile closes the book, his eyes twitching between me and Bren and back again.

"This is what we are meant to do, Xylia—together," Kage whispers.

CHAPTER EIGHT

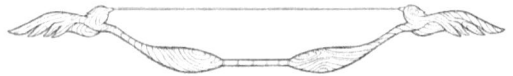

With our horses saddled and our bags packed, we await the rest of the group before heading on our long journey. It should take us a little over a full moon cycle to get to Jod, as long as everything goes smoothly. As we travel, I discuss the route with Hershaw, the large green orc, I spoke to yesterday. Kage and Bonji join in. Bonji is Hershaw's right-hand man. He's a gnome and could ride on Hershaw's shoulder if he wanted to. Their dynamic is hilarious but works. Hershaw is the opposing and dominant type, while Bonji is the soft and kind-hearted one.

"It'll be ready, and we be on our way once them get back here with food for the trek," Bonji chirps in.

"Wonderful. I need to grab something before we head out, so I'll do that now," Kage says, turning and walking away from the group.

"Care if I join?" I ask, not having seen more than the Slattern.

Kage nods with a smile, and I flock to his side.

We walk around the city, moving through the crowds until we come across an old, run-down building.

"I think this is the place."

I turn to him with a slightly confused look since a place like this doesn't seem like it would be on a Prince's list of places to visit.

As we head inside, the noise from outside fades away. The smell of lemon and lavender fills my nostrils. Looking around, there are shelves to the ceiling of different knick knacks, goods, and curious items. My smile grows as I approach one of the shelves. I run my hand across the coarse wood as I admire some of the ugliest-looking items I've ever seen.

Teapots with misshapen spouts, mirrors with horrific warfare as their frames, and books with humorously terrible titles.

I look back to Kage, who has an amused expression written all over his face. I drop my hand and raise an eyebrow at him.

He can tease all he wants; this place is something else.

It shocks me that a Prince, who lived in the Capitol the majority of his life, wouldn't find this fascinating.

As I am about to round the corner, a small, older, gnomish woman pops out in front of me with a very large broom in hand.

"What do you want?"

I glance down at her. She's wearing large round glasses, and her silver hair runs down the length of her back, tied at the bottom with a red string. She is wearing a yellow and red fota; the designs embroidered on her skirt are reminiscent of those we wear in the Adamina Clan. Rose knows this country's history well and integrated what she could into the Adamina Clan. It's not surprising seeing someone this woman's age wearing more traditional clothing like we do back home. Rose mentioned a long while ago that there is still a generation out there that clings onto the old ways.

I shake my head, bringing me back into the moment as

Kage steps forwards. The woman's eyes quickly glance over to him before returning to me with an even deeper glare.

I guess she didn't like that I was touching things.

"I apologize if we startled you. My Lady and I are here to see if your fine establishment would have any supplies for us. We are headed on a long journey."

The woman glances over to Kage again before hitting my leg with the broom lightly.

"What was that for?"

"This way," she yells, before she scurries away behind other shelves.

I look to Kage with wide eyes in concern and hilarity. He places his hand briefly on my shoulder with a chuckle stuck in his throat before taking the lead once more and following her.

After looking around corners and listening for her shouts, we find the woman at a large counter in the back of the store. In front of her, she has been setting out items for us to look through. She definitely didn't waste a second. Laid out before us are mysterious liquids, balms, food rations, waterskins, and packs. Kage looks over the items carefully, asking for prices and bargaining to fit these items into our limited budget.

As I listen to them chat, I look around the room again. Some weapons are hanging on the wall and different parts of creatures are mounted. I walk over to a glass display and take a peek at some of her higher-priced items. There are some gems and expensive-looking jewelry, but there is also a scroll with strange writing.

I have seen those similar markings hundreds of times before.

I quickly pull out my book, but my attention is drawn away when Kage calls my name to look at arrows.

"I'm sorry to interrupt the sale but the scroll in that case," I say, pointing in the direction of where it is.

Her tiny eyes suddenly turn large as she scurries over to where I'm pointing.

"This would be a rare magic scroll, from many sidereal years before even I walked this realm," she says.

It takes me a lot of strength not to ask her age, but I manage to push through.

"Do you mind if I look?"

She squints at me but nods slowly in agreement. I open my book and begin comparing the writing on the pages' borders to that of the scroll's content. A ringing begins to echo in my ears as I lean in closer, trying to match letters and handwriting. The pages are saying something; the golden text wasn't for decoration but a description of the images.

Before I can focus too much, I feel a wack against my head. The older woman is now standing on the counter, looking at me with concern.

Kage rushes over. "Xylia," he whispers, gripping me gently.

I look around. Items from a few of the shelves are scattered all over the floor, my blue book amongst them. Dropping the scroll, I take a few steps back. Kage lets go of me and picks up my book, placing it on the counter before putting his hands on my arms again.

I didn't even feel my power that time.

I had no idea I was even using it. I've never experienced something like this. The light has always felt borrowed, but my ability to move things was—is—has always been, mine. I control my heavy breathing before looking back over to the woman.

"I, I apologize," I whisper.

She nods her head slowly and hops off the counter towards me, holding the book in her hands. My heart drops seeing her tiny fingers grip it so tightly. Suddenly, she rips my cloak off, gasping as she stares at my ears.

"So, you are a magicae user, and an Elf at that," she exclaims.

The woman motions for me to kneel. Hesitantly, I do—Kage's hands never leaving my arms. She leans in, reaching out to touch my ears. As I lean back, she continues to lean forwards with a smile now spreading ear to ear, the wrinkles on her face more apparent than the first time I looked at her.

Kage tightens his grip around me as her face is mere inches from my own.

"You were most likely trying to absorb the magicae from the scroll. Normally, I don't need to worry about such things since there are very few of you left, and that applies to you twice," she says, her pointed finger in my face.

I look at Kage, who is scowling at her.

"Do you know anything about magicae?" I ask. If she has something that will help me, I'd gladly take it.

"Only what is really taught in communities like the one I grew up in. Magicae being a trait passed down by blood. Elves were the original ones blessed with the Awemother. The humans forgot that the doorways to the other versions of our Vitaterrium are what kept magicae alive in this one."

"We should just grab these arrows and go," Kage says, standing up and dropping more than enough coins to pay for a bundle of arrows.

The woman withdrawals herself and steps away from me.

"Do you think the scroll and my book could be from the same time?"

A bell rings towards the front of the shop, sweeping us all back to the present.

She looks back at me, though, and takes my hands. "This world is a dangerous place."

Just like that, she scurries off to go help her next customer.

As we return, Vasile and the rest of the caravan are just finishing their preparations for the journey. Kage and I don't say anything regarding the shop. I do my best to secure my hood to my head with some string I have left in my bag.

"It's such a shame you hide that pretty face of yours," Hershaw jokes as he gallops past me to take the lead of the group.

I roll my eyes and start moving towards our destination.

Vasile rides up to my left and gives me a 'can do' attitude smile. "Where did you guys disappear too?"

"Just some store to grab some arrows. How was your romantic farewell?" I ask, giving him a smirk.

"It's nice to know I'll be missed," he says with his chest puffed out, and head held high.

I walk up and ruffle his hair before grabbing my horse, the women's words echoing in my mind. I tighten my fist on the reins. I'm not exactly sure what happened back in that shop, but in that one moment, it tells me that I am just scratching the surface.

There's so much more to learn about the power I have running through my veins.

We ride until nightfall, where we find ourselves camping on the side of the trade route. The caravan stays right next to the road, but the three of us venture a little further towards the hill for some privacy. I get our fire set up while Kage rolls out the bedrolls, and Vasile hangs our stuff up in the tree near us.

Kage and I haven't spoken since getting back from the shop.

I hate that Vasile and Kage were right. I know nothing of the magicae that courses through me despite using it. Rye and Rose knew a few things, but it was all first-hand information they learned along the way while training me.

Vasile disrupts my thoughts as he throws me my portion of the provisions for the night. We all sit by the fire and begin eating in silence. Kage seems to be going over maps and reading out of some unmarked book, while Vasile hardly touches his food, looking out onto the hill lands.

"Everything okay?"

Vasile quickly recovers from his daze and looks over to me with his signature smile. He takes a big bite out of the jerky he has in his hand, his eyes squinting shut.

"Of course!" he says with his mouth full.

"You looked lost in thought."

"Was thinking of Madi."

Kage looks up from his book, closing it with a sigh. "Was this that boy you saw last night?"

Vasile looks to Kage with a curious look. "Do you care?"

"Not really, but if you miss him that much, you should probably just head back."

Vasile leans closer to Kage, who backs away. "Feeling lonely there, prince?"

Kage laughs. He throws the book he was holding at Vasile's head. Vasile catches it easy enough but starts joining in with Kage's laughter.

"Play nice boys," I comment with a smirk.

Vasile rolls his eyes, tossing Kage his book back. My eyes lock with Kage's emerald ones, my breath hitching. He smiles at me before looking down at the book in his hands.

That little boy I remember is a man now.

AFTER EATING, I begin cleaning up while Kage goes to lay down for the night. Vasile joins me, putting his arm around my shoulders, leaning his head against mine.

"Tell me, you said you were thinking about Madi. Were you imaging her realization when she finds out that we are no longer Adaminians?" I ask, genuinely curious.

Him flirting and slipping away for the majority of the night is not something new for him, but his affinity for Madi is beyond any feelings he has ever had for anyone else. When he came after us, I wondered if he thought about Madi.

"She is probably shocked and angry. Probably jealous that she didn't get to come on this adventure instead." He laughs, almost like it is to himself, and I just happen to be here. He grabs the utensils I'm holding and walks to put them away in the bag we have tied up in the tree.

"You didn't get to say goodbye to her."

"Nope. She was away on the trade job."

We both go silent until I hear him chuckle to himself again.

"She is gonna go find herself someone else, isn't she?"

"Were her eyes ever on you?"

Vasile walks back over, sitting down next to me, a seriousness overcoming him. "Madi and I are, were, dating."

I nearly have a heart attack hearing him say that. He doesn't look up, though. He just stares at the dying embers.

He lets out a heavy breath, the cold wind helping me visualize just how large of a sigh it really is. "She asked me not to say anything. Something about how a boy like me can't handle a woman like her and that it could hurt her position. The men she's working with seeing her in a way she couldn't afford them to." He smirks a bit now, meeting my gaze.

It takes me a moment to digest that he just took my constant teasing about her while being with her instead of coming clean. He must really love her to be willing to do that.

I smile back at him, seeing him a little bit clearer than I did before. "She is definitely a lot of woman," I say, grabbing his hand, squeezing it a bit.

"You were always right, Xy. I was jealous. I am jealous, jealous of what you and Codrin have."

"Had."

"No have." His eyes glare into me.

"Someone dying doesn't take all those memories and moments spent with them away from you, Xylia. I don't want you leaving here thinking you have no one and nothing, because you do. You have me, you have Codrin, Engle, Rose, and the whole Adamina Clan behind you. Whatever Rose told them, I promise you not a single one of them will believe it was because you were a coward or weak. You have given everything to this Clan, and they know that. Until the Feserpentline, the Clan experienced a peace we had not yet experienced. The Clan numbers nearly tripled, built several additional docks, and expanded our farming lands," he breaks, catching his breath.

"Thank you," I say nearly in a whisper.

I knew he held respect, but I didn't realize that he could think so much of someone like me. I didn't know he watched me that closely.

He relaxes back a bit. "I needed to say that for myself too, don't go and get a big head there."

I let a laugh slip through, now able to see that goofy smile of his.

"She will understand, Vasile. If you were able and willing to put her needs first, she will do the same for you."

He squeezes my hand tightly before bringing it up to his lips. He's not just missing his friend, but his other half as well. He's doing too much for me. I should have pushed him to stay; instead, I'm being selfish.

"We're gonna be okay, Xy." His words pierce through me. I really am selfish. He pulls me in and we sit like that until the embers die out completely.

Vasile and I stand, shivering now that the heat from each other is gone. We wander back to our bedrolls. Vasile offers to take the first watch. So, I shut my eyes and drift away.

"Xylia."

I quickly sit up, feeling Kage's breath on my face as he whispers my name. As I focus, he has his index finger pressed against his lips.

His body is close to mine. I glance around, not seeing any movements.

Kage tugs on my arm, making me look at him.

"What is happening?" I ask in a hushed tone.

Kage looks deeply into my eyes, and I right back into his. The emerald color is hypnotizing. I don't realize he's starting to lean in until his forehead is resting against mine. My heart beats faster as my thoughts freeze.

Kage reaches out and pulls my hood down, running his hands over my hair.

"Kage, stop."

"I need to say this."

I try to pull away, but his hand is firmly placed against the back of my neck.

"Since we met, it seems I've only caused you separation and pain."

"It does seem like that, doesn't it?" I place my hand on his, wanting to accept some kind of comfort despite the lump resting in my throat. I swallow hard and pause as I try to force the words out, "but there is not just one person to blame. I made mistakes that night, so did Vasile."

"Xylia."

I look up through my lashes at him and see an expression of complete guilt. My eyes travel down to his lips.

I don't want to be alone.

"What are you two doing?"

Both Kage and I freeze—coming out of the world only the two of us were occupying. Kage drops his hand, and I retract mine from him.

Re-adjusting my hood, I face Vasile whose charming smile is in a scowl. "We were having a discussion."

"Gotcha."

"Vasile, I—"

He quickly turns around, laying his head down effectively ending his shift to keep watch. I look at Kage, who lays down, before I grab the bow that is resting above my pillow, and bring it to my chest.

It was just a discussion. Nothing more.

THE SUN IS our natural alarm clock. The caravan crew begins packing up right away, breaking to eat some dried jerky for their breggy. Vasile is silently packing away his bedroll and adjusting his armor. I catch him glancing towards me every now and then, but more often, I catch him glaring at Kage.

"Vasile, can ..." Vasile turns his back away from me the moment the words leave my mouth.

I scoff in disbelief.

How am I supposed to fix this?

Vasile has never acted this way before.

I feel Kage's hand pat my shoulder, his lips pressed together, and brows furrowed.

"You two are close. I'm sure he will realize he is just being childish. It was just a conversation."

I nod.

Right. Just a conversation.

I'm hoping Vasile can realize that on his own.

Kage and I follow behind Vasile once the rest of the camp is packed up.

"Hey, guys! Them up and at 'em early, Hershaw! Hes thought you be sleeping till near noon!" Bonji says with a hearty laugh.

I just smile and look at Hershaw, who is downing one of his waterskin pouches.

"We can get a move on then! Get on up on your steads. Let's move."

We all settle our bags onto our horses and climb on, ready for the day's journey ahead.

Vasile's boredom must be winning over his anger because he rides up next to me.

"I don't think Codrin would have seen that as a discussion, Xy," Vasile mumbles.

"It does not matter what you or he would think, Vasile. It was about what was actually happening."

"Ha! Sure. Let's go with that." Vas huffs a bit, shaking his head, irritated.

"He was trying to comfort me. As a companion, not a lover," I whisper, leaning over close to him.

"You sure about that?" Vasile asks, giving me a side-eye.

"From what I gather, he is just feeling guilty." I straighten myself on my horse and sigh, tightening my grip on the reins. "Besides, I can handle myself. It shouldn't matter how he feels."

He gallops his horse to the front of the caravan, away from me. I let out a frustrated sigh and look off into the distance, trying to admire the highlands. Codrin would be talking about the large hills and small mountains that separate one side of the

Felguard Country from the other. He always found it inter-esting and more political than it is.

Codrin would have see it the right way. Right?

Vasile stays silent until we make camp at our next resting spot. He becomes more lively and starts talking to the rest of the crew as they play some music and sing quietly.

Vasile was right. Codrin would not have seen that as just some conversation. Jealousy was always Codrin's weak spot. I shouldn't have leaned into Kage like that, but his touch was what I told Vasile.

Comforting.

I feel a few tears slip down my cheeks, and I quickly turn my face down towards my bowl of mashed meat and potatoes.

Why couldn't I save him?

I close my eyes tightly, still imaging his handsome smile and beautiful eyes. Everything about him was perfect. He was always patient when I needed him to be and stern when I was too stubborn. Codrin was my partner, and I failed him.

Vasile and Kage are right. I need to be able to control my own power so when the time comes, there's no chance of fail-ure. I owe it to Codrin to give it my all. I'm sure Rose will understand why we needed to go to Jod instead of Stran.

Familiar hands wrap around mine, and I glance up through my teary lashes to see Vasile smiling. He moves his hands to my face and wipes my eyes with his thumbs. He leans in close and kisses my cheeks before kneeling in front of me.

"You deserve to feel some comfort, Xylia."

I bite my lip as it begins to quiver.

No, I really don't.

As we gallop down the road, a small village comes into view in the far distance. Vasile rides up behind me, a jaunty smile resting on his face.

It was awkward for a while between us, but I made sure to keep my distance from Kage since that night, which has helped Vasile and me get back to our Codrinless selves. I don't and can't blame him for feeling some way about it. Even I felt panicked and nervous having anyone that wasn't Codrin or Vasile that close.

"Think there will be a tavern or something?" More longing in Vasile's voice than him posing an actual question.

I sigh, longing, too.

It's been a long few days in the highlands. The perks of traveling through the largest country in the realm, that also takes its nature preservation seriously.

Orc man lets out a hearty laugh, apparently overhearing Vasile's whining comment.

"Don't worry yourselves. We will all be able to rest well and out of the elements tonight!"

"Thank **Mira's** holiness," Kage mumbles from behind us. His head hanging down, bobbing in time with his horse's trot.

I shouldn't feel amused by his indisposition, but I do.

"You might want to wipe that cute little smirk off of your face, My Lady. Otherwise, you'll need it to convince us a few rooms for the night," Vasile's whisper tickles the corners of my mouth until a bubble of laughter overflows from my chest, garnering Kage's attention.

"Mock if you will, dear Xylia, but your obviously loud-mouth companion is right. I like to think of myself as a gentleman, but I'm feeling far less so the longer I ride this monstrous creature."

Kage and I lock eyes, and my heart tightens for a moment. It's the same look he has been giving me the last couple of days.

Maybe it's the distance I've put between us, but he seems impatient and sad.

Even though Vasile is trying to hide his embarrassment caused by the Prince's comment, it's quite apparent. He never really was the stealthy type.

I roll my eyes a bit and mime that I'm sewing my mouth shut. For the first time since the night Vasile saw our small moment, I hear a small chuckle come from the depressing lump that has been our Prince. Vasile notices it too, and suddenly, the ride doesn't seem that bad anymore.

As we arrive in the village, I have to consciously close my mouth. Blackened wood and shattered glass fill our vision. I hear Hershaw curse under his breath before dismounting.

Shivering and cautious people are watching us carefully like they are trying to determine our motives; decide whether or not to run. The few buildings that are still standing seem too small to house an entire village, which means some were living in places not even suitable for doing just that. I look to the boys who are now both by my side, still mounted on our horses.

"What the infernum?" Vasile's smile is far gone, looking at this devastation.

I dismount quickly. Securing my hood, I approach slowly with my hands slightly elevated towards a small group of men. They appear to be trying to shoo their loved ones away.

One of the large men from the group approach, a broadsword strapped to his back. From the looks of it, I bet he would be the leader of what's left of these people.

I look back to Hershaw, who seems to be keeping his distance, which is probably for the best considering the looks of terror he appears to be causing. As the man and I get closer to each other, I hear someone dismounting from my group. I quickly hold up my hand to signal them to stop.

"My name is Xylia. I am helping to escort this caravan

through here and up to Jod. We were hoping to recharge and rest while here, but it looks like you all have enough on your hands."

"An' whos caravan does this belong to exactly?" His hand reaches up and grabs the hilt of the blade, a clear warning.

"It's supplies for a Forged Magic user up north in Ventra-ton. He hired these men to acquire the goods from Ko's market."

"Then where do your loyalties belong to?"

Looking behind me, I see Vasile dismounted, gripping the hilt of his swords tightly, his eyes not leaving the man's. I point to Vasile, garnering a quick glance from him.

Smiling slightly, I make eye contact with the man. "To those I trust."

CHAPTER NINE

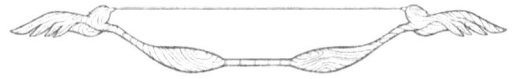

WE STAND THERE, unmoving and silent for what feels like a sunshift until the large man releases his hand from his blade and nods. I drop my hands slowly and look back to Vasile who's still watching him. His face is intense and nervous. Even from this distance, I can see sweat beginning to form on his brow.

"The name is Leon." Leon's voice is raspy and low.

Leon turns to another man who is smaller in frame and reaches out to grab his hand tightly. A wave of relief washes over them both.

Leon runs his free hand through his messy fawn-colored hair before looking back at us. "You mentioned a place to rest. We don't have much, but there's a house you can stay in. There are a few parts that are a little overcooked, but the roof is still intact. You can follow us."

"We appreciate your generosity," I say, my shoulders relaxing as the tensions have died down completely.

Leon and a few others lead us to one of the houses towards the inner village. He wasn't lying when he said it was over-cooked. Half of the lower side is burnt, and windows are smashed, probably from the fire's heat. Hershaw settles the horses and sets the guys up for patrol while Vasile and I look inside with Leon.

"My guess is that the village wasn't always like this?"

I elbow Vasile in the gut.

"No need to hit the poor feller. I'm not surprised none of you know about the attack yet," Leon says.

He tells us that the Fel Watch had recently laid the whole village to waste looking for any Magicae users. They took almost everything of value and claimed that there was a new tax raise that the village hadn't paid. The village knew it was just the fact the King needed more money to continue his search.

My heart tightens, thinking if we had been here, we might have been able to help them, or maybe they would have just taken me and left them alone.

"We haven't had any Magicae users here in a long while. Yet, they came anyway. I don't think any place is safe from that man anymore."

Vasile swallows hard, while I observe the room with a new perspective. This is the King's power; he takes what he wants. No one has ever been strong enough to stand up against him.

I shiver at the thought of being face to face with him. I know Kage believes that the book I keep close to me is about us, but my heart still doesn't want to give in to the idea that I am meant to be what I wanted to be: a hero.

Leon leaves us and lets us know where the rest of the villagers are, so if something happens, we know where everyone is. Vasile follows him out, leaving me in the burnt house alone.

I pull the blue leathered book from my satchel and run my fingers across it. Anger starts to build up inside of me. These people need someone who will stand up and shine bright, but I need to learn how to control my powers in order for me to.

Can I be who they need?

Kage walks in, seeing me caressing the book, and walks up with a slight smile. I go to put it away but he grips my wrist. My breathing quickens, and I feel the panic begin to rise again as a lump in my throat.

"I'm glad you are no longer running from me. Makes traveling a tad easier," he says with a laugh.

I give him a quick smile. Kage furrows his brow and leans in closer, and I purse my lips together. He smiles and strokes my wrist with his thumb.

"You feel it, right? A sudden surge when we touch?" he asks in a whisper.

I would be lying if I said I didn't feel anything for the person standing in front of me now. I've been trying to convince myself otherwise. I know it's Codrin who I wish was here instead, that it would be his touch. It's different walking with Kage though, there's an unspoken bond that I feel with him. Maybe I'm imagining it—I swear I see glimpses of that boy —but he was swallowed by a man who looks at me with an intensity I have never seen before. There is a craving there that is no longer disguised as guilt nor comfort.

"Don't lie, Xylia."

My attention draws back to him as he seems to read my mind. "Kage. Please."

He leans in closer, running his hands up my arms slowly. It sends warmth throughout my body. I shiver as his hands crest my shoulders, making their way to my neck, tangling into my hair. He moves his body closer, his chest now pressed against mine.

"Please, Xylia."

My lips quiver as his brush against mine, our breath intermingling. I let out a frustrated sigh as my heart flees the scene and into the arms of a lover I miss far too dearly. I push away, biting my lip and leaving Kage there holding a ghost.

Taking a few steps away, the warmth fades. "This is all too much ..." I whisper, my hand gripping my chest.

"I'll wait then, but I won't stop trying. I won't stop unless you can look me in my eyes and tell me you feel nothing."

I meet his gaze. I want to say it. Say that I feel nothing, but I'm feeling everything: my grief, my longing, my desperation, my loss. I want him in ways that I would have ignored if Codrin was standing beside me, but he's gone. I know he isn't coming back, but I'm not ready.

"Then wait."

He takes in a deep breath and runs his hands through his hair. Smiling wide, his shoulders relax as he lets out an over-joyed exhale of air.

"I'll wait."

Vasile and the rest of the caravan join us in the house that now seems far too cramped. Vasile glances from Kage to me, giving me a quizzical look. I give him my best smile and head towards the corner of the room to take a seat, but Hershaw grabs my shoulder and spins me around to face him.

"You were steller, little lady!" He hands me a drink that smells far too sweet to be something he would like.

Vasile and Kage are already indulging themselves, so I take a sip, the bitterness mild and the fruity flavor tingling my tastebuds.

"It's delicious. Thank you."

"You got us out of a nasty conversation, so have as much as you'd like!" He jaunts a few steps over to Bonji. They share a few words before a hearty laugh escapes the both of them.

I retreat over to the corner and watch the group interact. Kage and Vasile are surprisingly locked in on a conversation that has them both smiling. A few of the other caravan guards are playing a game of **Butcher**. I sip lightly on the drink at hand, trying to enjoy the noise and company.

Eventually, the sun gives way to her moon, and everyone seems to settle down. Kage and Vasile grab their packs, along with mine, and make their way over to me.

"Sorry, boys. This corner is all mine."

"You cannot just call the only non-burnt corner!" Vasile whines as he throws my pack at me and slides his body closely nestled to mine.

Kage places his pack on the other side, both of them squishing me.

"This was the best you could come up with?" I glance between them.

The boys look at each other, realizing I've already seen through their ruse. I slap them both in the face and spread my legs, pushing theirs aside.

Grumbling, they give me some space.

"My corner."

"Yeah. yeah."

"Of course, my Lady."

We all lay down for the night, exhausted from our travels on the open road. With the villagers keeping watch, we all can rest a bit easier and hopefully a lot deeper.

I close my eyes, but my mind wonders as I listen to the noises of the night. The wind blows against the boarded windows, and the house creaks as the cold settles itself into the wood. Snores erupt from the men we are traveling with, sometimes muffling the mumbles that escape Vasile's mouth.

As I drift off to sleep, I feel Kage's hand press against my back. I turn my head to look at him, but his eyes are closed, and his breathing is steady. I leave it be, trusting his words, 'I'll wait.'

I JUMP to my feet as a loud ringing stings my ears. My hands are firmly pressed against my ears. Looking around, everyone else is just as awake and mimicking my same body position. I run for the door, seeing flames and men marching. I feel Vasile grab my shoulders, Kage pulling my hood up for me. I hadn't realized it had fallen.

We all run out to get a better idea of what's happening. As we try to step out onto the street, we are thrown to the ground as a wave of heat and force push us down. I didn't even see the explosion, but I am on my back, ears bleeding, flesh burning as if it went off right in front of me. I try to sit up to gather myself. The villagers are scrambling, but I can't see what's really going on. A hand yanks me as a cloth is being shoved in my mouth, and a rope ties my arms behind my back.

"Don't touch her!" Vasile screams. He has left my sight and is now somewhere behind me. His grunts and shouts of protest are quickly muffled.

My eyes begin to water from the gag, my eyes widening, trying to take in my surroundings, but it's all moving too fast. I close my eyes trying to focus as I desperately try to call the light forwards. This is my chance to protect them. To protect me. I need to focus, I need to control my power, but the voice isn't coming to me.

A terrifying feeling encompasses me. I haven't heard the voice since the night I lost him. The last time I ever called upon the light.

I pushed it away.

I begin to scream against the cloth and begin to manipulate the rope around my hands to rip and snap. My restraints fall to the ground before they even realize I am escaping them. I shove my elbow back into the person holding me and throw myself towards the floor, ripping away from their grasp. I scramble and roll away from them, giving me enough distance to stand and turn to face them. I reach my hand out and will Vasile's sword to it, but it does not come.

Please!

Suddenly cold steel touches my hand, and I grip onto it for dear life. I refocus and finally take in the ten men standing in front of me. They are dressed in navy steel armor with gold lining and a symbol of a shield outlining a tree that is split down the middle with a sword at its center. At the men's feet, The Fel Watch have Kage and Vasile tied up and unconscious. I spit out the cloth and ready my stance.

This is going to be an impossible fight, but I can't go down without at least trying to save us. One of the men approach, a cocky smile taking up the majority of his face. Our blades clash, and I use the weight of his arm to push it to the side, causing his balance to falter. Dipping down, I swing my leg to kick his out from under him. He falls to the ground, his armor clattering as he does. I stumble back. Three other men run up, not giving me a second to recover. They all take turns slamming their blades against mine, knocking it from my hands.

One of the men laughs and grabs me by my hair. I yell out as he rips a few of my stands out. My hands are shaking, my eyes darting to meet all of theirs.

I have to keep trying.

I take in a deep breath, focusing on my intention and calming my self-doubt. The man holding me up winds back his fist, and the sword I had just wielded pierces through the chain-mail, entering in the small opening by his arm. He drops me and takes a few steps back as the sword rips itself out of him, almost like it is acting on behalf of its own free will.

The man falls to his knees, and his comrades turn back to me. This time all of them charge.

I begin to run, trying to put distance between them and me. The village folks are screaming and running every which way. Children clutching to their mothers and fathers as confusion fills the gaps where the smoke has not yet reached. My attention is still focused on the group chasing after me, only faltering when homes begin to collapse causing a thunderous noise to echo inside me.

They are losing everything.

As I reach the next street, another ring bursts through the air, slamming me against one of the other houses before I fall limp to the ground. All the air is expelled from my body and pain radiates throughout every bone. Blood trickles from my nose and I cough up some from my lungs. I try to force my eyes to stay open but the pain is overcoming me.

My vision goes black.

I'M SHAKING from the cold. I reach over, trying to find my blanket, instead, I touch soil. I quickly sit up, my eyes wide open. The sight catches my breath, the whole vitaterrium in front of me, burning. Everything is in the distance. I can still hear far off echos of thousands screaming as I stand on a hill, far from our bed. Looking down, I am wearing a blue dress with golden seams. I grip my book, which I find is somehow in my hands, and cling it tight against my chest as I begin to stand.

"Codrin?" I scream out, scanning every direction.

Large creatures are in the sky with monstrous roars further down the hill. People are running far off in the distance, trying to escape the flames and things that are chasing them. Guilt washes over me, and my knees feel they are about to buckle.

Where is Codrin?

I scream for him again, running towards the commotion. I

can't stop myself now as tears rush down my face causing my vision to go blurry.

Before I can reach the border of the flames, which are keeping me on one side and everyone else on the other, a hand reaches out from behind me and yanks my arm, jerking me backwards and away from my destination.

I turn around to Kage, his hair tied back, sweat on his brow. Kage. I was with Vasile and Kage. His lips are moving, but I can't hear what he's saying. All I hear are screams. Kage wraps his arms around me, tilting his head down so our foreheads touch—allowing my mind to drown out the chaos behind me.

A part of me wants to stay here and ignore the heat behind me, his lips, his eyes, and his smell all tempt me to stay. He leans in and kisses me, a rush of adrenaline coursing through my veins. I cave into his touch, not wanting to fight off the comfort he is willing to offer me. I want to feel okay. I lean back into him, feeling stronger in his arms even though I feel so unsure about what's really happening right now.

As I pull away to catch my breath, I find myself waking to see Kage's face looking at me with concern and realize that I am lying on a bedroll inside a half-burned down house. I quickly glance around the room and remember the attack. There is a strong taste of metallic in my mouth, and my body is stiff and sore. I try to sit up but everyone, even Leon, protests. There's only one person I do not see at my side.

"Where is Vasile?"

Kage places his hands on my shoulders, applying pressure to hold down my panicked composure. I yell, trying to break free from his grasp, but the pain in my leg and chest nearly paralyze me.

"Xylia, it's not your fault."

"Where is he?!"

I finally shove Kage off of me and stand up, my legs giving out as soon as I do. I land on all fours.

"Vasile!"

Kage grabs me, pulling me gently into his chest. Covering my eyes with his hand, he kisses the top of my head. "They took him, Xylia."

CHAPTER TEN

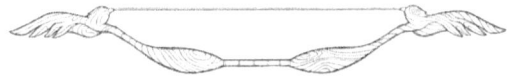

All I hear is static.

All I see is darkness.

All I feel is my racing heartbeat.

All I smell is burning wood.

All I taste is blood.

All I am is nothing.

I scream out, my hand extended forwards as the world begins to turn to ash around me—those invisible explosions echoing in my mind.

Vasile.

"Xylia."

I jolt awake at Kage's touch.

He is standing to the right of me, his hand resting on the top of my head. His brow is knitted with concern.

"Breathe. I am right here," Kage whispers, petting my head.

I settle back down into my pillow. Kage crawls under the covers with me, the frigid air making me quake as it touches my skin. He moves me slowly, so my head is now resting on his chest, his breathing still slightly elevated from the panic of waking up to my screams. Neither of us has slept well in a full moon phase. My dreams have become so vivid and life-like that I end up screaming both of us awake.

After the attack and Vasile's abduction, we are able to slowly make our way to Jod. Both the caravan and village were terrified and in shock to see an elf and Magicae user in their midst but offer their support in transporting me. I fractured my ribs, and one of my legs was broken. We found an inn inside the city, **The Snug Pillow**.

Kage has surprised me at every turn since our departure from the village. He has slowly nursed me back to where I am now able to stand and walk comfortably. Reassured me that Vasile will be alright, that he is the bargaining chip they cannot afford to lose. It gives me hope that the plan both Kage and I are putting together will work.

It will take a lot of persuasion, and there are many risks involved, but allowing myself to be taken in by the King seems to be our best way in.

Kage wraps his arms around me gently, still cautious of my still-recovering body. Taking a gash to the chest is a far better choice than being slammed with immense force into a house.

"Now that we are up, we should continue talking about what could happen once we get inside."

I nod in agreement.

"It's likely the King will force you to take a blood oath using a chalice that we recovered a few hundred years ago."

"A chalice?"

"It's a Magicae item. It allows the owner protection from any magicae user that commits a blood oath with it. You won't be able to utilize your powers against him or anyone in his bloodline."

"So if my will is to do him harm, I won't be able to utilize my power."

"Exactly."

"I can handle that."

Kage smiles and kisses my head, amused by my confidence. Though it's not confidence, it's determination. Knowing I have to let Vasile sit there is killing me. Every day I heal is one day closer to him, but it also means it's another day he has been there alone.

"We're going to save him, Xylia."

"I know."

THE SUN MAKES ITS APPEARANCE, the snow-covered city glistens. With my arm linked through Kage's, we make our daily round to the library. The streets are far less crowded and chaotic than Ko. The buildings are large, tall, and made of stone. Some are even built inside the mountains that make the natural border between the Felguard Country and Ventraton. It's a beautiful place. Codrin would have liked it here. Seems the further away the Capital is, the better off these cities are. They have suffered in ways, but they haven't had their world fall apart around them.

A charming, slightly older woman opens the doors for us as we walk up the stairs to the enormous building that is the library.

"Glad to see you both again."

She smiles warmly at us as we shake off the cold, entering the warmer interior of the building.

"We are happy to be back. There is just so much to learn!" Kage and the woman share a polite laugh before she begins to escort us to our normal spot.

The tall ceilings are covered with beautiful art of horrifying creatures and alluring beings of all races, including elves. The spiraling bookcases are filled with knowledge from across the vitaterrium. It's unbelievable that such a place has lasted in the current chaos taking over the country.

We head to a large stained glass window, one that reminds me of the artwork in my book, that looks over the city of Jod. Kage sits across from me at the large table we are given. He offers the woman a piece of parchment with the list of texts we are interested in reading. She hurries off to collect what we need. Kage relaxes back in his chair and looks around at the bookcases that stretch up to the top of the ceiling adorned with ladders to reach the top.

"You seem at home here."

He looks back at me with a large smile. "The library we have at the castle, nowhere near this size, was where I spent a lot of my time. It is how I got to be this intelligent, charming man who sits in front of you now."

I raise an eyebrow, making him chuckle. I take in his smile, the way it lights up his face. He is very handsome, the only flaw being the burn scar that I placed there myself. His hair has started to grow back out, but he's managed to keep up the clean-shaven face he insists on keeping. Even in his considered rugged state, he is beautiful in his own way. When I reach his emerald eyes, he seems to be studying me, too.

He reaches across the table and caresses my hand. I close my eyes and breathe, trying to control the desire I feel for him.

"You are by far the most beautiful thing I have ever studied, my Lady."

I open my eyes and pull my hood down a bit. "You should get out more."

He slaps his hand over his mouth, trying to avoid the burst of laughter that threatens to escape. As he calms himself, the woman comes back and places the texts at the end of the table before excusing herself.

We study and pour over the history of Magicae. The doorway that once connected the holy power of the Awemother was what gave life to the Magicae that lived in this part of the world. There are different ominous powers that used to infuse the rest of the realm, but since the war, they have sealed the doorways closed.

"I found it."

Kage steals my attention away from the text in front of me. He slides the book he is reading into view.

The Oracle, one who is born with a direct line to Magicae. A prominent position in the old country's parliament. They are able to guide the course of fate and offer enlightenment of the Awemother. A bright light is often seen illuminating the space of the Oracle. This light can provide immaculate healing abilities both physically and spiritually.

I hold my breath reading the passage. It's not a lot to go over, but it's definitely something to work with.

"You think this could be me?" I ask in a whisper.

He nods with a slight smile. "It would explain why you might not be able to completely control the light with the doorway being closed."

"How is it possible for an oracle to even exist with the doorway being closed?"

Kage furrows his brow and rubs his face a bit as he pauses, mulling over vast amount of information he has stored in his head.

"Magicae can be unexplainable. It could be that if you were born in the Vermilion Forest, the Magicae that still lives and breaths in those trees attached itself to you."

"Would make sense, since the only time the trees seem to

not grow back or heal is when it's my magicae causing the damage."

Kage closes the book and runs his hands through his hair, slicking it back. He keeps his hand up, pinning his hair under it. Looking up to the ceiling, he mutters. It seems to be a common thing he does when he's deep in thought.

"Don't overthink this, but why do you want to help me?" The question leaves my lips before I realize I'm asking it.

I understand he feels like he is fulfilling the promise of a young boy who wanted nothing more than to be free of the terrifying father who controlled his life, but to go back and confront his father is something I can't understand. I need to know why he is willing to give up his freedom to help me save a man he doesn't really know.

He drops his hand and looks down at me, a very serious expression resting on his face. He leans forwards, looking underneath the hood and into my eyes.

"Since I met you, Xylia, I have never stopped thinking about you. We were meant to find each other, meant to do something great together." He takes the silver ring off of his finger and places it in my hand. "I will do anything you ask of me."

"Am I allowed to be that selfish?"

"As long as I get to be by your side, Xylia, you can be as selfish as you want with me."

Kage stands from his seat and walks around the table to kneel down in front of me. He takes my hand once more and places it on his chest. I try to look away, feeling that panic lump raise up inside of my throat again. Panic that I could care for someone that isn't Codrin—want someone who isn't Codrin.

He turns my face back to his, pulling me forwards so our noses touch. His breath is heavy, and my heart is racing.

"All I need is you, my Lady."

My head begins to spin as I lean in closer, our lips gently grazing each other. His grip on my hand tightens when he takes a shaky breath, waiting for me to make a move. I bring my other hand up and run my hand through his hair. It feels so different from Codrin's, short and a lot thinner. He smells different, like peppermint and rosemary. Like Codrin though, he is kind and patient. I wonder what draws me in when it comes to him.

"Xylia," he whispers against my lips.

Right.

I part my lips, inviting him to consume me. He doesn't hesitate. Our lips begin to meld together as we take each other in. He stands, pulling me up with him, dropping my hand and wrapping his arm around my waist, tightly holding me to his chest. We melt into each other. My heart erupts with an ache for the love I once knew, but also for the one I am beginning to know. The hand holding my chin tangles up into my hair, deepening our kiss. My hands rest on his chest, feeling how sturdy and warm he is.

Kage pulls away, us both catching our breaths, but his face is turned from mine. I look over my shoulder in the direction he is looking—a very red-faced familiar woman is standing there. I didn't even hear her walk in.

"I apologize. I was coming to check if there was anything else I could get for you," she says, clearing her throat.

"We actually are going to call it a day. Thank you for your assistance again today."

He smiles at her, letting me go from his grasp. Kage takes my hand and the satchel he brought with, leading us out of the library. We don't stop or look back, just focused on making our way to our temporary home.

Walking through the door, he throws the satchel onto his bed before closing the door and sweetly taking me into his arms again. Kage pulls my hood down, allowing him to see me more clearly. He caresses my face, kissing my cheeks slowly and softly before resting his head against mine.

"You fit so perfectly in my hands," Kage admits, stroking his thumbs across my cheeks.

I'm sure they are beat red.

My feelings for Kage are not like my love for Codrin. I doubt any relationship or feeling will ever compare to how it felt when I was with Codrin, but this is nice.

"I'm tired of lying to myself. I'm happy to be here with you, like this."

I place my hands on top of his and squeeze them gently, slightly embarrassed to say something so romantic out loud.

"I'm happy too, Xylia." He lifts his head up and kisses my forehead. "Though as much as I wish we could forget about what is ahead of us and fall for each other, our time here is coming to an end, and we need to be ready," Kage says with a hint of agony hidden behind the responsible tone.

I smile and nod in agreement. "Here, I thought you were going to have a one-tracked mind. You certainly had us rush home fast enough."

Kage laughs a bit, and I kiss each of his cheeks slowly, but as my head settles in front of him, he leans in, so our lips collide. Kage's passion pushes me back a few steps until my shoulders are pinned up against the wall. He runs his hands down my back, wrapping his arms around my waist and pulling me closer to him.

"I'm still thinking about it, don't worry," Kage whispers against my lips.

He pulls away from me, leaving my knees weak and my breath shaky. Kage sits on his bed, reaching underneath it, and pulls out a small chest filled with papers. He looks back to me and smiles as I am still leaning against the wall, eyes focused on him.

I shake my head, blinking a few times before I join him.

He got me there for a moment.

We go over our strategy of writing a letter ahead of time, notifying them of our arrival. Hopefully, from there, we will be welcomed into the castle versus taken in by force. We will bargain that I will stay willingly, but only if Vasile is allowed to be escorted by Kage to the Adamina Clan. From there, Kage plans to negotiate with Rose about bringing our militia to help stage a ruse coup, where he will sneak back into the castle and free any and all who may be imprisoned in the cellar under the castle. While the Fel Watch is distracted, Kage can then find me, and we can escape. After that, Vasile can be free of me. I will begin to raise a large enough group to storm the castle once more and tear the King down.

After finalizing every detail, we crawl under the covers in our separate beds—our backs facing each other. I sit there, white-knuckling the sheets, trying to build up the courage to go over to his bed.

I've only ever shared one with Codrin.

I close my eyes and begin to count down from ten, though when I get to three, the covers are shifting, and I feel Kage wrap his arm around me.

I smile and nestle in.

"I thought I'd be brave enough for the both of us."

He is always reading my mind.

"I was working on it."

"Of course, My Lady."

THE NEXT DAY Kage leaves me at the inn to send out the letter we carefully crafted together. This will be the first step. Today will be our last day in Jod before we embark on our journey to

Fosa, the Capital. I grip my chest, knowing that I will do whatever I must to ensure Vasile's safety. The thought of him having been there all this time makes me sick. I want to save him the way he has saved me so many times.

I will not fail him.

CHAPTER ELEVEN

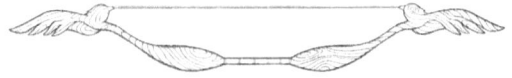

I KISS Kage's forehead delicately. I'm careful where I step as I sneak out of the room and down the stairs of the inn. Opening the main door, the freezing wind nips at my nose and cheeks. I pull my cloak tighter around me and step onto the street.

There is no reason for me to sleep. My mind only tortures me with images of those I love and no longer have. I thought I'd always have Rose and Rye, but I lost them both the night Rye died. Rose changed and hardened herself to the point where I stopped referring to her as my mother. I find it strange, though, how before I had Codrin, Madi, or Vasile, I had Kage. Now that Codrin is gone, Madi out of reach, and Vasile taken, Kage is the only one I have left. The thought that a stranger who didn't know me was willing to risk everything to set me free, and later gave up everything to come find me like he swore. Kage doesn't have to say it, but I am sure it was his digging that caused my location to be found by the King. The King then used that information and the fact his son was on his way to force his way into the Clan.

I shiver as the cold begins to settle into my bones, but

walking around on my own reminds me of the many mornings I spent out in the forest—the few shifts where it was just me. I pause, closing my eyes and inhaling the brisk morning air. As I open them, the sun is begging to wake up on the far horizon. The snowy sheets that rest on the hills and houses shine and sparkle.

I hear a door to the bakery open, a larger man carrying out empty bags of flour. Our eyes meet, he smiles and waves at me.

"Beaut of a morning, eh?"

"Yes, it is very lovely."

"Don't know 'bout you but, I find it to be the best time of the day."

He looks away from me and to the rising sun. We stand there, looking at the largest jewel we've ever seen and enjoying its immaculate beauty.

I look back at him, and he waves me a farewell before heading inside. The scent of fresh baked bread now reaching me.

I continue down the quiet roads, watching the city wake up. A few people wander out of their homes, beginning their day. To live a life like theirs was something Codrin dreamed for us. Being able to raise a family and live a life without constant worry for each other's safety. I would have loved that if it had been with him, but now I have a different dream. The one the little girl had. The one where I am the hero.

I know going to the castle now is a risk, but I won't be able to accomplish anything if I am worried about Vasile and Kage. I am going to take down this tyrant one day, and this will be the first part in doing just that.

Making my way back to the inn, an arm catches mine. Turning around, I see a distressed Kage, slightly disheveled and catching his breath. I stayed out longer than I was planning to, and he most definitely noticed.

"I thought you ... please ... wake me next time you choose to take an early morning walk."

He stands up straight, taking in deep breaths to settle himself. I reach up and brush my hand across his cheek. Kage caresses my hand, bringing it to his lips, blowing hot air onto it.

"Let's head back to the inn. We will be leaving soon."

Kage smiles and nods. We head back, hand in hand.

ONCE THE MORNING turns to mid-day, we head back out to the outskirts of the city, my bow and arrows in hand. After the fight at the village, understanding my magicae became a priority for both of us. I've trained myself how to use it, but I felt something completely different when the sword took over like it did. The light has yet to emerge, and the voice has been silent. Controlling the bow and arrows with magicae is as much practice and progress I have made. I normally have always held and fired the bow myself, but using magicae instead could help out if I am tied down. Kage always stops me at the point where I start to weaken, my body shaking, eyes furrowed, and aim a little off.

"Alright, soldier, we have business yet to accomplish. We will have plenty of time to continue practice on the road," Kage says, forcing me to sit. "Take a break."

Once I feel some of my strength come back to me, we head back into Jod and to the stables where we left our horses. Having to sell one of our steads for the amount of rations and supplies needed for our journey to the Capital is a sacrifice we need to bear. It will be a less comfortable ride, but we won't be able to make it without the supplies.

The small amount Kage had stolen, when he originally started his own journey from the castle, ran out after buying the room and medical fixings needed to get me back on my feet. My chest has healed very nicely, but my leg is still in need of the assistance the splint provides.

"Remember to grab the notes that are under the mattress."

Kage lifts up the cot and grabs the neatly tied stack of parchment we had hid there in case one of the owners came in while we were out. A detailed agenda of our plans to overthrow the King. Kage suspects that his father will be prepared for us to try something, so there is still going to be a great deal of improvisation on our end.

"All packed."

I stand slowly, making my way over to Kage, whose eyes are focused on the bag. I grab his shaking hand and squeeze it. He leans forwards, resting his head on my shoulder. I comb through his hair with my fingers, hoping to ease the tension I can feel building up inside of him.

"This is it. Once we leave, we are on course to Fosa," Kage whispers, a heavy swallow following it.

"Yes," I confirm, matching his tone and volume.

He looks up, lifting his head so his emeralds can look over the small room we have been preparing and recovering in. I place my hands on the back of his neck, drawing his gaze to mine. The terrifying desperation in his eyes overwhelming me. He leans in, his arms taking all of me in. His mouth encourages my lips to move and press against his. I wrap my arms tightly around him, bringing him closer, making our kisses even deeper. My heart begins to beat in time with his, our chests pressed tightly against each other.

I crave him too.

My lips follow his as he separates us for a moment.

"Xylia ..."

We kiss again and again until the fear that we both have fades into the back of our minds. We will have many nights to fear what that day will bring, but right now, all I want is him. I don't want to think of anything but the bliss that is filling my senses at this very moment.

His lips trail away from mine and onto my cheek, jaw, neck, collarbone before returning to my trembling lips. He moans as my tongue slips into his mouth, connecting us further. We entangle ourselves, enraptured with the feeling of being in each other's arms.

KAGE'S FACE is nuzzled into my neck, an arm draped across my chest, and a leg wrapped around mine. I pull my head away carefully, his head sliding from my shoulder to the pillow. I smile to myself and bring my hand up to stroke his hair back off of his face. He mumbles something under his breath, stirring slightly from my touch.

Codrin would want me to be happy. He would understand that I will always love and miss him, that I want him, and that I need some happiness. Codrin would approve of Kage, right? I'm not sure if Vasile will, but he didn't approve of me at first either. He loved me and was very jealous of Codrin giving his attention to me and me to Codrin, leaving Vasile all by his lonesome. I chuckle to myself, remembering how petty he used to be.

"Do I look silly?" Kage grumbles, one eye opened and looking up at me.

"Handsome actually, it's quite irritating."

Kage laughs and rolls onto his back, bringing his hand up to rub his face and eyes. "I doubt I compare to your beauty."

I lift my head up, grabbing the pillow I had been resting on, and smack it against his face. I hear a muffled laugh as he rips it from my grasp and throws it onto the floor. He climbs on top of me, grabbing my wrist and pinning them down on either side of my head.

"That was not nice, my Lady."

"You gave me no choice, my Prince. Saying such sappy words brings out the violence in me this early in the morning," I kid.

He kisses me, letting go of my wrist and taking my face into his hands.

"Hmm, I'll remember that," Kage whispers, now leaning back, standing from the bed.

I prop myself onto my elbows, my eyes following him. He gathers his clothes and begins getting dressed.

"Time already," I say, falling back onto the bed.

My heart begins to race just thinking about returning to that terrible place, even though it is a long journey.

"We are ready."

WE CREST the hill revealing to us the large walls surrounding the Capital. The tops of houses and shops just barely peeking over it. The castle, in the center, towering over everything, is just as terrifying as the day I first saw it.

I hold onto Kage tighter, pressing my chest against his back. It's all bigger than I remember it, if that is even possible. My spirit deflates seeing the mountain we plan to move. It has taken us over a full moon cycle to get here. Our bodies nearly frostbitten, and our minds are worn thin from the constant exposure. The few villages we passed were devastated and mostly barren.

The letter we sent a day ahead of our departure from Jod should have already reached the King's desk. The Fel Watch already awaiting our arrival. This is our last stretch before we hand ourselves over.

My breathing is labored, knowing I am just a sunshift away from being face-to-face with the King. My hands begin to shake, and I rest my head onto Kage's shoulder. I feel him shuffle a bit, perhaps trying to capture a glance at my embarrassingly weakened composure.

I'm scared.

"Xylia, this is what we are meant to do. Remember that." Kage leans back, his head turns towards me.

I stretch my neck and chin upwards, our lips meeting briefly before our attentions turn back to our mission.

He snaps the horse into action, and we move steadily towards the gates. The thump of the horse's hooves matches the rhythm of my racing heartbeat. Everything in my body is telling me to run, but Kage is right.

This is what we are meant to do.

Arriving at the first gate, it is already open. A few Fel Watch narrow their gaze as we approach. One of them holds their hand up, signaling for us to stop. As Kage rides up to them, they don't seem to recognize who he is with his rugged clothes and hair.

"What brings you to Fosa today?"

One of the guards slowly circles us as the other is focused on Kage.

"We have an audience with the King. I am The Second Prince, Bren Torrin," Kage states, loud and clear.

The guards look at each other shocked. The slightly bulkier guard who has done the talking thus far clears his throat and signals his counterpart, who immediately runs and rushes through the gate. Soon, there are more men and weapons around us than we can ever hope to fight off on our own. Kage squeezes my hand tightly.

They quickly force us down from our stead with most of their weapons drawn, before shackling our hands. I hold my breath to try and stop myself from showing them just how terrified I am.

I hate that I am scared.

I bite my lip as they push me forwards into the bulkier guard.

"We know who he is, now who are you?" he says with a light cackle. Kage keeps his eyes on me, as they pull down my hood. "Dear **Tempestas** ..."

A few of them jump while others lean closer, seeing my long pointed ears in person.

"Are those real?"

"This is what the King was talking about?"

"Disgusting elf."

"They look strange."

One of the guards reaches to touch them.

"The King will kill you for doing something like that," Kage shouts at them. The man quickly withdraws, the first guard who had stopped us, steps forwards to look Kage in the face.

"Speaking of, I'm sure he will want to welcome you home."

We are pushed through the gates and escorted through the merchant district, through the residential district and into the high society district. The only district with people out in the streets, walking around casually in gowns and jewels of immaculate beauty. They all move to the side, a wave of whispers crashing into us as we pass them.

Walking through the final gate, the castle now looms over us. There are Fel Watch everywhere, surrounding the castle and its grounds. Glancing around, I see a small girl dressed in a long navy blue coat, with a symbol I have never seen; a hand with a tree in the center, eight stars surrounding it. She looks up for a moment, meeting my gaze and her brown eyes widen.

She combs her brown hair down to cover her face a bit and hides her eyes.

My concentration is severed when I hear a thunderous clap coming from the castle's entrance.

"Welcome home, Bren. You miss me?" A booming voice calls out.

A slightly taller, more masculine-looking Kage, steps out from a large gate a few meters ahead of us with a very large woman following behind him. His jet black hair, just like his brothers, is nearly down to his waist. His eyes are gray, though, more suited for his cold personality. The armor he's wearing is elegant and made out of silver. He gives us a dazzling smile and opens his arms wide as he strolls up to Kage. He claps Kage's face between his hands and kisses his forehead.

"Brother," Kage says with an emptiness I have not heard before.

This is Elijah. He is not the little boy I remember from all those years ago.

"Don't sound so broken-hearted that your little rebellious stunt didn't work out the way you were hoping. Besides, I'm sure father will forgive you now that we have our treasure." He turns his brother's face to the side, looking at his scar. "Ouch, were you playing with fire? You should have known just how dangerous that is," he says, now looking over to me, giving me a wink.

Kage tries to grab his brother, but the large hulking woman standing next to Elijah slams Kage down onto the ground. I would love to see Madi kick the sense out of her. Kage grabs his leg reeling from the pain of landing on it so harshly.

I try to run towards them, but I have too many hands holding me in place.

"Still cruel, I see," I say, spitting towards Eli.

Kage starts to struggle against the women's grasp as the

First Prince Elijah Torrin steps in front of me. He walks over and looks into my eyes, excitement written all over his face.

"Xylia, it really has been far too long." Eli leans in closer so his lips are touching my ear. "I'd love to show you how cruel I can be. I have a few new tricks up my sleeve." He kisses my cheek before standing upright, glancing down at Kage.

"Keep your filthy self away from her," Kage growls, quickly whimpering as the woman puts pressure onto his now twisted arm.

Elijah laughs, arching his brow.

"You are the one covered in filth, my brother."

Suddenly the guards and Fel Watch surrounding us are brought to attention, their armor all clattering at one. All of their focus at the entryway.

My heart sinks seeing his silver hair step past the doorway's frame and into the sun. His withered face is covered with a long beard, blending in with his hair. He takes slow but proud and imposing steps towards us.

"Xylia, my dear it has been so long. You have blossomed into a beautiful woman."

He steps in front of me. I hate that he is taller 'cause saying I have to look up to him feels disgusting.

"It hasn't been long enough, your Majesty," I mutter.

"Ah, I see Rose has made you into a strong woman. I wonder how she is doing."

His breath brushes across my face as he leans in closer. Hearing Rose's name come out of his mouth feels like I just fractured a part of my body. He takes one of my braids, now half falling out, and twirls it in his old fingers.

I hear Kage get smacked as he yells out. My body moves towards him instinctively, but the guards hold on me is too tight. The King caressing my chin keeps me from even glancing towards Kage. I can feel the frown on my own face as the desire to vomit rises in my throat.

"Let go of me," I snarl at him.

King Torrin smiles, tightening his caress into a grip. I want to smack that smile off his face. He has no right to smile, not after everything he has done to this country. He has burned the homes of 'his' own people. Robbed the cities of their money. He has stolen people's lives by enslaving them for this magicae army of his. I want to watch him burn.

"Romana, let's take our guests inside," he shouts to the large woman.

Romana begins moving, picking up Kage as she does so. The King takes my shackled arms and sets them on his, guiding me inside.

"Father, please hear what I have to say," Kage's voice sounds low and angry.

The King stops and looks over to his son. For a moment, I swear I see shock come across his face.

Good.

"I will speak with you later. Be quiet until you are spoken to." His comment shuts Kage down.

One by one, we make our way through the iron doorway and into the interior castle. If I wasn't being brought here against my will and a tyrant wasn't the one living in it, I wouldn't mind saying it's beautifully elegant. A side of life I've never had but can admire. A large fountain rests in the middle of the walking path made of yellow stone.

I crane my neck, looking up at the large ornate dome sitting in the center of four towers that come to a teardrop point. Bars on the windows of the dome have beautiful harps illustrated and metal leafs surrounding them.

I feel a squeeze on my arm, I look and see a happy, smiling old face watching me admire his home. I turn my face away and start counting the endless amount of Fel Watch patrolling. Kage has his eyes on me.

Prince Elijah struts his way to my right and takes my other arm. Now sandwiched between two terrible men, we enter through large intricately crafted grand doors.

We are greeted by a beautiful raven-haired woman whose face is as still as stone.

Opening her arms, she smiles. "Welcome, Lady Xylia. I apologize for not making an appearance with your previous visit. I was feeling not myself at the time. Though I am glad to have made your acquaintance now," she says before slightly bowing.

The King coughs as if warning her. She rises, putting her hands together in front of her. She walks over to Kage and examines him, an expression of worry overcoming her stillness.

"My dear ..." she whispers.

"I'm alright, mother," Kage whispers in return.

Kage rarely spoke of his mother, but he only ever described her as beautiful. I can see where Kage gets his looks from. They both have slim figures and sharp features. It's stunning to see them together.

I stumble a bit as pain radiates through my mind.

"Stay calm." A girl's voice echos somewhere nearby. I look around, and everyone's face seems to be in shock seeing me shake.

"Xylia!" Kage screams rushing towards me. Romana quickly grabs him and throws him back towards his mother.

My eyes are darting around, trying to understand, and I see her. The small girl I had noticed outside has followed us in. Her hand is outstretched, and her eyes are focused on me.

When she notices that I have spotted her, she tucks her hand underneath her robe.

Eli clears his throat. "Kage, I'm sure, would love to retire to his room, and my beautiful, you will be joining father and me."

They're acting like nothing happened.

The Queen doesn't miss a beat and begins to assist Kage out of the room, heading straight forwards. Kage offers a few glances over his shoulder back to me.

I don't want him to go, but this is all coming together. Just like we hoped it would.

I immediately rip my arms free and try to run to Kage. Eli catches me mid-sprint, wrapping his arms around me, holding my body still. Stomping and kicking, I scream for Kage as he is being pulled out of sight. Romana silences me, her body towering over my own. She's at least a foot taller than me, but I don't back down. I push my chest out and raise my head, asking her to make the first move.

The King snaps his fingers just as I puff my chest out a little more, and she bows towards me.

What game is he playing, having his soldier bow down to me?

"How sweet. Father, it looks like she's fallen for a prince," Eli says, smirking with a wild look in his eyes.

"Let's retire into the other room, Xylia, my dear." The King offers his hand, but I shove Eli off me and walk into the room on my own, still shackled.

Walking in, there's a large chandelier hanging in the center with two smaller ones framing each doorway. There are several of them. We enter through one to the right, and as we head further in, the room is massive. It appears round with how the pillars are laid out, but if I stare at the wall, I can see the room is really square. The floor has a deep red carpet, and yellow and blue banisters are hanging from each pillar. On the walls, there are stained glass windows depicting the different territories of Limoria.

Damn it! I slap my face, startling both the King and Eli.

I grab my head in frustration, the pain ringing through it once more. I turn back to see a cloak disappearing behind one of the pillars.

What type of magicae is this?

"What is she doing to my head?" I ask, pointing to the pillar the little girl is hiding behind.

The King smiles and waves his hand. "She is here to make you feel more at home."

I turn away from them to hide the terror I'm feeling.

They are already breaking me.

They have a way into my head. I don't know if I can stop her from inviting herself in. I wonder if she can feel the pain and suffering I am feeling right now. Can she see the images my brain replays on repeat regardless if I want it to?

Focus!

She peeks her head out from the pillar when the King clears his throat. He opens his hands, inviting the girl closer. She hesitantly moves in.

He puts an arm around her shoulders. "We found Lily in a poor village, her talent being wasted. We brought her here where we could give her a better home and a place to use her talents to better her country."

I feel happiness pouring into my mind again. The king was able to provide her stability.

No.

"I've seen the poor villages you've created, and I'm sure there are poor villages like them all over this country, thanks to you and your families' greed. Sounds like you took her away from a place that needed her. She could have used her abilities to ease the pain and suffering of those around her. She is trying to do it to me now, but the difference is, I'm okay with the darkness I feel. I never thought I would be, but I am. So I will keep breaking her spell until this place is far behind me."

Listen to my words, Lily. Turning people like you against him is what will make this plan work.

Eli laughs at my response, but the little girl's eyes shed a few tears, though she wipes them away quickly, so they don't notice them.

I hate to say I feel happy seeing her tears.

"The darkness she feels, she says. Xylia, you have lived a sheltered life in the group of thugs Rosaria built. The only darkness is you."

I take a step towards him, but another calming wave hits me. I shake my head, trying to rid this feeling.

"I was a captive in my home for my entire life because of you, because of this world. All too afraid to co-exist with powers that supersede human intelligence. Your family cast my people and me aside hundreds of years ago. Now you stand here, you may look like royalty, but all I see is a desperate dog gnawing at a stubborn bone."

"You are special, Xylia," the King interrupts, "you are a part of a race we thought of as a threat but is now our only hope for salvation. I should have thanked Rose for protecting such an important piece of our history for the last thirty-some years. Though, I bet those years felt an awful lot longer to you. Don't you see the importance of what we are doing? Your role in the history we are currently creating? You will be what changes the future, Xylia. The blood that runs through your veins. I've been chasing whispers of magicae for far too long when I had you at the ends of my finger tips."

He's lost his mind completely. Enslaving is immoral, but breeding magicae users like livestock ... He wants me to be his livestock.

"So, you think mating the few magicae users left will somehow save you?"

"No, my dear. You will save us. Elves live an awfully long time. Your blood will ensure a new and improved human race. Magicae will run through us as it once did and with longer lives to learn how to utilize it."

I take a step back, his eyes widening and his speech turning from a veteran King into a mad man. I can see the fear in Lily's eyes as she hears him, her body stiffening and her eyes locked onto the floor beneath her feet.

"We appreciate your understanding and willingness to assist us," Eli says, a similar look in his eyes to match his father.

They are crazy, worse than what Kage explained. This is going to make the plan a lot harder.

"You really do resemble your adoptive mother, that fiery look in both your eyes. They look just like the flames that burned the Adamina Clan down to the ground," the King says, regaining his composure.

Wait.

"What did you just say?" I whisper, looking from one to the other.

"Well, when Rose lied about you and Bren being there, we had no choice but to treat the Adamina Clan as traitors." I lurch for Eli as he finishes the sentence.

The guards don't have a second to react before my hands are already at Elijah's throat. He smiles even with the pressure of my hands. The Fel Watch hastily pull me off of him.

"Playing with fire can get you burned, Xylia. I wonder if you have any scars?"

"Why?" My voice breaks as tears threaten to fall.

This wasn't part of the plan. Rose said the Clan would be safe if I left. The Fel Watch were supposed to leave once they saw we weren't there.

My home, is there anything, anyone left?

I feel that same paralyzing feeling come over me and the Fel Watch pull me away.

The plan, it's already falling apart.

"Take her to her room. I'm sure she's just exhausted from her journey. Let's get her comfortable for her stay," King Torrin commands, smiling at me.

I scream at him with every bit of anger I have.

CHAPTER TWELVE

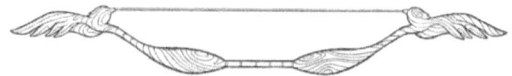

THE FEL WATCH drag me through the hallways. I try to memorize each turn; I *need* to commit it to memory. I'll kill him before I let him get away with what they've done. We head down a flight of stairs and take another right before a metal door opens. They throw me into the room roughly—magicae users, all wearing their matching robes, all awaiting for my arrival. They are surrounding the fireplace for warmth—my breath is visible in this room. There is nothing inside but a large bed and a small table with two chairs, not nearly enough space for us.

As I am taking in my surroundings, one of the taller users in the room starts to murmur and pulls something out from their cloak. The shortest among them grabs it from them and walks up to me. **The chalice**. Kage showed me drawings of it many times, going over how it worked. It is silver covered with symbols that remind me of the ones in the book; a single garnet facing me, pyramid in shape. The tip comes to a sharp point, just like Kage said. This is what the King means when he says 'get comfortable.'

I scoot away from her, but a paralyzing feeling washes over me. Their magicae has frozen me in place. They grab hold of my finger and prick it against the garnet jewel. They then hold my finger over the chalice, a single drop of my blood falling into it. As it splashes into an invisible liquid, a scream is ripped from my lungs as an overwhelming feeling to cower overcomes me.

"You'll feel better once you give in. It'll be painful until you do." Their words send a chill down my spine, and my brow begins to sweat.

Kage didn't mention it would be painful. My body begins to shake as I fight the feeling of something wanting to take over. I scream again and again. I can feel myself losing consciousness from just trying to stop this unseen influence. One of them places their hand on my shoulder as the paralysis wears off.

Gripping their wrists, I look into their eyes. "I will not fold."

The larger one rips my hands away and picks me up, tossing me into the bed.

⁂

I'm not sure how much time has passed since they left. There is no light to tell me how many shifts have or have not gone by. My body won't stop shaking. The pain hasn't stopped. There are moments where I think I might actually die or that I already did. A part of me wants to give in just so it'll all stop, but I can't. Every time I think of Codrin, or Vasile, or Rose, or Rye, or Kage, or Madi, or the Adamina Clan, or the stable owner, or the barmaid, or the lore keeper, or anyone who has ever crossed my path, reminds me I can't give in.

I won't give in.

I will never give in.

But it hurts.

No, just breathe. Breathe.

As my mind begins to lose consciousness again, the door bursts open. A cocky, smug-looking Eli comes walking in, a few magicae users close behind him.

You've got to be kidding me.

"I thought I'd come check on our newest little pet. That little toy we have seems to do quite a number on those who play with it."

He makes his way over to the bed I was thrown on. Eli grabs my wrists and pulls me up, so I am sitting upright. My body bellows at his touch and force of movement. He notices my pain, a surprised look on his face.

He puts his lips to my ear, his breath makes my skin crawl. "Still fighting it, I see. Hm, interesting."

Eli angles me slightly, sitting behind me. He starts to pull the bands out of my hair to loosen the braids. Twisting around, I slap him across the face and rip my hair out of his hands. I nearly blackout right there. I don't know how much more I can take of this constant pain on top of his visit.

"You will not touch me," I growl at him.

He laughs, touching his face where a slight red glow resides. In an instant, he goes from charming prince to devilish creature in seconds. Grabbing my shoulders, he shoves me to the floor. My head smacks against the stone, and I see stars.

He pins me down and leans in close, his breath on my face. "You belong to me. I will do whatever I please."

My vision blurs. I'm barely holding on, but I muster a scowl.

"So angry all the time. Why don't you smile?"

Eli releases one of my hands to cup my face. As he leans down towards me, I swing my fist back and punch him square in the jaw. He reels back enough to leave another opening for me to hit him again but that paralyzing feeling washes over me once more. I scream out the last bit of energy left in my body.

Eli sits up and pulls me up by my collar. He raises his fist before punching me in the face. I hear the shadows gasp as they watch him hit me. My body responds as the debilitating force leaves me, and I spit out a little blood. Pain fiddling through my face, I start to laugh, hoping to hurt his ego. He wipes the blood off my mouth and slams me into the floor. I'm still laughing, though, and I hear him start to laugh too.

Not quite what I was expecting.

Is he going to kill me?

I wouldn't be in this pain if he did.

No, he can't kill me.

"Maybe I should go get Kage. He always liked learning. I'm sure he'd be up for watching me beat you to see how an Elvish body reacts to pain. Or maybe I should get that rat of yours up here and make you watch."

I stop laughing and look him dead in the eyes. "I can't wait to see you dead at my feet." I mean it too.

His words oddly give me hope. Vasile is definitely alive. I just need Kage to work his side of the plan.

Eli punches me in the face again. He picks up my body and throws me onto the bed. Tugging my hair, he pulls my face to his, kissing my forehead.

"I can't wait to watch you squirm as I make that friend of yours cry out in pain."

He drops me and storms out of the room, shoving the two magicae users to the side. They look back at me and then each other. I watch them fade out of focus and then into nothing.

I took it too far.

I STARE up at the high ceiling, my breathing is shaky and faint. It feels like it has been days. Maybe it has. No. Elijah wouldn't wait longer than a day to return. He has a point to prove. Eli is right about one thing, I am the darkness. I've done nothing but hide behind others, and now I have nowhere to hide. No way to protect those I have left in my life to care for.

The image of the book appears in my mind. I used to wish so badly for those pages to be real. The stain glass to become my reality, so I could save the vitaterrium and rule. They would finally have a ruler who cared. It's funny now as I look back. Even within the Clan, there was never really a place for me. I tried to hide my ears. Tried to hide my powers. I tried to hide who I am. The voice terrifies me because I knew it made me even more separated from everyone else, but now that it's gone, I feel like I've lost a piece of myself.

I'm no longer going to try and be the girl I saw in that book. I'm going to be the woman I am now and want to be years from now. Being different is how I should be treated because I am different. I'm still riddled with guilt, and I don't know if I'll ever find a way to redeem myself—to erase that from me, but that's a part of who I am now too. I'll live and carry it with me. I'll do my best to find the moments where I think they would be most proud of me, and I'll hope that will be enough. Though I doubt it ever will.

⚓

THE DOOR BURSTS open once again. Eli is dragging a bloody mess of a man into the room. His hair is stained red, a mask covering his entire face.

Please don't be him.

Elijah looks proud, happy with the project he has been working on. It's monstrous. My heart is beating so loud I feel it in my ears. I want to hurt him.

"A gift, for you," Eli says, out of breath.

Eli points with his head in my direction, and a large cloaked figure walks into the room, grabbing my arms to pull me into a seated position. Elijah is desperate to make sure I get a good look at his 'gift.' Looking closer at the man, his hands are covered in blood and his clothing is nothing but tatters.

"Oh, my apologies," Eli says, taking off the bleeding man's mask.

I swallow the bile that is quickly rising in my throat.

Vasile looks up at me. "Xy."

I feel the uncontrollable urge to rip Eli's throat out, but the weakness and pain stop me completely. I begin to growl. Eli drops Vasile on the ground and comes over to me. He yanks me up by my hair and shoves me to the ground, so my face falls right in front of Vasile's broken one. I want to reach out, but my body will not move.

Vasile's eyes open again, shock and grief fill them. I whimper because those are the very emotions coursing through me, and I can't do anything to help him.

This is all my fault. I should have healed quicker, been here sooner, done everything in my power to rush here.

"Look at the two of you. Pathetic." Eli grips my hair, lifting me up once more. "My father spoke so highly of you—but you're a weak and puny girl. I don't see what's so special. Just another magicae user, except for your ugly ears. That's the only difference I see."

I hear a shuffle at my feet.

"You can't see anything special, because you are too dim-witted and too ugly to notice she is the greatest thing in this realm. Not to mention the mass of magicae users protecting you," Vasile says, spitting a bit of blood at one of Eli's boots.

Eli drops me and steps the same boot onto Vasile's face.

"Too ugly? Should I show you a mirror, rat?"

Eli chuckles as he puts more of his weight on Vasile's face. Vasile whimpers.

"Stop!" I push myself to move, this time yelling through the struggle of fighting the pain.

"Enough!" King Torrin yells, appearing in the doorway.

I grab onto Eli's trousers, pulling myself up. Eli takes his foot off of Vasile and rips me off of him. He knees me hard in the chest.

"I was only trying to demonstrate ..."

"That you are incapable of thwarting your urges," the King cuts his son off harshly.

If I did not also despise the King, I might've smiled. Eli storms out of the chamber like a child throwing a tantrum. The King points towards Vasile. A few guards come into the room from behind the King and drag Vasile out by his arms.

I bite my lip so hard, it begins to bleed, trying to hold back the sobs resting in my throat. I start to choke on it as he disappears, out of sight.

I'm sorry, Vas.

The King waits for me to compose myself. I shake and sniffle for a while, him watching me patiently.

"I hate you," is all I can muster.

"My dear, you just lack understanding," he says, stepping closer, leaning down, until I feel his breath on my face. "I am going to use you to start a new world. I will poke and prod that power of yours until we can wield it to take Limoria and restore it to its once former glory."

"I'm not giving in. I'll fight till it kills me." I spit in his face. "My power will never belong to you."

He smiles sweetly and turns away from me, one of the guards coming in as he leaves. I'm lifted up and placed back onto the bed. My mind, body, and soul going dark.

A COLD BREEZE rushes across me as I stand in the center of an old and crumbling building. My eyes open to see tall ceilings, intricate carvings embedded into the walls around me, gold tracing the seams of the stones as they connect. Taking a step forwards, the click of my heel hitting the stone echos through the large room.

A light begins to flicker, I must have awoken it. I freeze.

Where am I?

"Home," the voice whispers.

Did it just hear my thoughts?

"Yes," it whispers again.

I take another look around the walls that are now becoming more familiar as if I have been here before. Furniture appearing with flashes of light, voices belonging to glimmers that are dancing around the room. The feeling of arms wrapped around me tight, and tears dripping onto my face. I wipe the tears away. They don't belong to me but drip onto me from some invisible face resting against mine.

"Xylia."

I shoot up, my hand is extended, reaching towards her.

"Mama ..."

My eyes jolt open, the cold interior and bare room come back into view. I look to my outstretched hand.

The pain is gone.

I'm no longer shaking, no longer fighting for my soul. The voice, she's back. A smile emerges on my face, a comfort washing over me. A few of the tears slip through—my missing piece back now. My light is back.

I wait a few minutes, really testing myself to make sure I can handle what's coming next. Kage will be angry that I am going against the plan, but knowing the Adamina Clan is gone and seeing Vasile like that, I'm not letting him sit inside this terrible place alone a moment longer than necessary.

I march back over to the door and place my ear against it, trying to listen for any movement. There are two men quietly talking to each other and some shuffling. I look around the room to see what I can use.

The poker next to the fireplace.

I equip it and ready myself for a mad dash. I quickly reimagine the path they took here, heading the same way through the corridor Kage disappeared through. This place is huge, but if I can find him, we can rescue Vasile and get out.

Standing next to the door, I extend my hand and try to quietly bend and break the lock. I manipulate the matter of the lock until I hear a soft clink. I'm going to have to move quickly.

Take them by storm.

I take a deep breath and throw the door open, both men jump, drawing their weapons.

Don't hesitate.

I swing the poker and smack the sword from one of the guard's hands and tackle him to the ground.

"M.U. attempting escape ..." I grab the fallen guard's sword and throw it at the other, confident my magicae will not fail me. I guide the sword through the guard's neck, silencing his voice.

He crumples to the ground as I call the sword to my hand, looking into the wide eyes of the man underneath me. He puts his hands up, but I pierce him with the sword ending his life.

And Eli said the King spoke highly of me. Obviously not highly enough to post more than two guards.

I take the sword out of the corpse and look around, the hall is empty. I don't hear hasted footsteps or shouts.

I'll take that as a good sign.

As I step down the hall, I come across three different directions to choose from—my memory fails me. Tears build as I start to feel lost and hopeless. Two dead men are laying next to me, two men need my help, and two men want to use me. My legs weaken under the pressure, but I hear it—the voice is calling me.

I wait for the light to blind me as it always does. Instead, I see a light down the hall to my right. I hesitate for a moment, but it starts to flicker as doubt takes over my mind. It's the best thing I got, so I move towards it. The light shines brighter as I put my trust into it. The voice sings and hums in my mind, whispering my name here and there as it guides me through the halls, up the stairs, and around a large garden that rests in, what I think is the center of the castle. I am able to quickly hide from any patrolling Fel Watch behind lavish potted plants or window nooks.

Rounding the next corner, I see familiar raven hair draping down to the floor, a few braids woven in to add texture to her rather straight hair. I quickly lean back against the wall, hoping she didn't notice me peek around.

"Lady Xylia, you need not hide from me. Step back around so I can see you."

I pause for a moment, but the fact that she didn't immediately cry for help gives me courage. I step around the corner as she asks, and she bows towards me once more.

"I am looking for your son, Bren. As well as my friend," I state. I'm sure she could have figured that out herself.

She nods. "Of course. Bren has said some wonderful things about you, Oracle."

I hesitate at her words.

How long was I down there?

How much has Kage shared?

Can I trust her?

I shake my head. Regardless of if I can or cannot trust her, my fate is in her hands. I follow her graceful stride as she escorts me through the halls, my sword still ready to take on anyone wanting to stop me. We end up at a large wooden door with gold lining. She knocks but proceeds to open the door with no response.

"Mother, I said I am fine," Kage snaps as we both step through the threshold.

He freezes for a moment before shaking his head. "Xylia, what are you doing here?" he asks in a whisper. Kage looks from me to his mother, then back to me.

I rush over to his bedside, his arms outstretched. He wraps one arm around me while taking my chin into his other hand. Kage examines my face, which I'm sure is bruised from the hits his brother had delivered.

"I'm sorry, but I-" I start, but Kage puts a finger to my mouth and looks over my shoulder to his mother.

"Oracle, I will leave you two be. I'm sure Bren will see to your safety."

I glance back at her, brows furrowed, before looking back to Kage, who seems displeased.

"Kage. I couldn't wait. Our plan is falling apart, Vasile is in so much pain, and the Clan is gon-"

My lip trembles, just imaging the bloody crumpled mess he was and knowing that I may never see the home I helped build ever again.

"Xylia, we discussed the possibility-"

"He is alive, though. Elijah made sure I got a good look at his handy work. I know the plan. I remember our countless discussions, Kage, but none of that matters now."

"The chalice? You seem to be spirited, did they not use it on you?" Kage asks in a surprised tone.

I sigh and roll my eyes. "You should have warned me how painful that would be." I say.

"It didn't work?"

"Does that matter? We need to find Vasile, then we can get out of here," I say, stepping away from Kage. I figured he'd understand how desperate I am just by showing up.

"You are right. Now is not the time to ask questions. If we don't leave now, they will find us and stop us, Xylia. I know you want to save Vasile, but—"

"There is no but," I hiss, interrupting him. "We came here for Vasile. We are not leaving him here."

"I'm not risking our lives to save a dead man."

"He's alive, Kage!" I scream.

"Barely, from how Eli explained it, he won't make it much longer."

"Yeah, not under your brother's guard."

"Xylia!" Kage shouts, grabbing my shoulders and shaking me a bit. "Enough. We can argue later."

"Save yourself," I spit my words at him.

I'm not losing Vasile. My one piece of home. *My* best mate.

Kage drops my shoulders and rubs his face like he has something to be irritated about. He scratches his cheek and looks at me, a fire in his eyes. My heart flutters for a moment seeing him so intense. Kage's brow furrows, and he bites his lip before running his hands through his hair.

"Bloody Awemother ..." Kage whispers under his breath. "You stubborn, brutal, amazing, caring woman. You'll be the death of me."

Kage squares himself to me, cupping my cheeks, kissing me deeply. I lean into him, guilt rushing through my body as the pleasure wins. Wrapping my arms around him, he runs his fingers over my knotted braids. His breath hitches as his body presses harder against mine, causing me to melt into him. Kage's emerald eyes watch me desperately. I try to memorize every detail of his face. I don't know why but something clicks inside me like he's trying to decide on something I'm not even aware of.

Placing his forehead against mine, he sighs heavily with a small laugh. Pulling away from me, Kage looks me over. "We need to go. Let me just grab a few things we will need."

I nod in agreement.

Kage walks over to the table resting in the center of the large room.

My mind was moving so fast I didn't even realize I am standing inside of a room nearly the size of my old home. His bed is the largest I've ever seen, and the fireplace is decorated in silver and gold. I take a slow spin as Kage begins to pack a bag.

The wall that shares its space with a large bay window is just one large bookcase that starts at the floor and stretches up to the ceiling. I step closer and read some of the titles that are there. ***Vitaterrium History***, ***Languages of the Dead and Alive***, *and* ***Magicae Through Time*** are the few I read before Kage draws my attention back to him.

"Father and Eli were here just a moment before you arrived, I'm glad you didn't show up sooner, but my guess is they are on their way to visit you. They will notice your absence, and our chances of getting Vasile and escaping the Capitol start to narrow with every minute that passes."

Kage throws the bag over his shoulder and starts to make his way over to the door, pausing in front of me, taking my hand.

He sighs, stepping closer. "I'm sorry that I-"

I kiss him softly. He was worried about us. I understand that. Though leaving Vasile was never an option, I'm glad *he* understands that.

KAGE IS LEADING us down a hidden tunnel I remember faintly from my first visit to the castle. It leads us to the cellars. There are faint sorrowful weeps and cries for help that I'm sure normally never get answered, something that hasn't changed since I was a youngin. Kage's hand tightens on mine as we continue our hasted walk. Terrible memories of the things that are done to those down here makes me nauseous. Kage slows our pace as we reach a wooden door at the end of this tunnel. There are paths leading both to the right and left, but Kage rests his ear against the door.

"There are going to be a few Fel Watch posted outside in the main hallway. I do not think they are aware of our absence just yet," Kage whispers as he opens the door slowly.

He leans back so I can peek through. "They are going to be to the right."

I nod as I see three guards sitting around a table playing some form of cards. I extend my hand forwards and concentrate on the nearest guard's sword that happens to be leaning against the table. There is only a moment for any of them to notice before I will it alive and slash towards them. The owner of the sword crumples to the ground, and I take that as my cue to charge. I run forwards, Kage close behind me, and tighten the grip on the sword I stole from earlier and clash it against a blade identical to it.

"Kellen, run! It's the elf!" The man shouts, and the woman guard immediately listens to his command.

I push off of him to give us space and send the other sword after her. He leaves a nice opening for me to attack.

"Go for her!" Kage shouts as he appears from behind the male guard, a grunt escaping the man's lips, a panicked look in his widened eyes.

I run as the guard falls to his knees. The woman shouts, but I throw the sword, and it catches the small gap between her chest plate and her chausses. She screams as she collapses. I turn back to Kage, who seems to have grabbed her weapon.

Kage obtains the keys and opens the cellar door.

The twenty to thirty cells down here are all cramped with too many people shoved inside. The room is only lit by a few lanterns that are nailed to the ceiling, the floor damp. Nothing has changed.

As the prisoners start to spot us, they create more noise, begging for our help. Kage tries to contain them as I desperately search for Vasile.

He's not here.

"Kage." He looks directly at me as I fight tears. "He's missing," I say once I'm certain that Vasile is not here.

Kage looks at all of them before looking around the room. He glances at the different torture tools left out to intimidate and scare the prisoners.

"This is going to sound crazy, my Lady," Kage whispers, dangling the keys.

I cock my head to the side and arch a brow.

He begins unlocking the cages. "You all need to stay calm and listen to the plan. If you do, we are all going to get out of here."

My heart begins to race, seeing nearly fifty people of all ages, races, and I'm sure capabilities, stand together and listen to Kage. He has a calm disposition and commanding voice that Rose and Rye would be most impressed by. He's a man I'd much rather see ruling this kingdom.

"We are going to go through that door, take the Fel Watch out, and storm out of this place," he tells them the directions of where to go and areas to avoid if they get separated.

The tired prisoners take hold of the tools or whatever they can find to use as weapons, readying themselves for the fight of their lives. Kage opens the main door and the people go flooding out. I trail behind them, but Kage grabs my wrist and holds me back.

"You're just gonna let them run rampant with zero guidance?" I ask.

He just encouraged these people to fight, and now he is sitting back?

"For now. We have one more person to find. They will have to manage until he's freed as well," Kage says, leading me through the cellar door and back through the wooden door, turning left down the tunnel. "My guess is that he's in Eli's *special* cell."

My heart hurts, thinking he's had to be around that monster for so long.

We turn left, right, then right again, then deadhead it until we come to another wooden door. Kage listens through it again before opening it. We rush out and take a right until Kage leads us to a large door where I hear people talking. Kage looks back at me, and I nod my head.

"There are going to be more guards, maybe even some from the **M.G.A**."

"M.G.A?"

"The group of Magicae users my father enslaves. It's their group's name."

Kage opens the door, a bright light shines down, causing my eyes to adjust. Vasile is sitting tied to a chair, a small pool of blood beneath him. It takes everything in me to not run to him.

Instead, I focus on the four guards surrounding him and thank the heavens, there are no Magicae users here.

"Xylia, just run!" Vasile shouts. His head is now up, his eyes focused on me.

I know it's been moon cycles since he's been here, but Vasile should know that I cannot turn my back on him now that we are both right here.

"How cute." Eli laughs

Eli walks up from somewhere hidden in the darkness. He makes his way to Vasile and grabs him by the hair pulling his head back, putting a knife to his throat.

"Though, poor timing," Eli says calmly with a smile.

I scream in horror. Kage grabs my arms to try to turn me away. The light bursts from inside me, blinding Eli, the guards, Vasile, and Kage. I quickly extend my hand, using the surge of power to rip the dagger out of Eli's hand and have it fly over into mine. The light fades. Vasile and Kage look at me in shock as their eyes try to refocus. I charge forwards. The moment the guards notice, they charge after me.

I can hear Kage distract one of the guards as metal begins to clatter behind me. A taller woman approaches me, her blade already drawn. I duck under her heavy swing. I don't wait for her to wind up. I get in close and push the dagger into her neck. I kick her pelvis to push her body away and turn to a blade slashing towards me. It catches my shoulder. I scream as it tears into me and I fall backwards. The guards advance towards me, and I try to push past it. The shorter of the two lifts his sword upwards, ready to pierce me, but I kick his knee in. He still attempts, but it misses me entirely and he wedges his sword into the ground.

The other guard swings his sword down towards me, but I bring up my sword to meet his. He shoves me down, my back pressed firmly to the ground, our blades screeching as they rub against each other.

"Get off her!" Kage shouts, kicking the guard away from me before stabbing the wounded one.

Kage extends his hand, and I take it gratefully. He pulls me up, kissing my cheek before finishing the guard who had the advantage on me. I turn to Eli, whose face is a mixture of both fear and excitement. His eyes are wide but his smile is wider.

I step towards him when he meets my gaze.

"Quite the show," Eli says, applauding.

Vasile's breathing is rough and fast, his eyes teary and scared. The sting in my shoulder is nothing compared to the anger that I feel. To hurt someone so joyful, caring, and strong. I knew Eli was a monster, but now I think he's demonic.

"Let him go, Eli," Kage commands, but Eli just laughs.

Eli doesn't move as I am nearly arm's length from him. He looks down at me and tilts his head.

"You are gorgeous with a little blood on you. I bet I could make you beautiful," he whispers.

"Shut up, you bastard!" Vasile shouts.

Eli goes to grab Vasile, but I stab Eli in the heart, halting him. Elijah takes a step back before looking down at his chest. His brow furrows, and his hand grips the hilt of his own dagger.

"Kneel." I snap at him, putting a hand on Eli's shoulder and shoving him to his knees.

He coughs up blood, and his face begins to pale as his blood starts dripping on the floor. "I'm not the only monster in this room, Elf," he says, some of the blood spraying. Eli glances over my shoulder towards his brother. He smiles up at me, a devilish look in his eyes.

"We are all capable of being monsters. It's choosing not to be that means something." I push the dagger in deeper.

Eli's eyes roll back, and he collapses to the floor. I feel myself begin to shake from the adrenaline and pain.

"Vasile, we gotta go." I rush as I begin to untie him.

Kage walks over to his brother and rips the dagger out. He whispers something into his brother's ear and smiles. Kage closes his brother's eyes before standing, wiping the blade off, and throwing the dagger into his bag.

Loud bangs and echos reach our ears. This fight is far from over, and I am not done yet.

We need to move.

Vasile holds onto me as Kage leads us through the halls. I hate not having the sword in my hand, but I cannot carry Vasile with it. The fighting seems to have emptied the hallways, giving us time and space to move through the castle. Kage lets out a relieved sigh as we reach a door.

"This is one of the servants' exits. It'll take us through the kitchens and out the side of the castle." Kage opens the door and peers inside.

"Take him," I say to Kage.

Kage pulls his head back from inside the other room and furrows his brow. He rests our swords against the wall and takes Vasile.

"Is it your shoulder?" Kage ask.

I shake my head and smile.

"I'm going to finish this. The King won't allow this to happen again, Kage. If I don't strike now, we may never have the chance again." My sentence ends in a whisper, seeing the terrifying look both the boys are giving me.

A part of me never wants to leave Vasile's side again, and I know this means something to Kage, but I need them both to be safe.

"Xylia, I will not leave you," Kage says.

"I second that," Vasile adds.

I sigh and cup both their faces. "You are all with me, invariably."

Vasile whimpers a bit and brings his hand up to hold mine. I'm so happy I got him back. I am so grateful that he's alive, and I owe him for everything he's endured while waiting for me.

"Go," I whisper.

"Please wait!" A shout echos towards us.

I shove both the boys through the door, but they both begin to protest.

Before I can even shut the door, Lily's voice rings out, but now it is right behind me. "We wanna help."

I turn around and see her shaking hands wrapped around my quiver and bow. There are two just-as-scared girls standing behind her. I snatch my bow and quiver from Lily, quickly stringing both over and onto my back.

"Leave now, before you make me hurt you," I state.

I don't want to hurt them. They are children who have gone through the same pain I have and have been raised by a man who only values them for their power.

"We want to fight. That's what you plan to do, right? Fight?" Lily looks up to me, her hands laced together. She wants to be free from him too. "All of us do! We can help you." Lily confirms my thought.

"How did you do that?"

"Lily's Magicae allows her to hear and control thoughts and emotions," Kage says, stepping both him and Vasile back into the hallway.

"Raiden is the one who can track, though," Lily says, gesturing to the tall, lanky girl standing behind her.

Raiden raises her hand to wave. I smile briefly at her. That ability would have been handy in the Adamina Clan.

"Oh, and this is Shaw." Lily is now gesturing to the other girl.

"I can get us out quickly if things go bad," Shaw whispers.

"Raiden, where is the King?" Kage asks, setting Vasile onto the ground, resting against the doorframe.

"The throne room. He got trapped there. No one was really expecting the prisoners. We thought it would just be you two," Raiden says, pointing to Kage and me.

"Thank you. Raiden. Please stay with Vasile. There is probably a cart near the servant exit. Get that ready in case things go south, and Shaw needs to bring us back," Kage says.

Raiden freezes, looking at me first. I nod, and she moves around Lily and between Kage and me to help Vasile back up and into the kitchens.

"Xylia. I told you back in Ko that taking this Kingdom back was something we would do together. I meant that." Kage grabs my hand and squeezes it tightly.

"Then let's get going."

⇕

As Kage, Lily, Shaw, and I move closer to the main entrance of the castle, shouts and wails begin to echo through the halls. Complete mayhem is waiting for us ahead. As we gather in the domed entry room, Fel Watch and those we set free, are fighting each other. There are many improvised weapons from those freed, but they seem to be holding their own.

"It'll be a long fight before we can even get to the throne room," I comment.

I'll fight who I need to.

"There is another way in," Kage says.

Looking at his worrisome expression, I am not entirely sure if I want to go this other way.

He looks at Shaw, who doesn't really notice until all of our eyes are on her.

"Do you think you would be able to do that?" I ask Shaw honestly, not knowing the true extent of her powers.

"There's so much commotion, it'll be risky," Shaw says, unsure.

"She can do it," Lily says, nodding her head to her friend.

"Shaw, this is your magicae. Can you do it?" I know what it feels like to doubt your abilities, to be unsure if you can even rely on them.

If she doesn't, if she can't, it'll put us all at risk. Something I

174

wish I would put into practice. Shaw looks to Lily, who is beaming at her.

"I can do it. Ready yourselves."

I notch an arrow, Kage readying his sword, Lily takes a deep breath.

We all nod, and in a moment, I am surrounded by darkness, and it's cold, right before the light of day reappears. The room is filled with ten or more Fel Watch who are all taken aback by our sudden arrival. The King is at the other end, sitting on the throne.

I fire my arrow at the nearest guard who is readying his sword. It's fatal. Now knowing the amount and location, I grab a handful of arrows and throw them into the air, leaving my hand there extended. The hoard of arrows I will, each find their target, and I step past the falling bodies. I start to feel a strain, my shoulder now bleeding enough for it to drip down my body.

Shaw looks at me apologetically. Guess it wasn't as smooth as we thought. Two guards rush towards me, I raise my bow, but the strain makes me drop it instead.

Lily jumps in front of me, and they both slow their paces, dropping their weapons. "I can hold them for a while."

I nod, picking up my bow and moving around them. Kage shoves a guard off his sword, his shirt is ripped a bit and bleeding. Though, he reassures me with a smile.

We approach the throne that is now defenseless. Only a King and Queen standing before us. He sits there, his smile has disappeared. His happy, charismatic facade is gone. I can now see the man that has called himself a King for far too long.

The Queen is standing to his left holding onto his hand, but she is smiling, looking at us happily.

"Mother," Kage barks. His heart is still probably racing.

I know mine is.

The Queen rips her hand away from the King's and walks over to her son, taking his hand instead. The King's face reddens, and his fist begins to shake.

"You crazy, wretched woman!" He shouts.

"I warned you about the oracle, my love," she says, her face unchanging.

"She is no oracle," he shouts, his voice shaking with rage, "she's an orphan, an elf, something, and someone who is unwanted. You ungrateful little girl, I gave you purpose!"

"Then let me complete my purpose, Henry Torrin. Ridding the world of a Tyrant."

I raise my bow once more, ignoring the strain, notching an arrow.

"I hope you watch with pride, Bren. You've destroyed this kingdom and murdered your own family."

I look back to Kage, whose face has a small smile on his lips.

"I'm actually saving both, Father."

I fire.

CHAPTER THIRTEEN

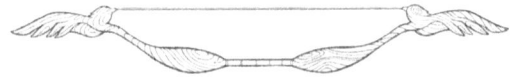

Ice and snow cover the trees of the Vermilion Forest. My boots sink in a few inches with every step closer I get to where the Adamina Clan once stood. After hearing from the Few Watch and the few magicae users that were here when the attack happened, we had to see it for ourselves. Vasile, now healed after a month of me treating him, was able to make the trek. It didn't feel right coming without him, and I'm the only one who would have been able to heal him enough to get back to normal. We both also needed the time to grieve and prepare ourselves for seeing our home in shambles.

At first, Vasile thought I was lying. He kept waiting for an Adaminian to burst through the castle doors, congratulating us. Rose's wish came true, along with every Clan member that joined us out of fear and need to escape the King. Though after a few weeks of waiting, he lost hope. Then both of our grieving could begin. I still didn't know as we prepped for our journey if we were ready, but being in the forest makes me feel more confident. Regardless of what's left, the memories we have are what will keep it alive. I hate to admit it, but some of what the

King said was true. Being able to run my fingers across the rough bark, I know this place was a sanctuary for me. I can be confident because I know it so well.

Hearing the crunch of the snow brings a smile to our faces, but the freezing winds do not. Of course, the day we arrive is the day of Lunamatrem. The day, once a year, where the moon goddess herself pours snow down onto those closest to her in the northern countries of Limoria.

"Remind me why we tied the horses up way back there instead of riding all the way in?" I look up into the trees, frozen leaves still attached to the tree's limbs. With the sun shining through the leaves, rainbows dance across us.

"So we could take our time," Vasile says, taking my arm as we arrive at the first chant markings.

"Right. Not rushing in." I smile at him.

We continue our cold and slow walk through the forest. Our first visit is to Codrin. It's easy to find, the hole never having been healed from the scorch that was the worst night of my life. The hole in the canopy had allowed the snow to find its way in with ease, as a hill of snow rests where he last was.

"He would be proud of you," Vasile says, crouching down.

I stay silent, not sure if Codrin really would be. The journey I've taken was one he never wanted me to.

I watch Vasile as he balls up the snow in his hands and smiles. "This was a day he loved to celebrate. He would cook that stew of his so that when we were done fighting and playing in the snow, it would heat us back up."

I wipe a tear from my eye and laugh, remembering how frostbitten we would all be. "He would be swimming in that hill of snow, I know that."

Vasile stands up and throws the snowball at the hill. "Yeah." Vasile takes my hand, it's cold and wet from the snow. "I can imagine it."

"Let's sit here awhile. I'm sure he's missed your company," I say, shaking Vasile's hand and arm.

Vasile laughs, though when he stops, we sit there and listen to the wind. The trees creak, causing an echoing sound that travels throughout the forest. Most of the monsters and creatures that call the Vermilion Forest their home, sleep while the Lunamatrem is here. It's peaceful during this time. I think that's why Codrin loved it so much. The hunting season would be over, everyone huddled in their homes, and warm food to eat.

Vasile brings my hand up to his lips and blows hot air onto it. His shoulders shiver, but he looks at me with teary eyes and smiles.

"Where's that stew when we need it?" Vasile jokes.

We should get moving. I don't mind the cold as much, not now at least, but we shouldn't stay out here in the open and without a fire.

"Ready to climb?" I ask, looking at his arm. Our matching fur coats cover him from my medical examination.

After the King had fallen, there was a lot of commotion. With the Queen still being alive and well, the guards were quick to stand down, and I was able to get back to Vasile. After being able to actually examine what Elijah had done to him, I noticed that his ribs, collarbone, his right arm, and left hand had all been broken, on top of dozens of gashes and severe bruising. His arm was by far the worst injury, though. Eli had cut through his skin and muscle to break the bone from the inside. Between every healer available and me, it took us three moon cycles just to get him back onto his feet. Once we got to that point, I was able to heal the rest with the light.

"You read like three books on medicine and made yourself my nurse," Vasile raises his eyebrow, knowing he is completely right.

I wouldn't be able to admit this to him, but it's out of guilt.

If I had been stronger, he wouldn't have been taken. If I was better, I wouldn't have taken so long to get to him, and if I hadn't lost control, I wouldn't have pushed Eli to take it out on Vasile.

"Well, I got you all healed up, didn't I?" I counter, arching my brows.

He laughs and shakes his head. He stretches for a sec, before freezing and looking into my eyes.

"I'll race you." Vasile jumps up high and grabs onto the icy branch.

My heart tightens, hoping he doesn't slip, but he throws himself up on top, safe and sound. Following his lead for a change, I jump up, and we both begin to race upwards towards the docks. As we see the docks still intact, my heart flutters. I, of course, reach the top first and pull myself up, which is a hell of a lot harder without a gatekeeper here to help. Cresting the top, I see the devastation. Carts, houses, shops. All burned and smashed. If I hadn't lived here for so many years, I doubt I'd recognize anything.

"Whoa, they really were telling the truth," Vasile whispers.

I nod, lost for words. A part of us was holding out hope, but it's gone now.

We walk through the little that remains. We pass Vasile's parents' place and walk into the shell that is left. I brush off the snow on the plaque they kept out front with all their names on it—a little chard but something he can take with him. I grab his hand as he starts to sniffle a bit but continues to walk around. Maybe I should have never left, they could all be alive if I hadn't. I know Vasile has been feeling the same way. He was meant to take over the reins and instead followed me. We were both selfish when our people needed us most. The Adamina Clan, though they never truly accepted me as an elf, still protected me from those who wished to use my heritage for personal gain. I was able to live in hiding without feeling hidden.

We continue through the residential district, passing the house Codrin and I once shared together. There's nothing left, no sign that it was ever there to begin with. Vasile walks away for a moment to give me space. I run my hands through the snow where our front porch would have been. I take a few steps forwards and turn, facing the direction our rocking chairs once were. The same beautiful view remains. Without the houses around, the view opens up even more—a sea of frozen leaves sway in the frigid wind.

I hear Vasile sneeze. We have only a few sunshifts before we start losing light and should probably start our long hike back to our horses.

I take one last look at my old home. "Bye," I mumble to the empty space.

FINDING the Command Post is harder. We had to find patches of dock to cross over; some of the old wood that held up the Command Post didn't withstand the fire. The building is still somewhat standing, though, on an island of dock, that I doubt would be smart to jump over. We stand as close to the edge as possible and look on from a distance. Being First Lady was a job I knew Rose was setting me up for. It would make sense for the Maresal to do so anyway—second in command taking over first command. The Adamina Clan was gone, though, and it would be a job I would never have to face.

Vasile takes my hand. "It was so scary to even think about," Vasile says, looking forwards. "That night, after I left your place. All I could think about were the words you shared with me outside of the detention center. I was somehow now having to be someone I didn't think I could be." He squeezes my hand even tighter. "I've always been in awe of you, Xylia. Since I saw that beautiful shining hair and those curiously tipped ears." I hear a small laugh escape his lips, remembering the moment he is retelling. "The first words out of your mouth, after Rose telling you to play nicely, were 'try to keep up.'"

I look over and see tears streaming down his face.

"Codrin and I used to talk about that first memory a lot. For him, it was the moment he fell in love. For me, it was the moment I realized how weak I was." He turns his face to me slowly, our eyes locking and a tearful gaze. "Every moment since then, I have pushed myself further, harder, and faster than I thought I could just to keep up with you, Xylia. So that night, I knew I still wasn't strong enough. If I were to ever become Maresal, I would somehow have to surpass you."

This time I laugh hearing that, not because it sounds outrageous, but because at the point of me leaving, I had full faith he was more than ready.

"I wonder if you would hold me in such high regard if it weren't for my power."

"The way you can just push through anything and everything. You lead with your head but never leave your heart behind. You show kindness, and it looks like a strength versus weakness. Sure, your magicae powers are super cool too, but I'm talking about you."

"He's right, you know."

Vasile and I freeze hearing her voice. We lock eyes, sharing a look of disbelief.

"Congratulations, Xylia. You accomplished my dream for me. I couldn't be prouder."

I slowly turn and see that fiery red hair, curls bouncing as she walks towards me. The way the sun reflects off the ice creates a ring of light, illuminating her hair. If it wasn't for Vasile holding my hand, I would think this is all a dream.

We both run towards Rose, our bodies crashing into hers when she opens her arms. I take her in, not sure if I am more thankful or relieved to see she is standing here with us right now. Feeling her embrace is something I did not think I'd ever feel again, but she's here.

"You're alive?" I barely get the words out with tears in my eyes. I barely keep my composure. I feel better seeing the same struggle on her own face.

"First Lady, how?" Vasile asks, amazed and undeniably happy that not everything, everyone is gone. There is still part of home—a piece that is alive and here with us.

She gives us both a kiss on the cheek, more motherly than what I've ever experienced.

"Madi, she was filling in as Maresal. She got a lot of clan members out while our militia and commanders fought. Your amazing evacuation plan actually worked. I should have listened to you. Maybe more lives would have been saved ..." her voice trails off.

A hug, kiss, and a compliment. This is a new Rose, someone I haven't met before.

She witnessed first hand the home she had built and promised to be a safe haven, burn to the ground.

"You said Madi made it? What about my folks?" he asks, a voice of desperate desire to hear her give him back a piece of himself.

"Madi made sure they were the first ones down and safe."

Vasile squeezes my hand tightly, his breath shaking with relief and happiness.

"They've moved on to Kel already. I think that might be as far as they go." Rose dips her head.

"The fact that there are any Adaminians alive means you

kept the promise you made to them. Their Lady did not fail them," I reassure her, putting my hand on her shoulder.

She puts her hand on mine and graces us with a smile. "You're like a whole new person. The little rebel I found in the woods all those years ago has ridden the disease that was killing this country. While Vasile over here has forgotten his manners already."

Vasile's eyes widen, and bows towards her, one knee down, putting his right hand into a fist over his heart.

We all laugh, Rose pushing his shoulder a bit.

"I guess I've grown a little slack on him. I'll pick the pace back up tomorrow."

Vasile sighs at my promise to get him back into Maresal shape.

We all head down, watching our steps and say goodbye to a home we all cherished and put our hearts into making ours.

Rose sheds a few tears. They freeze slightly in the cool wind.

"The winters were always the worst here," she mutters under her breath, maybe trying to force herself away with some distaste in her mouth. She's given too much to this place for me to allow her to do that.

"They were also the most beautiful. Millions of rainbows danced across our docks, kids chasing the rays trying to capture them in jars. The dances some of the older women would do from time to time to celebrate the Lunamatrem were breathtaking."

She nods at the memories, and we leave.

Descending the docks with no raft during the winter felt like any movement would send us to our deaths as our hands numb from touching the ice and snow. We all make it down safely, though. We take a moment to catch our breaths and continue moving towards the horses.

"Where are you staying?" I ask Rose, realizing that she is just probably following us.

She gestures towards the woods, slowly spinning in a circle.

"I've always felt most at home here. This is where Rye lives, where I belong."

My heart pings, and I slow my pace. I look off in the direction where Codrin took his last breath. She looks back at me and stops completely.

"But that doesn't mean you do," Rose says.

I stop, turning to completely face her.

"She's right, Xy. I know I haven't been the happiest for you with everything going on with Kage, but Codrin would be. As Codrin's oldest and closest friend, I can swear to you, he would hate seeing you so broken. He would hate seeing you turn away from someone just because of him not being here anymore, and especially because his death wasn't on you. A terrible creature took his life, and you did everything in your power to save him."

"It doesn't matter that you couldn't save him. It matters that you tried."

I take in a shaky breath, hearing Rose finish Vasile's thought. I look up to stop the tears from coming. After I killed the King, I thought a weight would be lifted. Like I put a balance back in my life, but nothing came. I felt heavier and darker, but hearing those words—I'll never forgive myself for watching him die, but it's time I stop feeling bad for myself because I couldn't stop him from dying.

CHAPTER FOURTEEN

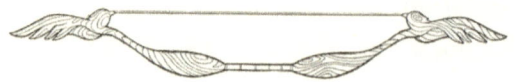

Rose joins us on our adventure to Ko. She catches us up on where the Adamina Clan stands now with the base being destroyed. Seems like, as of now, the Adamina Clan is disbanded and the Adaminians that remain are staying close. Now that the Old King is gone, the Felguard Country has slowly been rejoicing. There is still a lot of hesitation since the new King is the old King's son, but knowing that it was an elf he had with him during the coup seems to have earned a portion of the country's trust—strangely enough.

With the weather and horses having to work through the cold, it takes us an extra day to make our way through the snow and into the warm interior of the Slattern. Once we sit down, Rose orders us all something warm and a stein of ale.

"So you were the one to do it then?" Rose asks, some pride showing through.

"Yeah, though it wasn't what I thought it would be," I admit. I swirl my drink around, staring at the dark liquid.

"Change will come, Xylia." She touches my hand, drawing my attention to those fiery eyes of her.

I've missed them.

"The Queen, where is she in all of this?" Rose asks, pulling her hand back to grasp her drink.

"She retired as Queen. Kage and her agreed that having more than one Torrin could hurt the rebuild of trust," Vasile chimes in.

"She is living in Draco. It's where she was born and where her side of the family is," I clarify.

Rose nods. "That was a smart move. Even as well known as the Second Prince is, he is not as recognized. Felguardians may still be able to forgive and learn to respect him as a King."

She brings up the same point Kage did when we were all discussing it. Bran, Kage's mother, was very happy to go. Pleased to see Kage on the throne.

Rose excuses herself for a moment, giving Vasile and I a chance to look at each other and laugh. Having dinner at a tavern with the First Lady seems to be the strangest event either of us has experienced.

He becomes more pensive, though, and sighs. "Are you gonna say yes?" Vasile asks timidly.

My heart stops as I register his question, understanding his timidness.

"Would you?" I nearly whisper.

"He's not really my type but ... a castle, people waiting on me, the power, all that might change my mind."

"You truly do believe yourself hilarious."

We sit there in silence for a moment, knowing we have argued the good and bad sides of the arrangement Kage has proposed.

"This isn't my choice, Xy. Becoming the Queen of a country is definitely not something I'd ever be able to do, but you are more than amazing. I couldn't imagine a more capable person for the duty."

"You say 'capable' as if you have seen qualifying attributes." I look away before feeling his hand grip my arm gently.

"Don't try and erase the good things you've done for the Clan. Just because it's gone, it doesn't mean you didn't do your job well, Xy."

I pull my arm away. Vasile closes his eyes tightly, wincing from my drawback.

I take a deep breath and grab his hand, intertwining it with mine. "You are right."

Vasile's eyes dart, his mouth falling open slightly.

"I may have *some* qualifications to be Queen."

Vasile smiles that same childish smile he wears so handsomely. He squeezes my hand tightly and pulls me in, nearly yanking my body from the chair, wrapping his arms around me.

"Do you mind saying that again?" Vasile asks.

I push away playfully, laughing. "You'll have to earn it."

Rose returns and takes her seat beside me. She raises an eyebrow at Vasile, who is giddy in his seat from the praise. It does not help my choice, however.

I tug my hood tighter around me. How would the people react to actually seeing me now?

The decimated village we all were attacked at was in shock and kept their distance. They were kind, but the judgment was still there, or maybe it was all just disbelief.

"Hey Welma, a round for three," Rose whistles over to the same barmaid that was here when we first visited.

Her ever-beautiful sweaty frown slams the drinks on the table. I can say I'm pretty sure I'd lose in a fight with her.

"First name bases, huh?" Vasile asks, taking a sip of the sewage that fills these cups.

Rose laughs at the sight of Vasile's scrunched-up face.

"I used to come here often when we were first starting the

Clan, and it's been a good place to visit now that I don't have to be the First Lady," Rose says into her drink.

I swirl the liquid around in my tankard, still unsure if now is the time to ask her about *that* night. I'll get us rooms for the night. It'll feel great sleeping somewhere warm after the last couple of nights sleeping out in the snow.

After a few more rounds, Vasile starts to yawn, and the bed sounds even nicer.

"Rose, you said my parents went east. Did ... Madi ... accompany them?" Vasile tries to say slyly, back to old habits.

"Yes, she did. She wanted to make sure they were settled in before heading back here. She might be back already."

His ears perk up, and starts looking around. Rose puts her hand on his and laughs.

"I said might."

I've never seen her this touchy, this relaxed.

Vasile brushes the slightly embarrassing moment off his shoulder and excuses himself for the night.

Rose and I, as we finish our drinks, hear a group talking about the Vermilion Forest.

"It's never happened before, I'm telling ya. I swear I saw creatures looking at the town from the tree line. Some of them even crept closer!"

A lady sits on his lap laughing.

"Yeah, yeah. You sound like a parent telling their youngin a horror story! Those creatures are too skittish to even think about coming close to town, not to mention this time of year!"

The rest of the group laughs, nodding their heads. Rose and I look at each other with some concern. The Adamina Clans' presence kept a lot of those creatures deeper south and far to the east, not to mention the eighth King had the Fel Watch bordering the forest. If the creatures were to get loose, we would definitely would have a problem.

I pull out a piece of parchment and some charcoal. Getting Kage a letter will be much faster than me telling him myself. Rose smirks, seeing who the letter is addressed to.

"Must be nice being able to just write a letter and things get taken care of."

I stop writing for a moment to look up at her with an exasperated expression.

"We recalled the Fel Watch for the coronation. It's time they get redispersed. I'll advise Kage to keep the numbers small since the last thing this country needs is the feeling of a King cracking down on its people, again."

"It's we now, huh? And you are advising the King?"

"I was nearly explaining to you the situation. I've been raised to have a military mind and a protectiveness for others."

I go back to my letter, avoiding her gaze.

"That is true, but I'm sure the old King had plenty of military-minded people by his side. What makes you so particularly important?"

"Perhaps because I was a part of taking down the Tyrant?"

Rose gives me a sly smile and laughs. We go back to eavesdropping, hoping it'll maybe offer some more insight on what's been going on in the country and their opinions.

We hear a few grumblings about how the cities surrounding the capital are still packed, property line disputes, and missing boots.

"Is that actually right?"

"An elf? Here in the Felguard?"

I freeze. Rose and I meet each other's gaze.

"Well would make sense, taking revenge against the family that took 'em away from theirs."

"They used to live a long while, right? Is it possible?"

"They are weird with that magicae."

"The new King is still a Torrin, though. How's the elf handling that?"

"Heard that the elf was the one to put him in that chair."

One of the people talking jumps up onto their chair, swinging their arms around for attention.

"Elf, heh, they are all long dead. This is jus' a rumor to stray us away from the fact nothin's really changed!"

Suddenly the whole tavern begins to join in on the debate. With the truth still hidden about what happened, it gives room for people to come up with their own truth. Kage's reign can end long before it even begins if the Felguardians don't support him.

They need to know the truth.

I stand, Rose grabbing my arm and pulling me back down.

"Whatever it is you are thinking of doing, don't. I don't feel like watching my kin get torn apart."

I grip her wrist and pull her hand off of me.

"I merely want to show them the truth. I am terrified, Rose, but people are aware that I may exist," I bite my lip, "and if I agree to Kage, then there really is no more hiding."

"Agree to Kage?"

I step away and move towards the door. My hands are shaking as I reach for my hood and begin to focus on the light.

Am I really doing this?

This is dangerous, potentially suicidal, but if I even want to consider ruling alongside Kage, the people must see me. All of me.

I turn, hood resting on my shoulders, a bright ring of light surrounding me. The tavern goes silent as all eyes turn towards me. I even garner a look of wonderment from Wilma. My heart is pounding so loud it is all I can hear. Not even the voice is there to whisper to me. I let the light slowly fade out, taking a few steps towards the crowd that has slowly backed away. Rose is the only one still seated.

I brush my hands over my long-tipped ears and force my most comforting smile to appear.

"Do not be frightened. I simply wanted to garner your attention. I want you all to hear the truth about the rumors."

No one moves or says anything. Vasile appears from the stairway seemingly drawn back down by the noise the crowd was making just a moment ago. He turns his eyes towards the thing everyone is staring at, me. He is frozen.

"I am real. I am standing here before you, not above you."

The tavern is silent, waiting for more.

"Slaying the Tyrant King was not an action I committed alone. You were all—all of Felguard—was standing right there beside me." I swallow and take a deep breath. There are no angry mobs so far. I'll take that as a good sign. "Kage Felguard, formerly known as Bren Torrin, is a King for any who find this country to be their home."

I feel the blood rush to my cheeks. I have no idea what I just said or why those were the words I chose, but it's what came out.

I'm really playing into this oracle persona.

Whispers begin rolling off of everyone's tongues. Waves of nervousness and speculation crashing into me, threatening to drag me under.

I am drowning.

"Thank you, Oracle!" Rose shouts.

I look to see Rose now standing, clapping her hands. She nods to me with a smile. Vasile begins to clap too, shouting his appreciation. A few more hands begin to clap before the entire tavern is clapping and claiming their thanks.

"She heard our prayers!"

"An elf! An actual elf!"

"What does this all mean?"

"Look at those ears."

"Kage Felguard ..."

"A new era!"

"The Oracle?"

I raise a hand, smiling towards them all. They quiet down and wait for me to speak.

"I cannot ask you to follow my lead in supporting King Felguard. I only hope that one day you will see why it is him I give my loyalty to."

Vasile finishes his descent, making his way through the crowd to get to me. He extends his hand to me, that goofy grin adorning his face once more. I place my hand on his. He kneels to me, kissing my hand lightly.

I look back to the rest, them all kneeling now. My heart stops at the sight. My lip quivers as the tears begin to threaten. I bite down hard to stop myself.

My answer is yes.

THE PEOPLE all take their time coming up to me, wanting to touch my arms or hand. All asking questions about how I survived, how old I am, where did I come from, all things I am not too sure myself. I explain that I have been alive around thirty-six sidereal years, though my body seems to age a lot slower than a regular human's does. Tell them that I was found amongst the trees in the Vermilion Forest by my two mothers who raised me. I'm honest when I say that I do not know how I survived or how I am standing amongst all of them now. Some start chatting and gossiping, whispers start that I am born from the Awemother herself.

This was not what I was expecting, but Kage was right. The people are taken by my power and appearance.

I hate that he is always right. It's frustrating.

I'm glad he was right about this part, though.

We decide to call it a night and go to our rooms, but before heading to my own room, I follow Vasile to his. He gives me a cocky smile and looks at me. I arch a brow in serious interest as to what nonsense is running through his mind, but I'm sure I'll find out. He steps into his room, leaving the door open behind him. Reaching down, he pulls his tunic off. I do take a quick glance to admire his very well-toned body standing in the dimly moon-lit room. His copper-colored skin defines every muscle. The baggy armor he normally wears really doesn't do him much justice.

He crosses his arms and clears his throat. I look up into his brown eyes and see just a boy hiding behind them. I can understand why he is such a charmer, but, for me, that little boy is all I see every time.

"I knew one day you'd find yourself lonely and in need of some company. Always thought Codrin would be off on patrol or something, but alone is still alone. Here I am stuck in the middle between a beautiful woman and knowing she belongs to my best friend."

I smirk, letting him continue his fantasy.

"I can't say I blame you, Xy. We have always been close. It was only a matter of time as to when you'd start seeing me as a lover versus a friend."

I try to swallow my laugh, looking even deeper into his eyes and walking into his room. Closing the door behind me. I slowly make my way up to him, resting a hand on his bare chest, my eyes focused on his lips.

I lean in closer, so my breath is on his. "Keep on dreaming."

I shove him back, both of us laughing at the ridiculous thought of us ever being more than what we are right now.

"What can I do for you, Lady Oracle?" he asks with a little bow, a laugh trickling in after the oracle slips past his lips. "I've never seen you like that. So out there. A little theatrical in my opinion, but it made them happy, it seems."

My smile fades a bit. "I figured. If I am going to be a Queen, my people would need to see me. All of me."

"I know that wasn't easy, Xy. You've stayed hidden, been criticized, and judged because of who you are. Every time I think I am catching up to you, you come out and show me a better, improved, version of the woman I already admire." Vasile brings his hand up and brushes his thumb across my cheek.

I love you too, Vasile.

I smack him on the head lightly. He laughs and looks at me with an arched brow.

"I thought you were clever. You should know that I never expected you to become Xylia." His hand drops from my cheek, and places it into his lap. "I have always needed you to be Vasile."

He smiles to himself and rubs his chin a bit.

"You really know how to butter me up, huh?" Vasile laughs and scratches his head.

I like seeing him happy. I didn't think I would ever see that smile again after what Eli did to him. Though when we started talking about coming to the Adamina Clan, his mood changed. The Vasile I have known for years was back. I can't shake the thought that he could be happier. Throughout the whole night, even with being consumed by a mass of people. Vasile's reaction to hearing Madi's name is something I keep returning to. I know that Vasile could be happy staying by my side. I know that he is devoted and cherishes our relationship, but I want him to have his own dream. Madi has been that dream. I bite my lip. I don't want to have this conversation, but we have to.

He knits his brows as I hesitate. "Xy. What is it?" He still puts on the smile I love seeing, but his voice is a whisper.

"I think you should stay and wait for Madi."

He drops his smile for a second, mulling in his mind the words I just muttered. Maybe he's trying to make sure I actually said them because I am sure he's been thinking them since we found out she's alive.

"But the journey back, it's too dangerous for one person, and—"

I throw my hand up to cut him off. "I understand, but I'm a little bit stronger than your average person, and I can see your feelings for her are still there."

He looks out the window for a second before looking back.

"You told me, along with Rose, that I need to move on. I've been selfish enough, forcing you to stay by my side. For the first time since Codrin's death, I feel like I can do this without someone being next to me. Not that I don't want you beside me, but I don't need you at this moment. You have a life too and should live it how you want to. I'll always be your Maresal no matter where we are, and I'll expect you to come when I call."

I sit on the bed next to him, putting my hand on his. A faint smile spread across his face. He wraps both arms around me, kissing my cheek.

"Xylia, the day we met, I knew we were meant to be, one way or another. You were the first girl I ever loved and the woman I will always cherish the most. You taught me that it's not about what I can do but what I must do. My sweet Lady!"

He shakes me a bit before letting go and stands up tall, hands on his hips. His shoulders are shaking, his breathing uneven. His head drops, eyes trained to the ground as he starts to sniffle and rub his hands on his face before looking at me again.

"I'm going to miss the absolute craziness that follows you, Xy. If it ever gets too crazy, you come and get me."

I nod in agreement.

He steps up to me, kissing my cheek once again before resting his forehead on mine.

"And if you ever get too cocky, you come get me! I'll gladly put you in your place."

He kisses both my checks this time, and I leave with a taste of bitter-sweetness. I walk into my room, looking identical to the one I just left, and the one I stayed in the last time. I sit on the bed, thinking over just how crazy these last few months have been.

From the moment I met Kage, my life went into this spiral of chaos, but it was chaos that was destined. It allowed me to find my path and live out the dream I always had as a child—defeat the evil King and save the land. He made me a hero. Now, I'm an Oracle, someone who brings light and peace with them. Who would have thought, in this world, that an elf would be the one to bring peace. I don't have to fear their stares or judgment anymore.

Falling onto my back with a smile, I call the light forwards. Their normal hums and whispers are replaced with chatter in a language I do not understand. I listen, though, and fall asleep hearing them talk.

A LOUD POUND hits my door, and I jolt out of bed. I rush to the door and see that it's Rose on the other side. She steps in, a bow in hand, and a smile that means trouble.

"C'mon. Grab your stuff. We are gonna go hunt these beasties."

I give her a quizzical look and nearly close the door on her, but she grabs it

"Xylia. Please." This is not a demand, but a plea.

"I'd be honored."

I turn back into the room and throw on my midnight blue leather armor. Kage got me this set after my old set was lost. My thoughts are the old King burned them or something else that he figured would hurt me. Though it was sweet that Kage was able to burn the Adamina Clan's symbol on the right shoulder piece for me. He said he sketched it off of the mark I have behind my ear.

Grabbing my bow and quiver, I can hear her tapping her foot. Looking up, she has her arms crossed and she is looking down the hall.

"We should let Vasile know we plan on heading out," I say, lacing my boots.

"No need. Welma will let him know if he comes looking," Rose says, now leaning against the doorframe.

She waits patiently as I finish getting ready for our hunt. We begin our trek, sneaking out the back door to not get a rise out of any patrons still downstairs.

Thanks, Welma, for the hasty escape.

Rose takes the lead, and we start marching towards the Vermilion Forest.

"You are normally not so quick to jump on a rumor Rose. One person saying they saw something, not to mention no gold," I say, trying to cut the ominous air that seems to be sitting between us.

Rose seems tense, her gaze forwards, her disposition calm.

Maybe it's just the cold.

"How did it feel, showing yourself like that?" Rose asks, the snow crunching underneath her boots.

I was waiting for her to ask. I was wondering how it made her feel to see me being seen. She spent her life hiding me from the world. Rose and Rye found me when they were just children themselves. Seventeen-sidereal-years old. They knew I was different, and as I aged, my ears only grew longer. It was harder to hide them. Eventually, we moved to the Clan's base permanently, even before the residential district was built. They spent their youth creating a place for misfits to run away to, a place to hide me, a place where they could be together.

"Terrifying."

"It was scary for me too. I was worried I'd watch you get torn apart," Rose says, stopping at the edge of the trees. "But I am happy, Xylia. I was waiting for you to break free from the chains I trapped you in."

I stop moving.

"My chains?" I whisper.

My breath is thick like a mist, hiding Rose from my vision.

"Rye and I were never scared of the world seeing you. Being different was something we loved about you. *We* were different at that time. Though, that changed when we lost you, when the King found you." Rose turns around and faces me. Her hands are coiled and shaking. "Everything changed. You were wanted, a target. We swore the Adaminians to secrecy, and when we finally got you back, we promised ourselves we would keep you hidden."

"You fed into my fear ..." My words trail off at the end, realizing that they both wanted me there.

"If I had a choice—a say. I would have kept you there with me. Some things are going to come to light now that the world sees you, Xylia. I cannot lie any longer. Please remember. I love you."

Tears start to stream down my face. I haven't heard those words in such a long time. My legs shake, and before I fall to my knees, Rose catches me. She holds my weight, supporting me up.

"Mom ..." I whisper.

"I'm so sorry. The night isn't over yet, Xylia. I just needed you to know that my life has been spent preserving yours. Before anything else happens," Rose says, kissing my head.

I straighten myself out, rubbing the tears from my eyes.

CHAPTER FIFTEEN

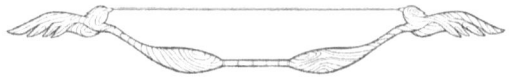

THE SNOW and freezing temperature are making it a lot harder for us to maintain our pace in the forest. There are no eyes to be seen in the tree line, so we can take that as a good sign. We will have time to climb before getting into any fight.

"Keep a keen ear," Rose whispers over her shoulder.

I respond with a chirp and take her right. I worry we may be getting in over our heads, but both Rose and I won't dive in headfirst with being short of manpower and resources.

As we finally reach the start of the forest itself, we begin to climb, swinging up higher and farther into the tree line. The cool rough bark chills my hands but feels familiar. We make our way carefully from branch to branch, calling out if we spot any ice or broken limbs. We search the western border, but we are not seeing any signs of these creatures, so we decide to head east. It could be just a rumor that there is anything here after all, but we are not going to just give up, nor are either of us ready to actually head back.

I swing down to a lower set of branches to try to get a better survey when I see a pair of eyes a few meters away from where we are. I make a few chirps and cry out to Rose.

In a moment, Rose is by my side, and now seeing what I am. We wait and watch for a moment, trying to gauge what exactly we may be fighting. I jump a few branches closer, now there are two more pairs of eyes attached to large shadow-covered bodies. Rose gives me the signal to move closer. I jump ahead, pulling my bow and notching my arrow.

Suddenly, Rose holds up her hand, making me lower my bow altogether. I give her a quizzical look.

"Do you think she has arrived?" a woman's voice whispers in the darkness.

I quickly scan, trying to find the source of the voice, seeing nothing but the eyes of the three beasts.

They can talk?

"We know of her return. We just need to remain patient. The Risen will be pleased," a deeper male voice answers.

I'm tempted to raise my bow once more. I look over to where Rose should be, but she is missing from her position. Scanning again, Rose approaches the shadowed beasts from the ground.

What are you doing, Rose?

I chirp as loudly as possible. Rose turns to me and waves me down. I look back to the creatures, and they are no longer looming there. They are at the base of the tree, looking up at me. I suppress my scream, noticing their eyes that have no lids and are as red as the crimson that runs through me.

Their heads bald, and ears as long as their bodies. They are short but lengthy things that at first appear to have fur, but are wisps of smoke emanating from their mouths. A foul stench is shorting my breath. I feel my eyes widen as it locks onto one of theirs.

What is happening?

I shoot down towards them, but they scatter back to where they once were, surrounding—"Rose!"

"Xylia," Rose commands. Her response lacking a hint of fear or hesitation.

Not only am I confused but terrified I'm about to witness my second mother's death. I shake my head, not knowing what has come over her or what my next move is. Codrin died in my arms because I jumped in. Rose asking me to do this now?

She points to the ground next to her. I glance back to the beasts that retreated to their previous spot and push my light out to see them. The forest that was in complete darkness lightens in an instance. The beasts wail and cower behind three humans standing there, who are also covering their eyes.

As I recall the light, it whispers something to me. I cannot understand what it is saying, but I feel somewhat at ease, despite the confusion I am still wrestling with.

I do as I'm told and descend to the ground floor, sprinting to her side.

"Who are they?" I whisper to Rose.

She grabs my hand, ignoring my question, as we approach the group and their pets.

"She is finally here!" I can see the shape of the woman whose voice I first heard. She is smaller in height and stocky.

They knew I was coming?

I look at Rose, who glances in my direction, before looking back to the group standing in front of us. I squeeze her hand tightly. She knew they were here. That look of worry I saw back at the Slattern was not for the people of Ko but because she knew why they were there.

My heart feels like it is being torn in two. 'Things will come to light,' she said. I'm seeing clear as day. Rose has cornered me.

Why?

"Our child, Rose, thank you for allowing us to gather here," another, more elderly-sounding woman says.

My heart sinks a bit hearing her call Rose in such a strange manner. Rose turns to me and strokes my face, but I pull away instinctively. She forces a smile and turns back to the group.

"She needs to understand our purpose, her purpose," Rose says.

All three figures nod in agreement.

She sounds like the old King.

"Rose, please explain." I lean over and whisper.

"Xylia, I'd like you to meet the high priestess, Agnetta," Rose replies.

The older woman pulls down her robe. Her gray hair billowing down, framing her shoulders. She extends her hand out towards me, as if I am to take it and bow to her.

Rose shoves my shoulder a bit, so I just shake it. Agnetta gives me a disgusted look but waits until I let go before retreating her hand.

"We have been waiting for this moment for quite some time, child. Rose has done a fine job safeguarding you all this time."

My head snaps to Rose, who is looking at me.

"Xylia ..." Rose grabs my hand. I lean back, eyes wide and terrified.

'My life was spent preserving yours.' That's what she said. It just wasn't out of love.

I thought I just got her back.

For the first time ever, I thought we could move forward from Rye's death, and have a mother-daughter relationship that wasn't dictated by our roles as First Lady and Maresal. Now I see there were roles I wasn't aware of.

"Rye and Rose both volunteered and were selected for their immediate attachment to you. They were both very aware this day would come. You are and will be the light of this country, this realm."

I shake my head, trying to gather myself. I rip my hand away from Rose. "I think I was left out on some of the details."

"Your name was given to you by your mother, who was the previous Oracle. Your name means the 'child born from the tree.'" The shorter woman now chimes in.

My real mother? Rose knew who she was?

I start fighting the frustration building up, avoiding looking towards Rose.

"You were sent here to ensure the survival of the Awemother's magicae." His voice startled me; it's low tone seems to whisper in my ear. "The only form of Magicae that has ever produced Oracles."

Ensure survival ... it seems all my mothers had a plan for me. A reason to be here, not that any were kind enough to share.

"Rose raising, protecting, and training you was by design so that we may bring you in to restore the country to its former glory." Agnetta smiles and opens her arms towards me.

I take a few steps back.

Being here, I'm starting to feel a tad ropey.

"We were startled to hear that you had disappeared. It had been planned for you to be escorted to us," the man says.

Stop talking.

"Very worrisome, indeed," the shorter woman confirms.

I grab my head.

Shut it.

"Though now that you are here, we can travel home together," Agnetta states.

Rose, tell me this is a lie. You didn't plan this.

"Xylia. This is part of the truth I needed you to know. It does not change our love, our history," Rose says, reaching out again.

Love. History. It was another job, another role to play, another insight as to why we have never been on the same page.

I take a few more steps back. "I think it changes plenty. It thinks it's time for me to leave," I say to the figures, readying myself to sprint to the nearest branch for me to get up into the trees.

I don't know who Rose is. How was I so blind?

"Now, child, all your questions will be answered if you come home," Agnetta says.

I can't even think straight. My heart is beating out of my chest. They are talking too fast and saying things they are expecting me to just accept.

I need to move.

I bolt for the trees as Rose yells after me. I'm fleeing the Vermilion Forest again, but this time there really is no place to come back to.

Not even Rose.

The man of the group whistles, and all three beasts are suddenly surrounding me in an instant, halting my escape. Before they can bite me, I burst with light causing them to cower and run—giving me an opportunity to do the same. I sprint, grabbing onto a branch, swinging myself up, but I feel hands tugging on my braid, pulling me from the tree. With nothing to grip, I slam back down onto the forest floor. The air knocked from my lungs; I gasp a few times and roll over onto my belly.

Rose's boots are standing there in front of me. My braids loosen and come undone as I gather myself back to my feet.

"Do not run from me," Rose says, with hurt in her eyes.

I push my hair out of my face. The figures begin to close in as well as their beasts. I flash my light again, everyone but Rose flinching. I quickly kick Rose's chest, sending her back into one of the figures behind her, before grabbing my dagger driving it into one of the beast's neck. The others scatter once more. It whines, collapsing to the ground, unmoving. I climb back up into the trees and begin making my way back towards Ko.

Rose recovers quickly and is right behind me. I hear an arrow wiz by my face.

Looking back, seeing her notch another.

"You'd shoot down your own daughter?" I yell at her, holding back the tears that want to come through.

She's going to hit me.

Just as she releases the arrow, a small hand reaches out, yanking my arm. The arrow nearly piercing my leg before everything goes dark.

"You're safe, Oracle," a delicate voice says, somewhere in the void.

Shaw.

Before I can respond, the interior of my chambers appears before me. A large fireplace glowing, cracking in its stone home. Books and paintings cover the walls.

Shaw holds my shoulders as I crumble to the ground.

CHAPTER SIXTEEN

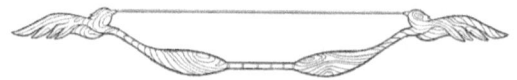

"Oracle? Lady Xylia?" Shaw calls out to me.

Leave me. Please.

I'm shaking, the dusting of snow begins to drip and melt off of my armor. I'm shaking, I want to scream. I want to cry.

"I'll return with the King." Shaw leaves me hurriedly.

My chest begins to burn, realizing I have been holding my breath. My chest starts to raise before deflating rapidly, like my lungs are trying to play catch up for the last few moments, but I can't breathe. I'm gasping for air, but there is no air in my lungs. I put my hands over my head, trying to breath. I feel like I'm dying. The weight of everything this year has brought me now physically crushing me. I bring my legs to my chest, trying to comfort myself.

"Augh!" My body rumbles as the screams leave my body.

Why Rose?

From the beginning, I was never the daughter but the object to keep for the opportune time.

Were they waiting for the King's death for the country to be unstable?

I don't care.

I'll kill them all.

No, I couldn't do that.

Maybe I could.

They have torn everything I had left away from me. The memories of Rye telling me stories, Rose training me, the rise of the Adamina Clan, being chosen as Maresal, it means nothing.

It has to mean nothing now.

I slam my fist onto the carpeted stone flooring. I recoil from the pain, but it gives me control over something. *Something.* I hit the ground repeatedly until I begin to lose feeling. With a shaking hand, I grip the carpet, bringing it to my mouth and scream again, and again, until my voice quits out on me.

The door bursts open, slamming against the wall.

"Xylia?" Someone rushes over and grabs my shoulders, pulling me tightly into him, nestling his face into my neck.

His breath on my bare skin is calming though, warm, and helps me take a few deep breaths myself. Someone approaches us, taking away my comfort as he stands, leaving me on the floor alone.

Don't leave me alone.

"Your Majesty," she bows, "they approached her just as you had expected. Seems they were waiting for her expected return."

He dismisses her with a nod and wave, but before she leaves, her eyes catch mine.

"A woman named Rose seemed to be the one who lured her out into the woods," she whispers, a little too loudly, to him.

I don't want to hear this.

He takes a step back, glancing over his shoulder towards me. Once Shaw exits the room and the door is closed, he turns to me, extending his hand to assist me up. I slowly stand, taking me a few tries to even get up onto my feet. I'm not sure if I am still shaking from the cold or being transported, or maybe because I nearly took an arrow shot by my apparent mother.

My eyes gloss over as my mind wanders back to Rose and the forest. The light begins to stir inside of me, sensing my uneasiness, just remembering her eyes avoiding mine. The look she gave me as she fired that arrow. I can't even hear the voice calling out to me as the light erupts from inside me, my voice screaming so much louder.

I don't care who hears this time. Let them hear me. Let them see me.

"Xylia!"

I feel the light fade hearing his voice come through. It's hoarse, like he's been sitting there screaming. He is shaking me hard. I flutter my eyes open, my vision blurry from the tears that are streaming down my face. I look around, the room is in tatters. Every book removed from its place on the bookshelf. Every painting torn. The bed flipped and broken. I turn to meet his emerald eyes looking straight into my panicked ones.

I shove Kage away and stand hurriedly, my body telling itself to move. I throw myself into the corner of the room, a shaky breath of air actually reaching my lungs.

Fel Watch guards are close behind Kage, looking at me with shaking hands and worried eyes.

I scared them.

Punching the wall, the tears rush even faster, and I crumple to the ground. Arms quickly wrap around me. I'm wishing they were Codrin's. Hoping that if I open my eyes now, the sight of the green light from the morning sun will be dancing across the ceiling of our home.

I just want him back, I want that future I was so scared of. Settling down, loving him wholeheartedly and forever. A future that would have been so certain.

Nothing is the same anymore, there is nothing and no one to trust.

"Sh, I'm right here." My eyes open, Kage reaching out towards me.

I turn away from him, causing him to pause. He takes a step closer, I run away from the wall, the guards backing away as I approach them.

"Leave us. Now." Kage snaps towards the Fel Watch.

They hesitate for a moment, but Kage quickly points towards the door, his face hardening. The guards exit, closing the door behind us. The one I begin to move towards.

"Xylia," Kage whispers.

My breathing starts becomes uneven once more. My lip trembling, watching him watch me.

Can I trust him?

I back up into the door, feeling around for the handle. Kage rushes me, slamming his hands on either side of the door, pinning me up against it.

"I'm so sorry." Kage's face buries in my hair and I lean into his touch, feeling the warmth of his skin on my own. He moves his hands from the door to cup my face. "You cannot scare me away. Scream, shout, use your magicae to the fullest extent."

I place my head on his shoulder and cry, scream, beg for this to be wrong. A misunderstanding. A dream. I want to wake up happy. I want everyone I loved and cared for in one room smiling at me. I don't want this pain. Our bodies slowly fall to the ground, Kage wrapping me into his lap. He rubs my back as I shake.

I thought I could be more. To be seen as more than just an elf with power. The endless training Rose put me through was supposed to be for the Clan's sake, not someone else's. Was I ever her child, or was I an object?

This doubt is eating me alive.

Kage kisses my head and neck, helping me control my breathing. "You'll survive this too. I know this. I have seen you break, but you will never shatter. Xylia, you are the definition of strength."

I left my head, sniffling. I take a few short breaths as I rest my forehead against his. He kisses my tear soaked lips.

"It hurts," I whimper.

Kage furrows his brow.

"Pain is temporary, Xylia, and not yours alone to bear. Put it all on me if you need to. I'll take it. You're mine, Xylia, and I am yours."

My eyes feel heavy, puffy and worn. I curl into his chest, readjusting myself on his lap. He holds me tighter, humming a simple tune.

I don't want to move from here.

"I'm glad you're back, my Lady," Kage whispers.

I listen to the beat of his heart, matching my breathing to his until I can clearly remember.

"You knew, didn't you." The whisper that escapes my lips is low and trembling.

Kage remains quiet. I sit up, pulling myself away from his lap, but still touching.

I need him here. I need answers too.

"I know for certain now," he admits.

"You knew."

"I was aware of the people looking for you," he says in his most honest tone. "From what I have learned, and from what you've said, they always had their eyes on you until Rose lost sight of you when you had to leave the Clan. I believe *them* to be a large and powerful group who call themselves the **Domi Nostrae**."

"Did I miss the part where I am not trusted?"

Kage widens his eyes, and his mouth drops open but

quickly closes. He pulls away just enough to let me know he is truly listening.

"Seems like it would have been important to inform me that you had someone following me because there is a group of people invested in my life and are tracking me down. Instead, you chose to leave me in the dark. If I had known someone was after me, I wouldn't have ..."

"Gone?" He looks away as the word slips from his tongue.

"We have already fought this fight. You know how important it was for Vasile and me to return home, to mourn, to look back at where we came from."

Kage drops his hands from my face, taking in a deep breath. He clenches his fist but quickly flexes it before placing it on my leg.

"Correct, but that doesn't change the fact that I was right, that you were going to put yourself into a situation that could potentially keep you from coming back to me," Kage says, trying to remain calm.

"It was you who put me in that danger, Kage, by not telling me what was really going on."

He bites his lip, running his hands through his hair. He is holding back.

"If you would have told me, maybe I would have agreed to some help, maybe I wouldn't have let my guard down so easily."

I hesitate, waiting to see what he will say. He just sits there, staring at me intently. He already knows that he is in the right. He knows that I know it too. Sharing country secrets is not something he can just do, even if he cares for me. This is how Codrin must have felt. Always waiting for an answer to a question he could never even ask.

I'll need to remember that.

I take my time steadying my breath. I feel like I will

collapse in on myself if I slow down, but I fear I'll combust if I don't.

"Finding out that my mother was still alive gave me back something I lost. Now, I have to live with the fact that everything I once knew is in shambles. A lie, a facade for some 'greater' purpose," I say, choking on every word.

He sighs, his breath just as shaky as mine.

We sit there in silence, again, just gazing at one another. I can see him mulling something over in his mind, not wanting to just blurt out what he intends to say.

"My father had always thought the Adamina Clan might have been influenced by the Domi Nostrae. The resources needed to create something like the Adamina Clan was far too much for three or four people to just begin. The group itself has been around since the beginning of the **Ancestry War**. A Cult, filled with both magicae and non-magicae users, who still to this day wish for the doorways to be open."

I rub my fingers in circles on my temples. I can't say his explanation of the situation makes me feel better about any of this, but at least I am able to talk it through with him.

He is trying to share something with me.

"The Adamina Clan regularly donated creatures and resources to what Rose called the 'benefactors'," I clarify. Though, I cannot say for certain who those benefactors were. "I won't be able to confirm your father's suspension, but the two must have some connection considering Rose and Rye were and are a part of the Domi Nostrae."

Kage nods. "Their leader is a religious figure in their eyes. They believe the doorways can and will be opened by him. I don't know why you are involved, but I'm sure it is your light and race that has attracted them as it did my father."

"The Adamina Clan has nearly a thousand members. If all

the members were a part of the Domi Nostrae, how large of a mass are we thinking?"

Kage leans back a bit, looking over into the fireplace. I stare into it with him, watching the flames lick the stone surrounding and keeping it in place. I thought the enemy of the country was gone. That there would be some peace. Rose would call me naive. She'd be right. Though, I would call myself hopeful.

"This cult spans across the realm, so my thought is many more than what the Felguard Country holds in population."

My heart sinks. This is so much larger than us. If they really want me, I don't know how we can starve them of that.

"Why now? If they knew where I was, raised me, trained me to be what they wanted, is it not strange they waited?" My question is an honest and confused one.

Kage thinks about it for a moment. "They did not succeed, though. That night you found me in the forest, your powers were unable to heal anyone without the risk of destroying everything around you."

I wince thinking about Codrin's last night once again. Kage must have noticed since he cleared his throat and shifted from his seat to a standing position.

"Question is, who inside the castle is with the Clan. Regardless of how well-known the rumors are of you, you taking every day to practice and heal Vasile was kept inside the walls. If we think on this rationally, your ability as Oracle would be an asset if they feared that opening a portal could be life-threatening. They have studied the doorways for, well … let's say a very long time. Coming across a healer Magicae user is most likely rare. Finding you must have been a miracle for them."

I find the will to stand. I'm no longer shaking from my emotions, just from the snow-soaked clothes I am sitting in. Walking over to the blazing fire, I warm my hands.

I don't want to talk about this anymore.

I told Vasile I was going to make a difference, that I was going to become a Queen. Their numbers sound terrifying, but Kage and I will be the victors in the end of it all.

I have to believe that.

Kage walks up behind me and takes my cloak off, hanging it on one of the drying hooks by the fire. He turns me to face him and points at my boots.

I raise an eyebrow, lifting one of my feet in the air.

A cheesy smile spreads across his face, with a small chuckle escaping past his lips. He leans in, lightly kissing my lips before trailing down to my stomach, then thigh, then knee, and eventually to the edge of where my boot begins. He unties the strings and pulls the boot off, tossing it to the side. My stomach stirs seeing him kneel in front of me, my heart fluttering. He points to the other foot. I switch feet, and he unties and pulls off the other one. The cold seems to have left my body, replaced with his warmth. He looks up to me, slowly standing, running his hands up against me until he tangles them into my hair. All I can focus on is his hands, his lips, his breath on mine.

"I want to tell you everything, Xylia. It burns me to keep you at a distance," he whispers against my lips.

I lean into him, our lips moving together. The pleasure I feel from him pushes the pain from my mind. I drape my arms around his neck, wanting to be closer, feel closer. I want these feelings to stay with me. To remember his heat, his care, his love. I'm vulnerable, but I'm okay with that as long as he is here.

Despite knowing he shouldn't, he was willing to share, to show me he trusts me. I know everything will come with time and status. I can wait for him, like he waited for me.

CHAPTER SEVENTEEN

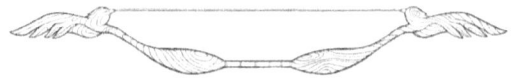

"Kage ..." I whisper. He stirs a bit in his sleep, hearing my voice.

I stretch upwards sorely, having fallen asleep on the ground. I wasn't ready to face anything outside this room. Kage stayed with me, talking about his ideas for the garden, the letters his mother has written to us, anything that was not Rose.

Don't. Don't think about her.

I turn back to Kage, who is wrapped around my lower half, still asleep. I brush his hair away from his face. There will be gossiping around the castle, but I'll take it. Having him is the only thing I am holding onto.

He stayed, even when I turned destructive. I didn't scare him away.

"Kage ..." I whisper again, this time waking him up enough to glance at me with one eye.

"Hmm," Kage mumbles.

"The King should not be asleep on the floor."

He smiles and slowly sits up, stretching as I just had. I lean in and kiss his cheek.

"Good morning to you too," he says, his voice raspy and low. "I like waking up next to you. Even if it is on the floor."

My heart flutters a bit, and I smile.

"Xylia, I mean that." He pulls a loose strand of hair and places it behind my ear. I grab his hand and hold it against my cheek.

He is going to have to leave soon. I need to keep talking.

"I should mention this to you," I start. His brows furrow, listening to what I am about to say. "While I was in Ko, there were rumors about me. Rumors about you and where this kingdom was headed. They were so angry and afraid."

"I expected as much."

"As did I, but I presented myself. I'm not sure what I was thinking, but I felt like I needed to do something, anything to help them. It was very terrifying, but by the end they believed in *us*."

Kage's eyes widen, and he looks at the dying flames in the fireplace. My chest tightens, not quite sure if he will take it the way I hope he will.

"I was not prepared to hear that, though I am happy to hear it ended well. A little sad I wasn't there to see it for myself." He turns back to me with a smile. "I asked you to be my Queen because I knew the people would love you, trust you."

I drop my gaze to his chest.

Right. I have an answer. I've thought about this for over a full moon cycle, but I am still nervous.

"Xylia. Come with me for a moment." Kage stands, offering his hand.

I take it and stand.

We sneakily make our way to the royal library. Only the immediate guards that were waiting outside the doors having seen us.

He excites me.

Kage opens the doors, sweeping me up into his arms, our lips parting enough for me to giggle. Kage sets me on the couch gently. I try to hold in my surprise at how effortlessly he made that all look. He holds up a finger before quickly running over to a locked bookcase. He pulls a key from the top of it and unlocks the case. I can't see what's inside.

"If you brought me in here to read, I might have to leave."

We both laugh as he makes his way back over to me. He hands me the book, and I freeze. Gently stroking the soft, worn blue leather with my hands. I look back up to him, a smile taking up the majority of his face. I thought it was lost, taken by a tyrant king, but it is now being returned by a kind one.

I open to the first page. These pages have guided me through my story that I never thought could be my reality. It's almost laughable to think pictures on a page could shape a world I did not believe could be a reality. I turn the next page, taking it in, as if it were the first time, looking at the beautifully crafted artwork. Though, I notice something resting on the next page, disturbing how the page lays. Flipping it over, a familiar ring is resting on top of it, only now a diamond seems to be set on the top of it.

I look over at Kage, kneeling before me.

Kage. You are consuming me.

My heart is racing, and my hands begin to shake. I pick up the ring, a ring that signifies our connection, the ring that is illustrated in the very book I just found it in.

"Kage," I breathe out.

I grip the book in my free hand tightly.

"Xylia. My Lady. My future. We have changed this country together, have traveled this country together, and now I am hoping to rule this country together. On that list of My's, I would like to add Queen. There would be no need for me to keep my secrets or hold my tongue. Even though I trust you with my life as we are now, the kingdom and castle do not. Saying yes means that I will tell you my truth, always." He stands slowly and extends his hand.

Even though he is more than aware of my dreams and thoughts of Codrin, he is here asking me to be part of not only his reign but his life. He's a strategic man, and I know he has more plans than to just win my heart. I also know I am putting him in a position to choose his country or me when I ask him for the truth. Codrin was, on more than one occasion, in the same position I find myself in now. Having someone higher in rank, ordering you to listen without the why. Only difference is, I wouldn't have been able to give Codrin the same luxury of being able to leave as Kage has done for me.

My heart yearns for Kage, yet it's not the same type of yearning I had for Codrin. Maybe because I knew Codrin was mine. From day one, he was on my heels and ready to be by my side regardless of the consequences or situations that would come his way. Kage was—is—someone that has shown me a world I never thought possible. Everything he does and says captivates me. His intelligence, understanding, and patience are just a few of the traits that I admire so dearly. The way he believes in the same dreams I have always believed in.

"I don't know how elegant and graceful of a Queen I'll be, but ..."

Kage lips crash into mine.

"I do not care to see you be the idealistic version of a Queen, but a Queen that is her King's strength. The same strength you have been providing to me since I was an exiled Prince." He kisses me again, and again until I am gasping for air for the best possible reason. Kage rests his forehead on mine and smiles brightly. "Marry me."

"Yes, my answer is yes," I say breathlessly.

A tear drops from my cheek, my body shaking from every nerve wanting him.

I take his hand and kiss him deeply. He takes the silver ring, slipping it onto my left ring finger before holding my hand.

"I want to change our world, together," Kage says, raising my left hand to his lips.

The smile he is currently wearing spreads even wider, his eyes now squinting. He picks me up and spins me around. We kiss each other, pushing away all the emotions that aren't pure blissfulness. Even if it is just for this moment, my heart, mind, and body are consumed with my care for him.

"You will make the perfect Queen, Xylia."

CHAPTER EIGHTEEN

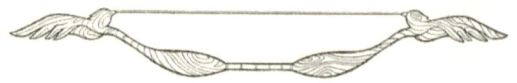

"Make sure you only give it to him," I emphasize to Shaw.

She smiles and takes the letter, placing it into her satchel. "I'll see to it, Lady Xylia."

In a blink of an eye, Shaw is gone. Already in Kel to deliver the letter to Vasile. It's been a week since the engagement was announced to the castle, and I won't hear the end of it if Vasile finds out from someone other than me. From what Shaw explained, he was shocked and confused about my disappearance. When she went back to grab my things, Vasile recognized her and was frantic trying to find me. She only explained that I was attacked, that I was alright, and that I was transported back to the castle. He wanted to come back with her, but Kage and I agreed that being alone and getting distance from those memories would be the best for now.

"Xylia," Kage calls out from the entryway.

I run up the stairs, and he opens the door a little wider so I can sneak in under his arm. He closes it and quickly pulls me in to kiss my cheek. He clears his throat and steps away as a guard looks towards us.

Kage wants to do things somewhat properly. He's kept us in separate chambers since he was made King, and keeps any form of affection between us. This I understand far too well. I was the same way as Maresal. Codrin hated how I would turn into a prude anytime we were outside our home.

"I want to introduce you to someone. Laura was a part of the M.G.A. She agreed to train with you, help teach you to control your power—perhaps expand it," Kage says excitedly.

"Something to keep my mind occupied, you mean."

I know he can see through my tired eyes. I have not been sleeping well. As soon as I am alone, Rose and the Domi Nostrae are all I can think about. Kage has already revealed too much to me about who they are and their assumed intentions, so I am left with my imagination.

"Give it a try," Kage says, squeezing my shoulders.

I smile and gesture for him to lead the way. He straightens a bit and guides me through the halls until we eventually descend down the main staircase and to a large metal door.

Opening it, a large training room reveals itself. Swords, spears, javelins, shields, bows, maces—every form of weapon is decorating the circular room. There's a large platform for where a sparring match can occur, and a beautiful brown-haired woman is standing in the center of it.

"Your majesty," she says in a bright tone, bowing towards Kage.

"Laura." Kage raises his hand, dismissing her. "This is Lady Xylia, future Queen of Fosa and the Felguard Country. She is who I was speaking of."

Laura's eyes widen a moment, her focus on my ears, but she smiles towards me. "He failed to mention that it was my future Queen I would be training," she says with a hesitant laugh.

"You wouldn't have agreed otherwise. Don't worry, Lady Xylia can hold her own." Kage winks towards me before pushing me towards Laura slightly. "I'll leave you two for a bit."

Kage exits the room while I step further in.

"Lady Xylia, it's a pleasure to meet you." She begins to bow but I quickly wave at her.

"Please, call me Xylia. At least while we are training. Seems I will be playing the student here."

This could be fun.

"Xylia, if you don't mind. I'd like to see what 'holding your own' looks like," she says with a smirk.

I hold out my hand and will one of the swords hanging to it. I grip the steel and slice the air in front of me. Laura nods, impressed.

"That's a nice trick!" she says, drawing her sword. "But can you use it?"

Laura rushes towards me. I raise my blade as she brings hers down. The steel clatters; her strength quickly pushes me down into my knees. I dive to the side, her blade slicing towards the ground. I roll back onto my feet before calling another sword, this one aimed for her throat. She stiffens as she feels the blade press gently against the neck. She sheaths her sword and starts clapping. I will both swords back to their place as Laura approaches me.

"Hm, not much of a student," Laura says, almost like she is admitting it to herself.

The door clatters open, a blonde tuft of hair rushing towards me. Laura quickly redraws her sword and stands in front of me. I'm taken aback, not just by Vasile's sudden appearance but that she jumped into action without hesitation —despite this being our first time meeting.

She's good.

"Laura, he's alright," I say.

Vasile doesn't change his pace—even with a sword pointed towards him.

Laura steps aside, and Vasile wraps his arms around me, spinning me around. He kisses my cheek and smiles.

"My future Queen!" Vasile shouts.

I laugh and pinch his cheeks. "You shouldn't be so forwards as to kiss me then!" I exclaim. "What are you even doing here?"

"I begged Shaw into bringing me back. I wanted to say congratulations in person! I also didn't get to say goodbye last time." Vasile's voice deepens, and his eyes focus on mine. "Please, don't disappear on me. I don't care about distance, but I need to know where you are and that you are safe."

"I'm not going anywhere." The words are there to comfort him, but myself as well. The Domi Nostrae will not get to me.

Vasile winks before even acknowledging Laura, who is standing right next to us. "Hi beautiful, I'm Vasile," he says, extending his hand out towards her.

Laura scoffs and rolls her eyes. "Hi, might want to keep your hands to yourself. Last man who reached for me lost theirs."

Vasile smiles wider. "Ooo, I like her, Xy." He takes me by the hand and starts moving us towards the door. "Don't worry, we will be back!"

"You better be! I look forward to kicking the piss out of both of you!"

"You aren't going to make me train, are you?" Vasile asks in a hushed tone as we exit the room.

"She is the mentor this time around. My guess is that you are going to be training," I say, trying to suppress my laughter.

Vasile and I head to the dining hall. On the way, he chats about how Madi arrived the following day to the Slattern and goes into too much detail about how they reconnected. He explains that she was angry at the both of us for leaving without a word to her, though her worry for us became more apparent the longer we were away.

"She still won't talk about the day the Clan was attacked," Vasile admits.

"I can't say I blame her. I haven't been able to talk to Kage about what it was like even looking at the aftermath."

Vasile wraps an arm around my shoulders as we continue our walk.

"Speaking of Kage, your letter mentioned he actually proposed? I understand he is a logical guy, but asking someone to wed them and become Queen at a table with four other people around is as romantic as a loo." We both laugh.

It was quite a stirring event for everyone at that table. He just blurted it out when we were discussing how to ease the tension with the Felguardians.

"He did. Using the book and the ring that really brought us together. Kage can be romantic and intimate when he wants to be," I say in his defense.

Vasile looks at my left hand, seeing my ringless finger.

"Getting it fitted to fit my hand. It was a little large," I explain, bringing my hand up for him to see it clearly. "What about Madi? She's okay you left?"

"Madi's fine. Shaw said she will be bringing me back today. Said that if Kage sees me, she might lose her job." I laugh hearing him say this.

"Kage is just becoming more worrisome, is all."

"Why's that?" he asks, slowing his pace a bit. "Because of what happened in the forest?"

"Yes, but that's all I can really say, Vas."

Vasile squints his eyes at me, leaning in. "I don't like this secret thing."

"It's not entirely her secret," Kage says. I turn and see him walking towards us. "Soon, it'll be back to the way things were when she was a leader in the Clan. Xylia won't be able to tell you everything."

Vasile drops his arm. "I said I don't like it, not that I don't understand."

I step in between them.

"You two are terrible."

WE ALL SPEND the rest of the day together, eventually returning to Laura, who promptly pushes Vasile to his limits. He keeps up that flirtatious spirit of his though. Kage shows Vasile something in his study that he has been working on, something I'm not allowed to see quite yet. Kage explains that it's his wedding gift to me. I've been wracking my brain about what I could even do or get for Kage. I don't technically have even a copper piece to my name, and I lack creative talents like Codrin. I'm already failing at being a life partner, and we haven't even wed. Whatever Kage shows Vasile, kindles some form of friendship between them. Which makes me even more nervous.

What am I going to do?

Vasile gives my cheek another kiss before Shaw takes him back to Kel, where Madi is awaiting his return.

Kage wraps his arms around me, kissing the top of my head as I watch them leave.

"He will be back when **Fons** arrives. The garden will be at full bloom. It'll be the perfect time and place."

"I know. Guess you will just have to keep me entertained until then," I say, turning around to face him.

He smiles, placing his forehead against mine. "I'll do my best, my Lady."

I lean up into his lips.

CHAPTER NINETEEN

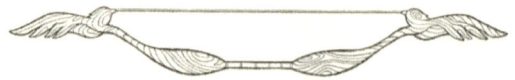

I BEGIN to focus on the sword resting in front of me, willing it to move. As it rises, Laura rushes forwards, coloring her steel against it. As I focus on each hit, I try to give it its own movement. I extend my hands, picking up another sword. Laura jumps back, readying herself. I push both swords forwards, them swinging in different directions towards her.

She pulls another sword from her belt. "Don't hold back this time," she shouts before her words turn into a battle cry.

Both swords begin to strike on my behalf as I close my eyes and focus inward, calling the light forwards to hide myself in. Laura squints, trying to remain focused on the now glaring blades coming at her.

As the light glows within me, I'm able to close my eyes and sense my surroundings, allowing me to have the advantage. In the spirit of not holding back, I grab my bow strung on my back and string it with an arrow. With my eyes closed, I line up the shot, aiming through the light itself and fire. The arrow buzzes through the air, scraping Laura's cheeks, sending her a few steps back.

I retreat the swords, so they are slowly spinning by my sides. I quiet the light that sings a melody to say goodbye. Lowering my bow, I smile towards Laura, who looks both impressed and defeated.

"How was that?" I ask, cocking my head and swinging my bow onto my back once again.

Laura lets out a hearty chortle before slicking back her brown hair. "You definitely didn't hold back!" She stomps her way over to me and slaps me on my shoulder. "I'm impressed with how good those swords fight."

"Yeah, cause shooting an arrow and hitting my target with my eyes closed is any less impressive," I brag.

We both laugh this time and set our equipment to the side for the day. Fenny comes up and begins to take some of it for us. His tall and lean disposition still surprises me. He is so quiet he tends to blend in with his surroundings quite well. Something Laura mentioned helped him with his previous career. She brought him in to help tend to the weapons and aid as another target for me to practice with.

"I have to say, it's a lot more work training without Vasile here. Not that he was any good," Laura says, poking a bit of fun at the end.

"He's good where he's at though."

"Hard for me to honestly imagine such a flirt even being able to sit still like he is gonna!"

I chuckle, grabbing a cup I had set aside with water in it.

"Oh, I doubt his love for people will ever change. He will just have more bruises when he's caught," I say before taking a drink.

Laura grabs hers, following suit.

The steel chamber door clangs open, Kage storming in. Laura quickly bows. He looks around the room, his eyes landing on me. He puts on a political smile and hastily strides over to me.

"I think you forgot something," he growls.

He grabs my left hand and places the silver ring on my finger. I bite my lip, trying to suppress my laughter.

"Or maybe I just wanted to see you get so worked up about it," I tease, knowing I took it off because I don't want to be treated like a Queen by everyone just yet. It is more comfortable being a soldier.

Kage squeezes my hand tight, trying to warn me not to tease him publicly. His personality is far more serious and tactful as King. It's almost like looking into the mirror back to when I was Maresal. If I hadn't had to change like he is now, I might worry, but I know what it's like to have the lives of others resting on your shoulders. Not to mention a reputation to uphold, expectations needing to be met, and duty to carry out for not just a Clan, but an entire country.

"How is the training coming along?" he asks, slowly releasing his grip on me.

"I think I've finally got it," I say, straightening my posture and tilting my head upward.

It has been a brutal full moon cycle training with Laura. Eventually, she brought in Fenny. Kage was right that training would keep my mind off things, but it's also gotten me to the point where if the Domi Nostrae does come, I'll be ready.

Kage smiles at my display of confidence.

"Care to show me?" he asks, gesturing his hand back towards the platform we were just training on.

I look back to Laura, who is already grabbing her swords.

"Enjoy the show, your majesty," I say, winking at him.

He raises an eyebrow, another warning.

I dawn my bow and quiver, placing them onto my back

once more before securing two swords on my hips, right beside my dagger. I walk over and step onto the platform. This time Laura starting right in front of me, one of her swords already drawn.

"Why don't you start us off, my King," Laura suggests, taking a slight bow in his direction.

He waves his hand in agreement and waits for us to get into our fighting stances.

"Begin!" he yells.

Laura quickly swings her blade up towards my face, but I turn to the side, feeling the air of the steel rushing past me. I slightly extend my hand, willing the blade to unsheathe itself from my belt. As it does, Laura swings again but this time colliding with my blade. I take this moment to retreat a bit giving myself the distance I might need to use my bow. Laura nods her head, looking over at Fenny, who has been sitting on the side watching our training sessions. He stands, grabbing a bow and notching an arrow. I extend my other hand, willing the second blade to come out. Laura is definitely pushing me right now. Going this hard after just ending a fight will take me to my limit. Fenny releases his arrow, but I swing the blade, cutting the shaft in half, causing it to lose its momentum. He notches another and fires it a lot quicker this second time.

I whip my head back and forth between Laura and Fenny as I need to be aware of where and what both of them are doing to wield my swords. I take a deep breath and try to not let all of this power overtake my senses. I grab my bow and reach inside to admit the light. It sings out, the heat that has been muted for awhile, now showing itself again. I begin to sweat at how intense the heatwave is.

Fenny closes his eyes for a moment, giving me the chance to rush him. I reach for my belt and throw my dagger at his shoulder before willing it to simply cut the seam of his shirt. I can tell I nicked him as he grabs his shoulder and kneels down knowing he is out. I turn my focus solely on Laura, who is trying to push through the blinding light. I will the second sword in her direction, surprising her. My second blade stops barely an inch from her throat. She drops her sword and raises her hands in defeat. The light fades, and I bring all three of my blades back to me.

Looking to Kage, his eyes are wide. He claps before approaching the platform.

I can tell he wants to kiss me by his excitement, but is holding back like the good King he is.

"That was incredible! You have improved so much. I am beyond impressed, Xylia." His smile is almost childlike.

I sweep my thumb across his cheek and return the smile.

He squints his eyes towards me, grabbing my wrist and putting it to our sides.

"I don't know what has gotten her so motivated, but her improvement is astonishing," Laura says, crossing her arms and nodding in approval of the King's praise.

Rose has a lot to do with it. Kage's eyes soften, knowing I must now be thinking of her once more. I never expected Rose to be the overly mothering type, nor to nurse my wounds, or even sugar coat her words, but for her to corner me like that ... pulling me down by my braids and taking a shot like she did ... that is something I'd only expect an enemy to do.

I bring myself back and turn towards Fenny. "Sorry about that," I say, pointing towards his wound.

He smiles and waves his hand, his way of telling me he's fine. His smile is small, just like his frame. Fenny and Laura, at first glance, make an odd pair, but their fighting skills are both quite impressive, so I can see why they partnered up.

"I should say congrats to you, Fenny as well, you are quick to the draw," Kage says.

Fenny's eyes widen a bit and his smile becomes more shy. He quickly nods in thanks and turns, putting away his equipment.

I blush on behalf of Fenny.

"Well, with his Majesty's approval, I think we can call it for the day, Lady Xylia," Laura says, sheathing her sword.

"Fantastic, we do have another engagement," Kage says, then turning to me.

I nod and make my way over to Kaitlyn, who is already waiting to take my armor and weapons from me. I peel off the training chest plate and bracers. While she takes my belt, I grab the dagger and its sheath before she can take it away. I hope our next engagement is a—sweaty, simple white blouse, and trouser wearing future Queen—appropriate event.

Kage extends his hand towards me when I am no longer dressed to attack. I take his hand happily, and we leave, quickly waving towards Laura and Fenny. The heavy doors are opened by the guards Kage keeps in his company. Sampson and Ananias, I think Kage said their names were. They don't talk much, which doesn't really bother me. They both are large, strong, and decorated guards; maybe they think that speaks for them.

Kage leads us through the halls, making one turn after another.

"What is this engagement we are rushing off to?" I ask, hand still entangled with his.

He looks over his shoulder and smiles devilishly. I immediately lose the luster I have and sigh. If I had known saying yes would mean day after day planning and discussing this ceremony, I might have just dealt with the secrets. The way we wed in the Adamina Clan is simply by reciting a phrase in the old tongue, saying you have chosen to be tied to this person by flesh, bone, and soul. It wasn't anything that needed to be public. Once people saw the wedding bands, that generally meant they had performed the ceremony.

I told Kage that's all I wanted, but being Queen and King means it's not just for us, but our people as well. *Our people*. When it was just the Clan, those two words were important and meaningful. Gave me a sense of pride and duty, but when I know I'm speaking of the entire country, my head starts to spin.

"This is the fun part," Kage says as we arrive at my chambers.

Sampson opens the door, and a crowd of women are smiling and looking at me expectantly. I look to Kage, who is wearing the same smile, and I can feel my stomach fill with dread. There are golden, white, and navy blue dresses that seem to cover the room top to bottom.

Kage ushers me in, more of a shove than anything.

I put on a small smile and nod, acknowledging the packed room. "Where should we start?" The question slips out, and suddenly the room comes alive.

Four different women show me dresses, claiming theirs are the best in the Realm and tell me of all the different people they have dressed. Others are already trying to strip me from the clothes I currently have on.

I look back to Kage, terrified, but that same smile is on his face.

"Have fun!" he shouts before closing the doors.

Sure, he gets to escape from all of this. He should have just picked the dress himself. This is all so fast. It has been a little over two full moon cycle since I agreed to be his Queen—Felguard Country's Queen—and the ceremony is in two weeks time. I suddenly wish I had enslaved Vasile forever so he could be here, making this more enjoyable than a pain. I can imagine a goofy grin asking if he could try on a dress himself.

"Lady Maresal, would you mind looking at this dress?"

My heart stops for a moment, and I turn to see a familiar old lady. One with white hair and wrinkles. Her reservations and apologies digging in my memory after we had collided on the deck back in the Adamina Clan. I nod and push through the sea of women to view her dress. It is long, has a loose-fitting top, and a cinched waist that leads back into a flowing skirt. A familiar pattern is sewn on the top as to what I had worn every day of my life in the Adamina Clan. The embroidery is navy blue on top of white, and the flowing skirt is golden.

This hurts.

I smile towards her, even though my heart is pounding. The dress is beautiful, I cannot deny that.

I bet Codrin would have loved this dress.

"This is perfect," I say, running my hands over the complex pattern.

It would have taken her many hours to put such a dress together. Even with the lies, seeing something so familiar brings happiness to me.

She smiles back and steps closer to whisper something. "She wants you to have this."

She?

A note is placed into my hand. She pats my shoulder, leaving a parchment on the table for the cost of her dress. The other women in the room now flood me saying I shouldn't be so hasty. I look back towards them with the kindest stare I can muster.

"I made my choice. Please gather your belongings. I'd like a moment to myself."

They all quiet down and quickly pack their things. Once

the mounds of dress and women disperse, I sit on my bed and open the note that was handed to me.

Xylia,

    I can't imagine what you must be thinking or the hurt you might be feeling. I meant what I said that night. Both that the Adamina Clan was built out of love for you, but also that you deserve to finally know your story. They will be coming for you, as your only living mother, please heed my words, and allow yourself to be taken from that place. It is far darker than you know.

I bust through the door and quickly run through the halls to the library, where I know Kage normally works. One of the Fel Guard jumps in front of me, seeing the concern on my face. I slow down to confirm my future husband's whereabouts.

"The King, take me to him."

The guard nods and begins running ahead of me. My guess was right, the library is where we are headed.

'Darker then I know', saying it as if she made a mistake. More secrets. The more I am left in the dark, the louder the light seems to scream inside of me. The guard pushes the door open and moves to the side for me to rush through. Kage looks up from his desk and stands seeing me so disheveled. I hold out the note towards him before either of us mutter a word. Sampson and Ananias are resting a hand on their weapons, looking around, as they notice my panic.

"Who gave this to you?"

"She's already gone. She was a seamstress for the Adamina Clan. Brought a dress for me to look at."

I'm sure he will be a little angry that it's her dress I chose, but it had been prior to the note before I knew it was from *her*. He slams the note down into the desk and rubs his eyes. He mumbles something to himself, takes a deep breath, and then opens his arms towards me. I walk into them.

He lifts my chin up with his hand, so I meet his gaze. "I won't let them take you.

CHAPTER TWENTY

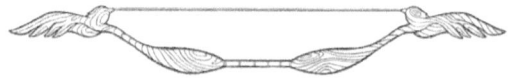

Kage takes action and starts barking orders at the guards that are in this room. I reach for the note that is sitting on the desk, but Kage takes my hand gently.

Shaking his head, he says, "leave it be. You'll torture yourself if you keep it."

I nod at his instruction—begrudgingly—because he knows me well enough that I don't just let things go. Sampson looks to me with his hand out, his way of asking me to step ahead so he can escort me back to my chambers.

Kage kisses me quickly on the cheek, holding me there for a moment with his hand in my hair and his chest still pressed against mine. I am out of his reach, and I can see the displeasure this is causing him, but it is his choice to make. He's said in the past that until I am Queen, there are some things I am going to have to be left in the dark about.

I can't not put my thoughts out there, though. This is about me.

"We should speak soon. We think better together," I say

with a small wave and even smaller smile, my eyes only parting from his to glance back at the note.

We are always better together.

That night in the Vermilion Forest was real. It wasn't an act. Rose was and has always been with the very people threatening the life I now live. I place my hand over my heart, suppressing the light that wants to burst and console me. I feel Sampson's eyes on my back, so I straighten and shake off the hurt that continues to build inside me.

Reaching my chambers feels relieving, but it quickly fades when Sampson invites himself in, locking the door behind us.

"Sampson, I appreciate your escort, but you are dismissed," I say, waving him off.

As I turn from him, I see the dress still here. I walk over to it, running my hand over the embroidery once more. Even though I am confused and somewhat terrified of what's to come, I want to be able to appreciate this.

"It is lovely," Sampson says with no waver in his voice.

I look back at him, surprised he spoke. He has always been quiet, and if I'm honest, this is the first time I think I have heard his voice. He is admiring the gown, me admiring his piercing gray eyes. He seems to stiffen as our eyes lock onto each other. He turns from me and stares off into the corner. It's apparent I will not be left alone.

I pace the room back and forth, growing more and more frustrated as I am not sure what it is I am supposed to be doing. I bite onto my nail, staring at the wall where Sampson is, who is keeping me from leaving this room. Every time I even look to the door, he takes a step in front of it. I cannot just sit in this room doing nothing. There has to be something I can do. Kage's words were meant to put me at ease, but there was so much unsaid, and not being involved in whatever conversations he is having is driving me mad. I know I am not Queen yet, but with me about to be Queen, I should have some sway and permission.

I walk over to the bay window that resides on the other wall. The view is a breathtaking sight of the castle gardens. The large fountain, where Kage and I found to be a quiet spot for us to spend time together, where we will eventually vow ourselves to each other, is now in sight. One of the garden trellises is to the left of my window. The cool Fons wind howls against the glass that is now beginning to fog because of my breath.

I need a plan. A reason to escape.

It seems obvious that Rose is a small player when it comes to this group, so talking with her directly about the issue doesn't seem to be the best course of action. Though the letter she had delivered leaves me with more questions than answers. There are more secrets she is keeping.

Wondering about personal curiosity and grudges won't do, though. That older woman, the priestess, seems far more important. She mentioned that I was to be escorted to them. Rose must have been under the impression that Kage was involved. Though Kage may have been able to bluff for answers?

It was one thing for Rose to walk me up to them, but now that they are coming after me? I am risking more than just my freedom.

I trust that Kage told me all the information he had on the Domi Nostrae, but maybe his conversation with Rose at the start of all this held more than what he shared. I need to speak with him. Maybe something Rose said could tell us more. He's smart but can overlook things when it comes to someone who is naturally intimidating, like Rose.

Maybe just giving in all together might be the other option. The thought of being the reason any more lives have to be lost is beginning to dig in.

I tighten my boots strings and tuck my shirt into my pants. I look back to Sampson, who has averted his gaze.

Now.

I push open the window quickly and jump for the trellis that is farther away than I was expecting, though all those years jumping from branch to branch is coming in handy. I grasp onto the trellis for dear life, my grip breaking the fragile wood. I fall a bit but quickly catch myself.

"Lady Xylia!"

Sampson is at the window, his arm outstretched towards me. I give him a wink and quickly begin my descent. Sampson disappears from the window, likely to be sending people on my heels.

I know that a normal Queen wouldn't even be able to climb something like this, but Kage said himself that he didn't want just another ordinary Queen.

I'll make sure to note that when he tries to get mad.

As soon as my feet hit the ground, I begin running towards the library, where I am hoping Kage is still located. The wind feels nice as my overthinking has my body in a blaze. My boots sink into the muddy earth.

"Lady Xylia, stop!"

I'm impressed with how quick Sampson is. I don't turn back to look, knowing that will only slow me down. I reach the window where the library resides on the first floor. I extend my hand, willing the window to unlatch. I pull them open and crawl through quickly, but am disappointed as I see an empty room.

"Damn," I mutter breathlessly.

"Lady Xylia."

Sampson crawls through the window and reaches for me but quickly drops his hand. I begin to walk ahead of him, ignoring his pleas to stop.

"Where is the King?"

Sampson quiets himself. I look over my shoulder at him, his eyes filled with something I can't quite describe. I start wondering the halls calling out for Kage as I go. Sampson dismisses any guard from halting me, even ordering one to step away when they approached me. I face forwards and begin heading to the strategic room as my early guesses begin to fail me. I made sure to take careful note of all the rooms in the castle when Kage gave me the 'royal' tour. I pick up the pace as my frustration and confusion builds up again.

As we reach the door, Sampson actually grasps my arm as I go to push open the door. My eyes narrow as I look at him, challenging Sampson to make his next move. I will open the doors without moving a muscle or thinking twice. His hand drops immediately, and Kage and the two military heads are in front of us.

They turn expectantly, surprised when they see my appearance. Kage walks around the table, his eyes glaring at Sampson. Kage places his hands on my shoulders, guiding me back into the hall, shutting the door behind him. He looks to Sampson again, who turns around himself and begins walking down the hall a bit, still in eyesight.

"Xylia, I ordered you to your chambers. I thought we discussed the importance of you understanding my duty of King ..."

"I do understand. Though I think that me being directly involved with this issue changes the arrangement."

"It does because a threat against you is a threat against the crown. Us being near each other is a danger."

"Being apart could be more of a danger."

I trip him up on that as his mouth opens and no words come out. I put my hands on his shoulders and lean in closer to him. I want him to understand. I can't just sit this one out.

I can't wait.

"In that letter, she said that here is where the danger was. That I will be taken by force. The old lady being allowed in here, when I overheard your order that any clan members were to be kept out ... I'd be lying if I said I wasn't happy to see her, but it was out of nostalgia. Rose knew that would stop me from calling the guards right away. She knows how to make me cave. If I hadn't been in shock back in the forest, I might have gone with them. Now I am going to need your help Kage, convince me to stay."

"You want to leave?" The hurt in his voice is heartbreaking.

"If it means saving lives—your life—you know I will do anything."

I don't want to go. I've been happy here with him. Leaving would break me, but I won't risk someone else's life to ensure my happiness.

Kage nods in understanding. He pulls me in tightly, his chin resting atop my head. I nestle into his chest. His heart is beating fast, but his arms and body feel steady.

"As long as we are together, Kage, we will work this out," I mutter into his chest.

I can feel him shake for a moment before he takes in a deep breath. "Okay."

We pull away from each other. His emerald eyes staring into my eyes.

"We will marry tomorrow. The title itself may be enough to delay them. The clock will start to tick then. Once we have the people on our side, they will have a strenuous time trying to take the people's Queen."

Tomorrow? Married?

"You just came up with that?"

He lets a small laugh slip through his lips but nods. "The

Marshal and Colonial will want to have a say, but if they think it could work, then we will do whatever it takes."

"Married. Tomorrow?"

My heart rate picks up.

We had two more weeks. I figured we could talk more, I could ... explain Codrin. How present he is despite being gone.

He kisses my forehead, his lips lingering there. "Please do not tell me that I convinced you to run away instead of staying."

I laugh nervously, knowing that I will be here. He leans back to look at me once more, but I pull him down, so our lips connect instead. Kage leans into it, allowing our kiss to deepen.

He cuts it short, though, putting his hand on my cheeks and pulling away. An apologetic look in his eyes. "Sampson, escort Lady Xylia to my chambers and this time, make sure she stays where I put her." Kage pinches my cheeks and turns away from me, back into the room.

I'll get him back for that one.

I sigh as Sampson approaches me. I swear I hear him sigh as well.

At least we are on the same page about our feelings towards each other.

We walk slowly but surely to our destination. Sampson opens the door to the King's room. I nervously step in, not having been in this room before. It is far grander than his princely room. The large bed that could hold four of me on it. The drapes, the same navy color as the flag, the large balcony overlooking Fosa. Two large chairs partly facing each other with a short table in front of them, where there are piles of books resting.

The fireplace is nearly my height and has a blazing fire roaring inside of it. Kage has a few things resting on its mantle, one which I recognize. I reach up for the decorative sword he once adored, though Sampson beats me to it. It takes everything in me not to punch him as he hands me the sword. I understand his intent, but it feels demeaning nonetheless.

I turn it over, a terrifying memory wanting to take over my mind. I hand it back to Sampson, who actually shows a look of surprise that I am not attempting to just put it back myself.

I walk around the rest of the room, browsing the book titles and feeling the satin bedding.

"Would you retrieve my book for me? The blue leathered one."

"I'm afraid you have lost my trust in your ability to follow orders, Lady Xylia."

"I don't believe it is your trust I need."

Sampson pauses for a moment before turning and walking out the door. He returns far too quickly though, but I now realize that he must have asked a guard nearby to retrieve it for him.

He's clever. I'm starting to like him.

I sit on one of the chairs once my book arrives. Every time I flip through its pages, I obtain a new feeling about and towards them. The thought of Codrin fills my mind, but so does the connection it shares with Kage. It's exhausting thinking about them both. I desperately miss and want Codrin here, but I am so thankful that I have Kage ... though I wish he were with me now.

As if on cue, Kage walks through the door. Him looking as exhausted as I feel. I glance out the window and see that it has already been four moonshifts since I saw him.

Kage dismisses Sampson to the outside of the chambers with a simple wave.

"He doesn't listen to me," I say, just loud enough for Sampson to hear as he exits.

"Good." Kage smiles at me as he joins me in the chair I am currently sitting in.

I readjust myself to sit on his lap, placing the book in mine. He leans his head back, resting it against the head of the chair.

"Are we getting married?" The words come out the way I feel, nervous.

"You think I would let anyone stop me?" He tilts his head to the side to glance at me.

"I haven't even tried on the dress, and speaking of the dress ..."

Kage laughs at my comment and rubs his face with his hand. He leans forwards and picks me up, taking us both to the bed. He drops me onto the bed and jumps on top of me. Kage nuzzles his face into my neck and sighs happily.

"It'll just be the castle present," Kage explains. My heart tightens, Vasile won't be there. I understand not bringing anyone in, but I'll ask about Vasile in the morning. "They won't say anything if it's a little too tight."

I smack him over the head, hard.

"Try again."

"I mean, loose, of course."

"I was going to say, maybe I should wear something else."

Kage picks up his head to meet my gaze. "A bride in armor will not work."

That wasn't what I was going to suggest, but I don't want to add more stress to this. I'll wear it. Tomorrow won't be about her or them. It will be about Kage and me.

"The dress it is then."

I SET the book down onto the nightstand after reading it for the hundredth time. Kage is already fast asleep beside me. I close my eyes, listening to his soft breathing. It still baffles me at how soundly he sleeps. Or, I think it might actually bother me. Here I am tormented by every death I've caused and every death I've witnessed, but he can close his eyes and forget it ever happened. I poke him in the chest as a form of justice. He groans and turns away from me a bit. I stifle my laugh and scoot down under the quilts.

Turning from Kage, our backs facing each other, I stare at the book for a while until I feel Kage stir awake next to me. I turn over, but it's not him laying in bed. I see a brightly smiling Codrin laying next to me. My eyes begin to water, and my smile spreads across my face, just as bright as his. He runs his hand through my hair, and I close my eyes to take it in gratefully.

As I open my eyes, we are standing in the Vermilion Forest; a dark light is being cast over us as both the sun and moon are dancing above us. Codrin takes my hand and twirls me around before pulling me in. I laugh and take him all in. I take his face in my hands and feel the heat from his skin.

"I can't believe you are here," I whisper to him.

"Actually your belief is why I'm here," he says, nuzzling his nose against mine.

My eyes burn as tears come to the surface, realizing this is all a dream. When I wake up, he will be gone again.

"You're wrong. I've been here, I'll be here," he whispers, kissing my head.

Of course, my thoughts aren't safe from him. They never really were. He always could see what no one else could.

"Even though it's not you who I'll be wed to tomorrow?" I ask, though I know the answer.

"Not even death could separate us, Xylia."

"I see that now."

He lifts my hand and kisses it lightly. I blink twice, and he's gone. The low-lit interior of Kage's chambers fills my gaze. I immediately take a shaky breath and hold it in, knowing that if I let it out, I'll scream.

Sneaking out from under the covers in my nightgown, I grab my leather boots that are sitting by the fireplace, all before tip-toeing out onto the terrace. The cold wraps itself around me, and I'm forced to release my breath from the shock of its embrace. Tears stream down my face, whimpers escaping my lips. I fall to my knees, wrapping my shaking arms around me. I'm enjoying the cold, though. It lets me know what is actually real, even if this reality is not what I'm entirely yearning for.

I reach inside me and bring the light just to the tips of my fingers, welcoming the soft hum it brings with it. This was the thing I was most terrified of, and now it is the thing I hold most dear. This light is the only constant. Everything else has flipped over on top of me. I can hardly breathe with the burdens weighing me down. I wish I could let it all go, but letting it go means letting go of them—of Codrin—and that seems even more painful.

What am I supposed to do? How do I make any of this better for those I've lost or hurt along the way? I let out a scream that turns into an uncontrollable sob.

The door to the terrace opens. Kage wraps a blanket around me, pulling me into his arms. He stands us up and tries to move me inside, but I pull away from him, rushing to the bar and holding onto it, so I am immovable. The blanket silently falls to the ground in between us.

"Xylia," Kage says, shaking his head in confusion.

I look at him with my swollen eyes filled with anger that I know should just be directed to myself.

"I miss him so much," I whisper.

"Vasile?"

"Codrin."

His confusion turns into hurt. He bites his lip and looks out towards the eastern castle wall. He doesn't say anything, just crosses his arms and looks off into the distance.

"He was a home I thought I would always be able to return to."

I want him to understand, even if he can't right now. I want to say it, so maybe one day he will.

He finally looks over at me.

"A lovely thought. I had one of those once. I thought my devotion to this country might mean I could have saved it without taking it by force, but it was just that, Xylia. A thought."

See the difference, please.

"No matter how much I develop my abilities or come to understand the power I wield, it's my heart that is weak. There's no exercise for that. Only time can help me, Kage."

"Time is not something we can ever get back, Xylia. You cannot, will not, wallow in it while time passes. You are too important to this country, to this era, to me." Kage staggers back a moment, almost if he is admitting something to himself for the first time.

I hate that I understand what he is trying to say.

He picks up the blanket in front of him and starts folding it.

"I know. That's why I haven't wallowed, why I have put one foot in front of the other every single day. I haven't slowed down. I've been holding my breath for months, knowing I cannot wallow. Tomorrow is something Codrin and I spoke about quite often, but now it's not him I'll be tying myself to."

I gasp as it all comes out. I haven't even admitted this to myself. Kage is hearing it raw, without thought, just emotion.

Kage furrows his brow, and he twitches his nose. My heart aches watching him. I let go of the bar and place my frozen hands onto his chilled cheeks.

"I am not saying I do not love or want for you, Kage."

"Is that what your words are portraying? That you have love for me, but that love is nothing compared to your love for him?"

"I'm saying that I'm breathing for the first time. Let me wallow tonight so that I do not wallow tomorrow."

Kage meets my gaze, those dark emerald eyes piercing through me. He stops folding and unfolds so that he can wrap me up once more.

"Then wallow, I'll hold you until you're done."

The tears immediately begin again, and he tightens his hold. I scream into his shoulder and weep for the man I've loved, the mother I could not save, the mother I've lost, the mother and father I've never met, the loss of a home I once thought was my cage, and the loss of the person I once was.

It's not until I feel Kage jerk away that I notice the figures surrounding us. I try to reach towards him, but darkness succumbs my consciousness.

CHAPTER TWENTY-ONE

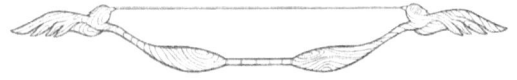

MY HEAD HITS A WOODEN SURFACE, jostling me awake. My hands are bound and are resting in my lap, my feet manacled and chained to some part of the carriage I am riding in. The jostling lets me know the carriage is moving in some direction. I try to take deep breaths, but they are shaky and dry. I feel naked and more vulnerable than I have ever been. I'm only in my nightgown. I have no armor or weapons, not even regular clothes.

This is a nightmare.

I try to peer through a crack in the boarded-up window, but all I see is dirt and grass. It's daytime now. The wedding. The Domi Nostrae. Kage.

They wouldn't hurt Kage.

Right?

I need to focus on getting out of here before I can worry. The Fel Watch will have noticed my absence if Sampson wasn't already there at the sound of a thump. The rope on my hands is easy enough to untie, but the manacles are going to need a little more work. I extend my hands and focus on breaking the lock, but nothing happens. I shake my head and try again, it's like I cannot see the manacles while using my magicae. Kage said that the Domi Nostrae had many magicae users in their group. I'm going to assume that one of them can negate other magicae, or at least can make an object immune to it.

I'm stuck.

I lean my head back, letting a few tears roll down my cheeks. I thought we were safe, that today would come and we would have peace. Kage seemed sure too.

Codrin. You even came to me, came to tell me it was okay. That you would still be with me even if I was with Kage.

At least I won't have to deal with an angry Vasile. He would be heartbroken knowing I got married without him. I smile, imagining Vasile throwing a fit over every little thing, wanting the day to go perfect. He would think nothing would be good enough. He still doesn't think Kage is good enough. Vasile nearly killed Kage when he found out that we had shared a bed.

They are all with me. Even now. I don't need to be scared.

I watch the day turn to night before the carriage stops. There are a few voices that come into earshot—all whispering. A few moments pass before someone quickly opens the door. I extend my hand outwards, facing the door. I doubt I'll be able to do much, but I'll try.

I always need to at least try.

The door quickly opens, and a numbness consumes me. I slump to the side, and my eyelids feel heavier than steel. Forcing my eyes to remain open, I see a blurry figure enter the carriage. They turn my head and pour some disgusting thick liquid down my throat. I start to cough, but they hold my mouth closed, forcing me to swallow.

"It's food. We have a long journey ahead of us, so I'd recommend getting used to the taste," Rose says.

I choke again hearing her voice. She's right here.

Why? Why is she here? Why is she with them?

Once the *food* is down my throat, Rose gets up and leaves.

"Thanks for the dress," I shout.

She doesn't turn around. She just leaves me there. The carriage door slams shut. I bite my lip, holding in the sob I feel building inside of me. I thought I was done with this grief, but her betrayal is like a knife twisting in a wound.

Rose is no longer a person I know. A stranger inside of a body I recognize.

THE SOUND of the carriage door opening stirs me away, and I sit up quickly just in time for a bag to be placed over my head.

"Don't try to run. If you do, those legs will become nothing but bags of flesh. Understand?" a woman's voice calls out. It sounds deep and low.

My heart sinks. They are hiding their numbers. I have nary a clue of where I am, and my magicae doesn't seem to be reliable at the moment due to whatever magicae they are using on their side. Running is not even an option. The chain connecting me to the carriage clatters against the wood. I'm pulled from the carriage and thrown into the mud. I start to crawl forwards but I'm picked up, my feet now trying to catch up.

"You'll stay out here with us at night," the woman says into my ear.

I'm turned, and my back is shoved into a tree. I slide to the ground, the bark scratching my back.

They won't kill me. I'm not going to die. I'm going to live. I'm going to find a way back to Kage.

Someone grabs my arms, metal clamping around my wrists. I hear chain dangling and being moved around, my new confinement. I tug a bit once it quiets down, I'm chained to the tree. I try to will myself free, but nothing happens.

Come on. I didn't think it would work, but I wanted it to.

"This is going to be your life until we reach our destination. Get comfortable. Let us know if you need something, but don't always expect an answer." Her voice starts to fade as she walks a bit.

Is Rose watching this? Watching me be humiliated, threatened, tied to a tree, like some mutt or beast.

I cry silently, wanting this to end.

I LIVE that same routine as promised. Pulled, tied down, jerked, and forced to do as they wish. I haven't heard the voice, been able to wield my magicae. All that training, every thought and plan to keep me away from the Domi Nostrae mean nothing.

How much farther?

How much longer until I am back in the carriage?

How much longer until I am back outside?

Why must I sleep out here?

Where is Rose?

I wonder if Kage is okay.

Is he chasing after us—they are in no rush, so I doubt it.

He will come.

It's gotten warmer.

How long has it been since I've been in the sun?

Vasile is going to be mad. I said I wouldn't disappear.

I feel ill.

My back hurts.

Whatever they have been feeding me must have made me sick.

Kage, where are you?

I lose track of how many days pass by. The carriage rattles and my body shakes. I wait for them to feed me, to let me out, to let me sleep. My body is weak, and so is my mind.

The carriage stops. I look out the boarded window and see the sun still shining. Something is happening. The carriage door opens, a bag placed over my head, the chains undone, and I am pulled once more from the carriage. A numbness washes over me.

"Welcome home, Xylia," I hear Rose whisper before I drift off.

CHAPTER TWENTY-TWO

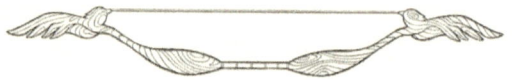

I FEEL SICK. My body is slowly spinning in the air as it is suspended. All I can see is darkness. My hands are tightly bound behind me, the taste of blood in my mouth. I try to extend my hand out, but they even have my fingers wrapped together. There are soft whispers in the near distance, but I can't understand what they are saying. I start struggling against my bindings, but pain rings through my body. The bodies in here must hear me wake because footsteps start to clomp towards me.

"Good morning, Xylia."

Rose.

"You can drop her."

It only takes to the end of her sentence before I plummet to the ground, my body slamming into what feels like a cold stone flooring. My body twitches from the pain, my lungs finding their breath.

"Couldn't have opted for the gentle set down?" I ask with what little air passes through my body.

Rose pulls the blindfold off of me. As my eyes focus, I

notice hers look a lot darker than the last time I actually saw her. Two guys pick me up from the ground and sit me in a chair behind me. Looking around, there is nothing but old ruined walls with moss covering some of the stone flooring I had just become well acquainted with. There's a slight glimmer from a small pool of water that is collecting in one of the corners, and a portion of the ceiling is missing, allowing the moon to shine in.

No sign of Kage.

"Xylia," Rose says, extending her hand towards me.

Her fingertips brush against my cheek, but I pull away, making sure to maintain our eye contact. She recoils her fingers into the palm of her hand and turns from me. She nods her head in the direction of the door to the men that are standing with us in this room, letting them know she's heading out.

They nod their heads in understanding.

Rose heads for the door.

"You could have told me."

Rose stops, looking over her shoulder. "I wish I had been strong enough to do that for you."

Nausea quickly returns to me, and within moments, I lean forwards and vomit.

The guys jump away from me in disgust. Rose looks at me with not only disgust but anger as well. She storms out of the room, the men standing nearly on the other side of the room.

I lean my head back, taking in the fact that neither of these men are armed. They must know my fighting capabilities. Hand to hand is not my specialty. Even though I could easily escape my bindings, escaping *them* would not be as easy.

"... Oracle ... now?"

"... child ... must ... Priestess."

I can hear bits and pieces of their whispered conversation, but they are too far away for me to hear what they are actually saying. Though, it is obvious they are talking about me.

The door creaks open, a new face appearing from behind it.

"Um, it's time, now. Please bring her. Please." The quiet and nervous voice belonging to a small adolescent.

They pull back from the door as the two men approach me, picking me up and walking me to the door. They follow their underling through the old and now crumbling halls. I hear a soft hum in the back of my head, along with the echos of voices I think I remember.

As we come to an intersection, my eyes are drawn to the right, where I see a figure of light opening their arms to me. I shake my head, not sure if I am witnessing this. I am taken left, and the figure leaves my view.

We enter a chamber; a wardrobe, chest, bed, fireplace all accounted for. Though, it is the steam and smell of oils coming from the connecting room that everyone else focuses on. They set me on the bed and untie my hands. I try to suppress my confusion. It is apparently obvious from the laugh of the younger figure in front of me.

"Um, binding your hands is not necessary anymore. I, I'm, I mean, I can do things. Painful things. So, please do not, you know, run?"

I look to the two men who are now standing a lot closer to the door. I furrow my brows, not sure how to handle this. She seems honest, and her evident awkward nature would make her a poor liar.

"I will take your word for it."

They smile and clap their hands together, pleased with my 'trust' in them. The men leave the room quickly.

"Um, please, you know, remove your clothing. We need to get you ready."

They point to my body, their finger scanning up and down my body.

"I would rather n—"

A scream is ripped from my lungs as a deathly pain sears through my chest. I grab the left side of my chest, falling to the ground. My eyes feel like they are about to bust, my heart feeling like it is no longer beating, my mind is racing.

"Now."

The pain stops.

My body is shaking.

Vomit on the floor.

They were not kidding.

I begin stripping slowly out of my nightgown. I'm sore and still nauseous.

Once my body is bare, they walk me over to a bath that has been already prepared. The room we are in is large. Broken windows, looking out onto a large mass of water, take up the entire far wall. All forms of plant life seem to have made their home here in this room. A red moss tickles the bottoms of my feet.

I get in, the hot water boiling my skin; it feels good on my worn body. I hope they don't think this will somehow forgive the rough accommodations they provided getting me here.

What did they do to me?

"Um, you can soak for a bit."

I lean back and look up to the tiled ceiling, pieces of it missing but the overall design is beautiful. It reminds me of the book, the same intricate patterns that incorporate symbols from a time period long before this one.

"Where are we?" I look over to them, surprised by my question.

"Um, the old country."

Do they mean the old Capital?

I sit up. "Where is the King?"

They glare at me.

"That imposter is likely sitting on the throne built by his

ancestors who only achieved their means by the death of those who it truly belonged to."

I'm taken aback by their words and the intensity behind them. Kage is safe, which means he's going to try and figure something out. I'm not alone here, though. I look down at my hands, red from the temperature of the water. This power inside of me cannot just be taken away. I can take comfort in that, and hopefully, Kage knows that I won't just sit here and wait.

"Kage is nothing like his father."

The door in the other room swings open, hitting the wall. Their glare now entertained by the sound. They get up and go to inspect, leaving me in here alone.

I hop out of the tub, the water coming alive as I do so. The splashing on the ground brings their attention back to me. I don't dare look behind me, and without a second thought, I race towards the broken window, leaping onto the windowpane, willing my nightgown to my hand.

Looking down into a dark abyss below me causes my heart to quicken and my stomach churn.

Jump.

The cold water and darkness envelop me. I hope the direction I am swimming towards is in the direction of air as the shock of the cool water takes all of mine from me.

I expel the light, the voice sounding just as panicked as me. It illuminates a path to the surface. I breakthrough, and gasp for air, hastily swimming to the bank. I won't have long, they are already aware of my escape, and now my light will draw in their attention. Reaching the bank, I climb onto it, the grass and mud feeling warm in comparison.

Going from a hot bath to cold water was not an amazing idea.

I slip on my soaking and nearly tattered nightgown, trying not to show everyone exactly what I'm packing.

I try to take in my surroundings through the profuse amounts of shivering. It feels like my arms and legs are going to fall off, they feel so weak, but I cannot stop now.

The old country—the ruins of what once was—is exactly that. Ruined. Stone, iron, wood, all torn and burned to asunder. Some of the structures remain but in pieces, like the main building I was just in. Mostly, it's the eastern side that looks demolished, while the rest has been eaten away over time. There is a small shelter a few hundred meters ahead, and I dash towards it as shouting starts behind me.

The voice is still screaming. I open the door and enter the small structure. Hay lays out on the floor, a subtle creak as the boards take on my weight.

I won't survive out here. They will find me sooner rather than later. Making my way back inside might be my only chance. I will just need to stay out of their sight. I look towards that eastern side. It's dark, meaning it's likely quiet.

The shouts outside seem to be misdirected towards the body of water. Thinking I might not have made it out.

At least I have that going for me.

Peeking my head out of the door, there are a dozen figures looking for any signs of me. Thankfully, they are all searching in the dark of night.

I sneak out of the shelter, my body pleading for comfort as my skin touches the mud and colder wind. I painfully—slowly —make my way through the rubble. My bare feet and hands are growing numb from the chilled rocks scraping and cutting them. Calling the light to ease the pain would be easy, but it would mean I could lead them straight to me.

What am I even doing? I could be making this all worse for myself. What if Kage actually comes? What if they find me regardless of my escape?

I collapse onto the stone floor and huddle myself into a dark corner. I'll stay here long enough for them to assume me, either dead or escaped, then I can grab some clothes and hopefully a horse. I'll have to wait until morning to sleep. They will either give up on searching or give me an opportunity to find a better spot to hide.

The old country, the ruined castles, we had to have been traveling for longer than a few weeks. It would have taken us a full moon cycle and then some to get to the northern part of Nymph Lake.

I've missed a chunk of my life. I've missed my wedding. I wonder what Kage must be feeling. I smile a bit, thinking about Kage's furrowed brow and darting eyes. Something I find so charming, an expression he does anytime something doesn't go his way. It's in those moments I can tell he is really a prince, but as soon as his hand is in mine, that selfishness fades into that beautiful smile of his.

A tear rolls down my face at the thought of not seeing his smile again. After everything I have lost, I found something to cherish and hold onto. The thought of remaining here, dying here, never being with him again ... sounds terrifying. My stomach begins to churn again, and I gag. I throw my hand over my mouth to try and stop myself. My stomach has to be empty. They have fed me nothing but that liquid mess.

The sound of footsteps echo inside the room. I press myself against the wall. I cover my mouth to try and hide my breathing. As the footsteps pass, my light emerges. My skin is illuminating.

Stop. No, control it. Control it!

Swirls of light dance under my skin. Panic sets in as I

cannot stop it, the voice humming sweetly. The footsteps begin to get louder. I'm out of options.

A taller man peeks his head into the chamber, the room too dimly lit to see him clearly. He steps through the large crack in the wall. As the light is illuminating my body, it begins to showcase his face, familiar features reveal themselves.

CHAPTER TWENTY-THREE

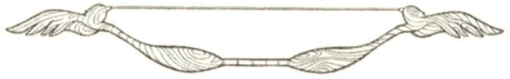

WHEN THE MAN steps into the light, we gaze at each other. I recognize his familiar features as they are similar to mine. Light fawn-colored hair, his eyes matching mine in color. He has sharp features, making him quite handsome. His ears look like every other human.

My guard is down.

I can't move, though. I am frozen in fear, or is it awe? His hand reaches out towards me, stroking my face with his thumb.

Memories of shining lights fill the sky far brighter than I've actually ever seen. I hear laughter in a distant time that is filled with love and happiness—the cry of a small child, but the joy that comes with it.

My eyes flutter a bit as my head spins. I stumble back, and he grabs my shoulders to hold me steady.

"Xylia," he says with a shaky breath and a desperate smile. He places his forehead on mine. His voice seems familiar, the accent similar to the voice that comes with the light.

"Who are you?" I whisper.

He pulls away, a look of both shock and sadness washing

over him. He looks down to my arms, where the light is still dancing around.

"My name is Baron." Baron bows with his head towards me.

He stares into my eyes. Obviously, he has a thousand questions threatening to spill out as he opens his mouth, but he quickly closes it. Pressing his lips together firmly, he makes sure nothing escapes.

My heart aches, and the voice hums.

"You're with the Domi Nostrae."

He nods hesitantly. "There is someone we both have been looking for on the other side of all of this."

Heavy footsteps begin to approach us, Baron looks over his shoulder hearing them too. He looks back to me with his hand extended. I know this is not what I should be doing, but the light and my heart are betraying me in this moment.

I take his hand, not sure what my next move is.

BARON HOLDS my right hand tightly as the different sized, shaped, raced, and gendered crowd around us begins to follow his lead. We walk deeper to the western side, where the damaged ruins look far less ... well, ruined. The light is still dancing around, now concentrated into my right hand. I start to feel light-headed as we continue our journey.

"Please bring her some clothes. We will retire to my chambers for the evening."

The panic sets in again. I instinctively pull away from him, the crowd behind us ready to smite me.

He quickly raises a hand and extends his other once more. "I have no ill intention, believe me."

Believe him? Does he think trust can be won over so easily?

"I don't really have a choice. I'm outnumbered here, and I'm not sure I have the strength to run again." I take his hand and he opens his door to a large—not crumbling apart—room.

There is a large bed with carvings of creatures and trees that make up the frame. A long lounge chair sits in the corner near a tall, full bookshelf; the books all have a worn-dyed binding. It feels like my book could be in there somewhere.

There are drapes covering the windows view and carpeting that comforts my torn and sore feet. The large fireplace that is warming my bare arms. Baron takes a seat on the chair while gesturing for me to take a seat with him. I turn my gaze away from him, walking to the bed. I run my fingers over the intricate design, poking at the **Eelgers** pointed teeth. Looking more closely, most of the creatures are aquatic. Most likely due to the proximity of the largest lake in the Realm.

"Do you like it?"

I look over my shoulder to Baron, who is nervously fiddling with something in his hands. I nod in response, knowing that it's really Codrin's taste I am thinking of.

"It took a while, though having to stay within these walls gave me plenty of **tempus**," he admits, his accent thickening more towards the end.

He made this himself?

"Tempus?"

He furrows his brow a bit. "Our word for time. I slip back into my native language now and again. I apologize."

Why did he bring me in here with him?

Who is he?

How am I going to get out of this?

I grab the blanket off the bed and wrap it around myself, feeling too exposed.

He turns his eyes from me seeing this and looks up at the bookcase. He skims over some of the books before grabbing one.

It looks just like mine, except more worn and even older. He holds the book up as almost a peace offering before approaching me.

"Every time you look at me, I see an even more confused expression than the last." He laughs awkwardly.

My eyes are glued to the book, remembering exactly where I put it last. It can't be my book.

"I am confused."

"About who I am?"

"About everything that is happening. Though yes, starting off with who you are is the priority.

He sighs, a light smile playing on his lips.

"You talk so formally."

"Seems appropriate."

He suppresses a laugh and nods. "My name is Baron. I am, how do they put it, an important member of the Domi Nostrae. Meaning that they are using me to achieve their means."

"Looks like you are choosing to be here."

"I am. Like I said, there are things I have been looking for. The Domi Nostrae, in exchange for my Magicae, are assisting me in my search."

I get a little more uncomfortable, now feeling like I am one of those things.

He sits down on the bed, leaving plenty of space between us. He must have noticed me pull away because he throws his hands up once more, a concerned look on his face.

"I'm looking for my family."

"That's nice."

What does he want from me?

He chuckles a bit again at my response, but his brow furrows and his jaw tightens. We sit there, staring at each other. He opens his mouth to say something but closes it again, tapping his fingers on the book he has in his hand. We listen to the fire crackle and the wind quietly howling outside of the windows. I shiver a bit, remember the cold.

Baron pats his book, drawing my attention to his hands.

"Well, I can tell you a story if you would like."

"Would it be the truth?"

He nods. "I'm not very good at make-believe, so true stories are what I have always told ..." he says, cutting himself off.

"Will it be interesting?"

He laughs outright this time, his smile returning. "I hope so."

I furrow my brow and lean up against the bed frame. I have no trust in his words, but it looks like waiting is now my only option.

It's frustrating. He found me almost too quickly.

It's like he was able to call out to me, or my power at least. Maybe that is his Magicae.

He looks strong and capable, something Rose would have admired in a commander. He seems hesitant, though, almost afraid of breaking something.

I've already learned enough to know that he is willing to join a group like this one just to achieve his objectives. Maybe this story will reveal just a little more.

He clears his throat and wraps his hands around the book tightly, glancing at me once more before fixing his gaze onto the fireplace behind me.

"This story takes place a long tempus ago." He gives me a wink, using the native word he just taught me.

"There was a very skilled soldier, who could wield any weapon. He became so connected with these weapons that eventually, he no longer needed to hold them to wield them. The weapons would slay his enemies for him."

I shift a bit as he describes a power similar to the one I have.

"He fought for money, mostly, until he wandered deep into

a reddened forest. There was a beast that had a pretty high bounty on it, which was very appealing at the time."

The Vermilion Forest, I'm assuming.

"Eventually, a noise attracted his attention, but it was not a beast. It was the most **pulcherrima** woman anyone could have seen—dazzling like light itself. She was dancing around. The moment he spotted her, though, she spotted him. There was a connection that felt so surreal."

He smiles widely, looking at me. His eyes tear up a bit, but he deters them by staring back into the fire.

"They loved each other so much, but she was an Elvish woman, royalty on top of that. Her family did not approve of this boy. Even a showing of his Magicae, though impressive enough to earn him a spot as a top guard, was not enough to win her hand. However, despite this, they continued to meet. Eventually leading to the birth of a **paulo puella**. She had golden hair that matched her mother's and eyes just like her father's. Her cry was the greatest song ever composed and she was deeply loved."

I hadn't realized I was crying until his hand touched mine.

"Her name was Xylia, child of the tree. Named after the love that was born in the forest. What allowed us to have you."

I shudder, hearing him say my name, not out of fear but a longing.

I wasn't expecting that.

CHAPTER TWENTY-FOUR

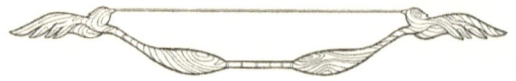

A KNOCK at the door startles us both. He pats my hand before standing and answering the door. An unfamiliar woman looms in the doorway, holding garments in her hands. I quickly move from my seated position, more than ready to get out of this gown and into something more fitting.

"Thank you, Lilith," Baron says, taking the clothes from her.

I keep a close eye on the clothes, and I hear Baron chuckle before he hands them to me over his shoulder.

I eagerly take the clothes from Baron and head to a far corner.

"I'll step out a moment," Baron says as he exits the room

I begin putting on the pair of tan trousers and the white tunic they have spared. I hear the door open and close as I am finishing tightening the leather straps around my waist.

"Better?"

I am feeling a lot more confident.

"You mentioned something about the group's means. What exactly are they so desperate in needing me for?"

"Opening the doorway. I have tried opening the doorway many times, and it has nearly killed me every time," He admits, shaking his head. "We tried different types of rituals, Magicae users assisting, and nothing was working. Eventually, we came across some text about how they closed it. It seems having a direct connection with the Awemother is what was necessary." He gives me a soft glance before looking away. "Being part elf, you have that direct connection."

Part elf. Right.

If he is truly my father, I would have to be part human as well.

"I thought that was going to be the end of my journey, and I would be stuck on this side while you and your mother were on the other," Baron continues. "Then they told me that they had you—" he bites his shaking hand. "I cannot explain how angry I was. I nearly tore this entire place apart, hearing they had been hiding you from me, but it meant that we had a chance at bringing your mother back."

"The daughter connection thing is good. Great way to create sympathy," I say, walking around him, watching his reaction.

I want to believe him. I can feel something inside me telling me that he's right, but I can't risk my heart again.

Baron steps closer, his arms outstretched. A desperate sadness washing over him. "Xylia. Look at our eyes, our Magicae," he starts willing the books off the shelves. "The moment I saw you, I recognized you. It took everything in me to not wrap you up into a hug and never let go. I have waited for this moment for nearly thirty-seven sidereal years."

I want to believe him.

"Coincidence," I whisper.

"I don't want to put you in danger. I am sorry for taking you away from whatever life you have lived up until now, but please. This is the happiest day of my life since we were reborn. Once your mother is here, I'll follow you wherever you take us. I don't ever want to be apart from you."

I believe him.

"What do you plan on doing with me in the ritual?"

He sighs and sits on the chair once more, running his hands through his hair. All the books retire to their shelves.

"Hopefully nothing much. Just being close by may be enough. It's likely the doorway will absorb a part of your Magicae, but I cannot be sure."

"You are not worried it will kill me?"

He shakes his head.

"It's more likely it will kill me. It will take everything in me. The Domi Nostrae will join in if they see me falter though. Only one Magicae user can start the ceremony, but it takes more than one to open or close it. I'm sure it would kill me otherwise."

I nod, trying to get a grasp on what exactly is happening.

"It's interesting though. That light inside of you. Even in the prime of Magicae, I've never seen a user with more than one power. It's how I found you. It called out to me just like your mother's did. Seems like my Magicae wasn't the only Magicae you picked up."

I furrow my brow, not quite understanding. I look to my hands that are still dancing with light. This power was inherited by her. An oracle's power cannot be inherited, though. Maybe Kage and I were wrong, but Baron is not wrong. A Magicae user having two inherited powers has never been recorded.

Wait a moment.

"I need you to clarify something for me. The door was sealed nearly five hundred sidereal years ago." He nods at my accurate statements. "You are telling me my mother is on the other side of that doorway." He nods again, leaning forwards resting his elbows onto his knees. "Elves are known to have lived a long time, but there is no possible way for her to have been put through those doors after being sealed."

Baron laughs as he stands, an eyebrow raised.

"Xylia, your mother protected us. She hid us away in the very trees we ran away to, the very trees we had planned to raise you in. She was dragged and forced through that door after giving us time. We were reborn nearly thirty seven side-real years ago. Though when I woke, I could not find you."

Rose.

She must have found me first. Rye mentioned that the day they found me, they had headed into the forest after hearing a woman's voice echoing through the woods, in a language they could not understand. They said it looked like the whole forest was glowing.

I need to sit down.

I walk past him and sit on the chair he just stood up from. This is all too much. He is my father, I'm actually over five hundred sidereal years old, and I was born out of a tree.

I can't have just one normal thing about me.

"But we are together now." He places his hands on my shoulders, the light traveling to where his hands are now touching.

"We are going to open the doorway and keep it open long enough for her to pass through and come over to us. I don't plan on destroying the land I care for. Once Evanora is with us once more, the door will seal once more."

"Evanora?"

"Your mother's name."

My breath hitches, the light's voice sings in a soft tone. I place my hand over my heart, telling me that this is all real, all true.

"They will not be happy when you close it."

He laughs with a nod. "That is true, but your mother is far more powerful than any of them. Even combined. That forest, I believe you call it Vermilion now? Evanora's magicae is what created it. Only her magicae can destroy that forest."

That's why only the holes that have remained are those ones I've created. Even with the attack on the Adamina Clan, the trees grew right back, like nothing had happened.

When the King tried to chop down the trees, they grew back almost instantly. Though when my light burned a hole through it, it stopped growing. I place my hands on top of his. My mind is screaming at me to not get sucked in, but my heart is telling me everything he is saying is true.

He is my father.

The father I had thought about for so many nights while growing up. I look up into our identical eyes. There's a love there, saddened, but there.

"Xylia?"

"You really are him."

He smiles and nods. "Yeah, **amare**."

I wrap my arms around him. Sobs slipping out as years of emotions rise to the surface. He strokes my hair as cries slip through his lips just as often as mine. He never gave up on me, he fought for me. I gave up on him, though. I even ran away from him. Even though I was unaware of it being him, I stopped searching.

"I'm sorry."

He pulls back a bit to look at my reddened, wet face. He shakes his head as if understanding every thought I just had.

"You are here now." He kisses my cheek and pulls me back in.

I feel weak, exposed, and unnerved, but safe and comforted.

He tells me more about our home. How it was a small meadow near the much smaller forest that was originally called **Rubrum Silva**. Boren had built a cottage, using the very same magicae I have. He explains he also put this room back to its original state. It was my mother's room.

He tells me about the family I will never meet due to their deaths which came at the hand of the First Torrin King. Despite the fact that he was never accepted by my mother's family, he talks very highly of them. Saying they were the most beautiful people, as well as the wisest. They had been through the beginning of the doorways opening to a communal land where all could live together. Where we had one King above all others, who kept the peace.

He hesitates but eventually talks about his family and the sadness that washes over him. He speaks of his absent father and sickly mother. How he swore he would be there for his child, but now barely even knows who I am and that he missed every moment.

I tell him about the Vermilion Forest, about the home I helped build. I tell him about the Adamina Clan and how I gave them everything I had. How badly I wanted to be the strength of the Clan, to be what they all needed. I tell him about Codrin and Vasile and how they were the only people I ever dropped my guard around. I tell him about Codrin's love for me and his obsession with carving. I tell him what little information I have on Forged Magicae.

He asks about who raised me, and I tell him about Rose and Rye. He recognizes the names and shifts uncomfortably as I tell him about who they were. How they did their best, and that there were points where it was unbearable, but there were others where I had felt incredibly loved.

"Though, I'm sure hearing that it was all for the sake of keeping you from me or from the world must have been painful."

I bite my tongue and nod.

Of course, that would be painful.

His eyes dart away from mine and towards the door, clenching his fists.

"Continue, please. I want to know more."

I explain their roles in the clan; how Rye was the previous Maresal and that I had been designated Maresal after her death. I explain that Rose was the First Lady and kept the whole show running despite losing the love of her life and being trapped inside the very place she had chosen to run to let others be free.

I tell him about the previous King, who he already seemed quite informed about. His dislike for old King Torrin made me nervous on the next subject.

"What do you think of his sons?"

"I think anyone who was raised by that **homo malus** could never be good, honest, or respectable."

I look over to the fire, trying to avoid his gaze. I can recognize that Eli was a terrifying creature that I was happy to put down, but Kage is not like them.

"Do you know?"

"That you killed the old King?"

I look back at him, a smile on his lips.

"The Second Prince, what was it I heard people are calling him now, King Felguard?"

News travels fast.

Kage nearly buried me in the snow when I told him what people are going to start calling him, thinking it's foolish to take the country's name for his own. Though, I made the point that he technically did not take it, I gave it to him. He liked it a bit more after that.

"From what I've been told, he seems to have your support. Though, as your father, as a man who has killed evil men, be wary of him, Xylia. Regardless of how you see him, he is a man who was raised by darkness."

"I am actually marrying him."

Baron's face goes pale, his eyes wide. He coughs a bit, shuffling in his seat. He rubs his face with his hand before looking away, up to the ceiling.

"Xylia. Please do not tie yourself to him quite yet." He looks back to me, a seriousness in his eyes. "This group has plans for him, and I do not wish to see you get hurt due to an attachment."

My heart tightens—hardens—hearing his words. "What do they plan to do?"

He turns completely towards me, making sure that I am intent on his words.

"Is this arrangement out of anything more than security?" he asks.

"Yes."

He inhales sharply and closes his eyes. "Then I will keep this to myself."

I grab onto his hand. "If they are going after him, they are going after my heart, Baron."

"That's why I cannot tell you, Xylia. You will try to stop them, and they will not allow you to."

My eyes start to well up with tears of anger. "Is it already in motion?"

He nods. I stand up and start pacing the floor.

There has to be something. Sampson is with him. Right? He will be fine.

"There is nothing to be done, Xylia."

"That cannot be true!" I shout, my body shaking from the frustration.

I bite onto my thumb, trying to think.

What can I say, what can I do, where can I go?

"Xylia, they want us on that throne."

"I will be on that throne. I am going to be Queen."

"You are going to be *his* Queen."

"What about the people? They wanted him."

"They wanted him after seeing he had you, Xylia."

I crumple to the ground. "I don't want to lose him."

Baron rushes over and wraps me in his arms. I shove him away, but he grabs for me once more. We fight each other, separating and being brought together.

Kage needs me, and I need him. I cannot lose anyone else. I won't be able to handle it.

The knock on the door breaks up our struggle. I am able to effectively push Baron away and shoot myself across the floor. He looks hurt and lost as he stands and answers the door. A large group of people are now outside the door.

My heart drops. A few of the figures turn to look at my disheveled self, so I stand and straighten myself out, turning my back to them.

"Xylia. It's time."

CHAPTER TWENTY-FIVE

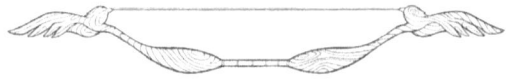

My heart is beating out of my chest as we walk down the different hallways.

Does this mean he is already dead?

How could I have not thought about this? I should have risked everything to get back to him. I was too weak, but I would have just ran if I had known—I should have known. I won't see him again. I failed—again.

I want to die.

Baron grabs my hand, shaking me from my daze. I look up at him through teary eyes.

"He's fine for now."

I take my first breath hearing this. I look down at my empty hand. This power is incredible, but what is the purpose of having it if everyone I care for has died?

We head down hall after hall until a grand opening comes into view. The stone entryway is carved into large trees that appear to have faces. Their leaves are large and shaped like pears—the intricate detail makes them look alive.

Walking through the doorway, I am greeted by a large mass

of people, all staring towards us. They bow, and Baron raises his hand to dismiss them from their greeting. There are three large chairs sitting on a stone platform down the aisle we are walking on. The walls have stained glass depictions of all different races. Elves, Orcs, Gnomes, Humans, and a few I've never seen before. Baron tightens his grip on my hand as we approach the end of the maroon carpet, leading us to where I assume we sit.

A familiar older lady steps out in front of us, bowing towards us. She looks up and removes the hood from her head— the priestess from the forest. She smiles towards me; there is something devilish about her. She escorts us the rest of the way, asking us to take a seat.

"I am so glad you could finally join us, child. We were worried that the false King was going to keep you from us."

Baron quickly moves his hand from mine to grab my wrist as I jump at her. She laughs lightly when my father pulls me back down into the chair to his left.

I am not your child. I was supposed to be Queen. I was supposed to be with Kage, her King. He wants to save this world, not rip it apart.

"Are the preparations ready?"

She nods. "Of course. They are ready for your address, my King."

She quickly bows and steps away from the throne. Once she is in line, Baron stands and opens his arms to the group of nearly a hundred. They are shoulder to shoulder, but all looking up excitedly.

"Today is the day we are reunited with the power of the Awemother. Let her power wash over us."

They clap and holler, almost at a deafening volume. Baron smiles and turns around, facing the back of the throne room. He pushes his hands outward. Stone begins to crack and crumble as he wills the wall to tumble apart. I stand, watching the effortless destruction. He looks over to me and nods, asking me to join. I shake my head, afraid of the uncertainty of this moment. He reaches down and grabs my hand, raising it now with his.

As the dust clears, a hidden chamber begins to reveal itself. I feel something inside me being jerked awake as I feel my power begin to merge with his. We pull out a large mirror hidden deep within the chamber. The colors of the mirror are vibrant and glowing. The image is not a reflection of us but of a land that has purple and pink skies and blue grass. A tree shifts from its resting place, moving, so it faces the dotted suns.

"She's right there," he whispers to himself. A tear sliding down his cheek.

The voice calls out. Baron notices, turning his attention from the mirror to me.

The crowd begins to cheer again, drawing Baron back to the mirror. He spreads his fingers apart, letting go of my hand.

"**Aperi ianuam ex hoc mundo ad, Awemother.**"

The light erupts from inside of me. I'm pulled forwards towards the mirror. I grab onto the chair to keep myself from being drawn any closer. As Baron is shouting in pain, a blue semi-liquid seems to be sucked from him.

His Magicae?

His hands are shaking, and blood is trailing from his nose.

Fear sets in. This is really happening. How will he know when to shut it off? Is he going to be strong enough to close it? The mirror begins to ignite with the same light I am producing. The walls and floor around us begin to quake.

"Baron!" I scream.

He doesn't hear me as blood is now coming out of his ears. He's killing himself.

Suddenly, I feel something brush past my head. An arrow flying through the gap between Baron and me, aimed directly at the mirror. I turn and see navy blue robes surrounding an armored Kage. My eyes go wide as both relief and terror wash over me.

The room comes alive when the Domi Nostrae realize they have company. Screams and shouts that were once of excitement turn into anger and fear.

I feel a hand suddenly on my shoulder as Shaw is by my side. I shake my head, pleading, and point to Baron standing next to me.

"I cannot leave him. Please, buy us time. We need to close it!"

She nods and evaporates. I turn back and see her now standing next to Kage, who is currently swinging a sword, slashing into one of the Domi Nostrae. He holds up his shield as fire radiates from one of the other Domi Nostrae. An invisible barrier covering much more than just the physical shield protecting him from the flames.

He leans over and listens to Shaw's words, his eyes quickly finding mine. He nods, agreeing to my plea, and I give him a brief smile.

"Baron, we need to close it!"

My light ignites even brighter as I say his name, looking at him. His fawn-colored hair has turned gray, his hands now skeleton-like. I grab his arm, but as I do I feel the drain he must be feeling. I collapse to my knees at the unexpected exhaustion. The voice is screaming now, the light trying to fight against the pull of the mirror.

Creatures begin calling out and crawling through the once calm-looking image.

"Xylia! Run!"

I shake my head and grip onto his arm again. He won't be able to do this himself. I focus this time, expecting the pull. I focus my will onto closing the door, to cutting the draw to the doorway, from the Awemother.

I can tell there is a resistance though.

"She isn't here yet."

He's waiting for her.

"If you don't stop, you will die!" I scream.

He looks over to me and smiles. "Not if you help me. We can do this together, bring her back together."

"Xylia, close it!"

I turn and see Kage now making his way towards me. His eyes are full of anger and desperation. He is fighting his way through the crowd, trying to get to me.

The Domi Nostrae are distracted by the creatures making their way around us and to them. I look back to the mirror as one of the trees is now crawling through, its face similar to the ones that are made of stone. It moans and creeks as it squeezes through.

Her voice is clear this time. I know it's her. I can feel that it's her.

"**Prohibere eum**," she pleads.

The light is wavering and beginning to flicker. She is fighting him on opening it.

I grab onto Baron one last time. Fighting him as well. He can sense it and turns to me.

"He will only hurt you, Xylia. Do not side with him."

I shake my head desperately. "She's not on the other side. She is here with us, right now."

I place my hand on my heart. His eyes begin to water, understanding what I mean instantly.

"No ..."

"She's trying to stop you. We need to close it!"

He closes his eyes and nods, his heart now shattered. He

takes my hand in his, and we focus on the doorway together. As the mirror begins to drain us once more, I can feel the blood drip from my nose. My knees begin to buckle, and nausea returns.

"Agh ..."

I look over to my father, whose eyes are wide and hands have now dropped. His eyes are trained down where a blade pierces through him. The light flickers out. I step towards him, and the blade is pulled out of him. I follow the blade's hilt to its wielder's hand and scan up to see Kage's face, blood dripping from his brow. His breathing is heavy, his eyes fuming with rage. He looks at me, and for a moment, his rage is replaced with confusion. Shaw's hands quickly grips onto Kage and me.

In a moment, darkness succumbs me before I am vomiting onto a grassy hill.

No.

"It did not close," Shaw says, backing away from Kage, who is pacing back and forth, muttering curses under his breath.

"I know!"

Shaw disappears, leaving just me and him.

We hear an explosion go off at the ruins, screams quickly following after. Terrifying creatures begin to fly from bits of the rubble and out into the open sky.

Kage grabs my wrist and pulls me up. We start running, not sure in what direction, but we are running. Reaching the decline of the hill makes us pick up the pace. Kage trips, not being able to see where we are going, pulling me down with him. We roll down the hill until we reach the bottom of it. I shiver in the snow, Kage's hand still wrapped around my wrist, but his grip has tightened. He stands up, before helping me up. He throws my wrist, slapping his face with both his hands.

KAGE

"It was all for nothing!" I scream out into the abyss.

It's ruined. I'm ruined. I rip off my cloak and throw it to the ground. I look out to see the ruins, which are ablaze, a trail of fire leading to the city of Stran. I clench my fists, trying to stop my shaking. Everything I've done, everything I worked for, gave up, nearly died for is all for nothing. I feel a hand press against my shoulders.

Don't touch me.

"Kage ..." I hear Xylia whimper.

That's not my name. It's not it. I'm not this Kage you've built up in your head.

"My name is Bren! I'm not that pathetic little peasant boy. I cannot take another moment of you truly believing I was ever that pathetic little boy who sat there and cried a river about his life. He's been dead for years. Killed right after he freed you. I only ever kept him around before that because he would tell me about you, how beautiful and exotic the elf girl named Xylia was. It wasn't hard for me to find you either. I spent years speaking to different folks from all over, convincing them to confide in me about the strange, almost elvish-looking girl. Let's be honest, I'm far more charming than the rest of my family. It was only natural I'd be able to find you first. That stupid little group gave me one of their beasts, not realizing that we were both after the same prize."

I feel like I am breathing for the first time since I was eleven. I've been planning this, working for the moment of becoming King. I turn to her, and I watch her face contort into someone I don't even recognize. Someone weak, someone who cannot bear what I have had to bear.

She's supposed to bear this with me. Cry for my loss. She is going to bear it.

XYLIA

"After Codrin was out of my way, you were so vulnerable and in need of something to live for, so it only took a letter to my dearest late father to set the rest into motion. Once you killed him and the cup was mine, that meant you were mine too. Accepting my offer to be my Queen was the last step, but I knew after my heartfelt speech of love and happiness, I had you wrapped around my finger. I thought it would be harder, honestly."

The tears streaming down my face begin to pool at my feet.

How could I be so stupid? How could I have overlooked it?

"Now it's all gone. It was all for nothing. All that time wasted chasing you, convincing you, deceiving you, all of it was for nothing! Nothing!"

My heart beats faster. I take a step back, though as I do, Kage yanks my wrist.

"Where in the inferno do you think you're going?" His grip gets tighter, and I can feel myself bruising. "You cannot leave me. You are all that's left. I'm not losing you too."

I try and pull away, but he pulls me in, slamming his lips against mine. He wraps his other hand around my waist, our chests pressing against each other. I bite his lip. He pulls away instinctively, leaving an opening for me to twist his arm behind his back. He releases my wrist as the pain hits him. I kick him to his knees.

Slamming his head into the ground, I take off running. My heart turns to dust with every step I take. This is all my fault. Everything I've done wasn't for me, it was for him. It wasn't for the people, it was for him.

I chased the dream you told me I shouldn't, Codrin.

My vision is blurry, and I reach forwards, screaming, "I'm sorry! I'm sorry!"

KAGE

I try and focus my vision as my head begins to spin. Blood filling my mouth. I slowly sit up and grab my jaw.

She broke my tooth.

The taste of crimson is on my tongue. I try to focus on finding her in my daze. I look towards the ruins and see her running towards it, away from me—no, towards danger.

Xylia. Do not leave my sight. Please.

"Xylia!" I shout.

I need to stop her.

XYLIA

I don't let my legs quit even if my will to live does. I run straight past the screams and fighting, creating a shield of stone around me. I head into the ruins, a home I once belonged to.

In my heart, I know his words were his confession. They may have been out of anger, but I'm hoping it was his heart crying out for help. He said it himself; this is not what he wanted. He wanted to bring peace to the Felguard Country. He has been using me as his weapon this whole time. As blind as I may have been, lives were taken. The pain caused was all for a purpose that I could not see, or more so, he could not share. I was too afraid back then, too attached to ever possibly realize my role. He did what he thought was necessary and made me believe it was too.

I start running towards the throne room we had just fled.

I will close it.

As my feet carry me, I imagine Codrin running by my side. The way he had the majority of our lives. He was always right behind me, eyes fixed on the back of my head, watching me closely, waiting for my signals. He moved when I moved. He was everything I had imagined—the person who I'd always have by my side. He was strong, intelligent, capable, but even more so caring and kind. Yet, even in this moment, when my thoughts are on him, Kage is the one my heart is breaking over. Codrin was warm and safe, but Kage was mysterious, like cold waves crashing onto me. His words entangled me, enticed me to walk beside him. He made me feel stronger at a moment I had felt my weakest, encouraged me to embrace my fears, and made my dreams a reality.

Even if it all started for his own gain, somewhere in the middle, it was I who started to entice him. Letting me and Vasile find closure, his patience with my stubbornness, his tenderness, his understanding, all of that was done for the sake of us. Not this crusade. Though even those moments, my feelings for him, my desire to be with him, does not forgive everything he has done, everything I've been a part of.

I reach the ruins, the screams ringing in my ears. They all give me the last bit of courage I need. The fighting has been taken farther out to give them space from the very doorway they were all so excited to open. I rush past them, running to the center. The ground begins to quake as if feeling my presence.

I can feel it too.

The doorway, which has grown in size, is hovering in the center of the throne room, vines and roots now decorating the walls and floor.

The cool winds swirl around me, sending my toes curling in my boots that are placed firmly on the stone beneath me. I stretch out and grasp the mirrored door with both hands. It reacts to my touch, sending a bolt of bright light into the sky, piercing the stone above me. The light it's now producing dances across my face in its own intricate ballet. I'm currently responsible for the chaos I hear echoing through the ruins—a place once occupied by a family I will never know.

I inhale the scent of ash and death, which feels oddly

encouraging and pushes me towards my goal. This moment gives me peace, knowing it wasn't for nothing. Codrin's death, the fall of the Adamina Clan, my father's death, my mother's death, and the deaths of thousands Kage has possibly tallied. Looking back over my shoulder, he's running towards me. I smile, knowing that I tried not to love him. I tried keeping him at bay, but I'm glad I did love him. Otherwise, I would have just been a fool.

I close my eyes to him and reach out for the light. I can hear her soft hum and the warmth comforting me in these last few moments. Even with my eyes closed, I can see her hand outstretched towards mine. A smile appears, allowing me to see the source of all this light. Her golden hair matches mine, flowing around her, three braids framing her face that are far too beautiful to describe. I can feel the drops from my eyes evaporate as they touch my cheeks in the heat of this light. *Her* light. It was never really mine, a borrowed power I could have never controlled.

"**Mame.**"

"Xylia." She wraps her arms around me and nestles her wet face into my hair, taking me in.

"Will you help me?"

A happy sob leaves her, and she pulls away, cupping my face.

"**Etiem. Incunctanter.**"

My heart lightens hearing her words.

She pulls me in, and I am enveloped in Evanora's light once more. Unafraid of the flames, willing to accept the fire, and the bliss of this moment. Everything I once knew washes over me and drifts away, not into darkness, but into a blaze of redemption and purpose.

CHAPTER TWENTY-SIX

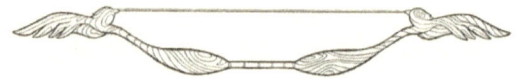

KAGE

My feet carry me towards her. I thought I could just watch this all transpire, take what I need to save this country and the people it once betrayed, but no position or reason is worth losing her. As I reach the edges of the ruined palace, I see a beam of light erupt from its center. My heart, that I've slowly developed, drops into a pit I did not know I had. So many first because of her and a part of me hates that.

I pick up the pace, pushing myself to reach her, passing the violence that is surrounding me. I shouldn't have killed the Risen, but when she reached for him, my blood boiled. The fear that she was choosing him over me superseded any trust.

Whatever God is in my head and listening, please just keep her alive long enough for me to reach her. I've convinced her to do far harsher things than to live.

I quickly navigate through the halls, but the walls begin to shake. I lose my footing, the ceiling now dropping in. I pick myself up out of the way as a thunderous clap pushes me forwards, and I find myself on my knees once more. I stumble but manage to carry on, even with the ruins collapsing on top of me.

I need to hurry.

I veer left into the throne room, and there is a perfect silhouette of her standing there, reaching out to the mirrored door. I cannot stop myself from pausing and taking in the sight of her enveloped in such elegant light, reaching towards power, of course, only she can understand.

Focus.

"Xylia!" I scream her name, but the sounds of death outside, the collapsing of this place, and her mere determination are screaming far louder than me.

I put one foot in front of the other and begin walking, jogging, sprinting towards her, knowing if I don't stop her now, I'll lose her. I should have never told her. I should have lied and lied until she resented me, until her arrow ended my life just like it ended his.

She glances back at me, those eyes piercing me more effectively than that arrow would.

"Xylia!"

She closes her eyes, shutting me out.

"Look at me! Don't turn from me!"

I force myself to move faster until my hands grab her waist. I let out my breath I hadn't realized I was holding. I wrap my arms around her waist and try prying her back into my chest, but she doesn't budge. I look down to see what may be impeding me from my goal. Her hands and feet are turning into the very stone she is standing on. I can feel panic rising in my throat.

I take a step back, brushing my hand across my wet face.

Am I crying?

I shake my head.

Focus.

I go to step closer, but her light expands from her, nearly blinding me. I shield my eyes and scream out in frustration.

Why am I so weak?

"Xylia, listen to me!" I take a few steps towards her direction, eyes still covered.

I stretch out my arm and wait to touch her arm, feeling her leather armor with my fingertips.

"I swear, from now on, I will only give you the truth, love, blissfulness, happiness—everything I couldn't or wouldn't before. I am no King. I would have never even gotten this far if you hadn't been there pushing the directive. My mind means nothing if I don't have the strength you've provided me. I thought I could become something I was never deserving of, but something you have always been. Take my place, become the ruler these people deserve! Xylia! Listen! Hear me and let go! Please just, please, please let go."

I crumple to the ground, feeling the heat and the strain of the light fade. The smooth surface of her armor is replaced with the cool feeling of stone. I drop my hand from my eyes and see the most beautiful statue resting in front of me. I start to shake my head and slam my fist into the floor.

She closed the doorway.

"Xylia, I cannot do this on my own. I cannot do this without your warmth. I cannot do this."

Just say it.

"I love you, Xylia."

I stare intently, waiting for her to move, her eyes to open, and that smirky smile to spread across her charming face.

In every way, she's bewitched me.

"For the last time, I swear, do this for me. There are no lies, no tricks, just my heart. I love you, and I'm begging you to please just come back to me." I thought I could just use her, manipulate her, play her in my game of **Witend.**

I should have been stronger, held all of that guilt and burden in.

No. She deserved to know.

A part was the heat of the moment, watching it fall apart, but the other part was because I started to hate myself. She was gone, ripped from my own arms. I failed to protect her, so I couldn't continue lying to her. Seeing someone as strong as her fall apart and break so many times yet still able to pick herself up for the sake of others is far too powerful to watch and continue to be the one behind it all.

I hear the sound of crashing and turn to see the ruins falling apart around us.

I nearly forgot, or maybe I just don't care.

I make myself stand and wrap my arms around the stiff frame, one hand stretched outward, taking hold of the mirror, the other open and offering itself for me to take it. I kiss the stone lips, my last resort, hoping maybe those fairytale stories were real too. Though, she still stands still and cold.

Footsteps draw my attention once more. Shaw looking scared and panicked, running up towards me.

"Majesty, the Oracle."

I glare in her direction.

I don't want to hear it. I cannot hear it.

"My King, I cannot leave you here to die."

She reaches for me, and before I can protest, I'm pulled away from Xylia. I swear I can see her flicker away into the darkness before my eyes close and open to my empty throne room that is far different than the one I had just been standing in.

A wave of anger and guilt washes over me. I raise my hand

to slap Shaw, but I pause and take in a shaky breath. "Leave me."

Shaw's face saddens. The Queen they had all desired is gone.

Now, there is only me.

"When the ruins have settled, take a team, and retrieve her," I mutter, catching her attention before she leaves.

I march towards the throne I traded everything for.

I will sit in the mess I made, closing my eyes, seeing the flame I once had now flicker out. I am enveloped in darkness that is filled with regret and longing.

"I'm sorry, my Lady."

INDEX

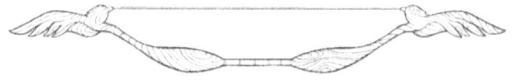

The World

The Ashen Land Territory - A country located south of the Felguard country. Known for its blackened earth and uninhabitable landscape.

Ancestry War - After the doorway to the Infernum erupted open, killing the True King, the Old World's Capital, creatures spilling out, the creation of the Ashen Land. The world went into a craze. Every race turned on each other, stating who truly belongs on this plane and who should go back through the doorways. This caused the world to go to war. Humans, Gnomes, Orcs, Dwarves, Passerinnet, Piscesfolk, Reptilians, and Grimlens were granted the heirs of the Material Vitaterrium. Any other race was either slaughtered or forced through the doorways. This war took place 500 years prior to the events of Light of Evanora.

Awemother - The mother of Magicae. She is believed to have created all of the doorways that lead to the different planes of Vitaterrium. She is more feared rather than praised due to the Infernum doorway expulsion that caused the death of the True King and the creation of the Ashen Land.

Birdsmen - A position the Adamina Clan posts at various crows nests that litter the Vermilion Forest. This allows them to have eyes and ears across the expansive terrain.

Command Deck - The first deck the Adamina Clan ever built.

Command Post - Where the brain and heart are of the Adamina Clan. It was the first building ever built in the Adamina Clan and is where the First and Second Lady are generally seen working. Few higher recognized commanders can also be found.

Crows Nest - Hidden, and often small, observation points, utilized by the Adamina Clan, all located in the Vermilion Forest.

Fel Watch - The Felguards Military guard.

Fons - Spring.

Forged Magicae - A way for those who are born without Magicae to practice a form of magicae. It deals mainly with the elements, natural minerals, and metals.

Gatekeeper - A position the Adamina Clan posts at all climbing posts. This allows the Adamina Clan to monitor who is coming and going, as well as assist the elderly, farmers with livestock, and trading caravans up by working the rafts.

Healers Ward - A location in the Adamina Clan where they can perform first aid, surgery, and can help the Adaminians with their other medical needs.

Hunters - A position in the Adamina Clan that was first used to feed the few clan members that existed when the Clan first started. The position later became an honored role in taking down any threats or capture beasts.

Ignis Troopers - Skilled hunters whose main priority is putting out any fire that may occur in the Vermilion Forest.

Infernum - Hell.

Ko's Forest Border Headquarters - Made mostly up of volunteers and the Fel Watch who sit around the perimeter of the forest to keep an eye out for beasts and fugitives. Their base resides just on the border of the Vermilion forest.

Lunamatrem - The mother of the moon. She is praised most openly, for she is believed to be the birth of everything. The world's calendar is based on her 29-day cycle.

Magicae - Magic. It's magic.

Maresal - The highest military title the Adamina Clan can appoint. There have only been four Maresal's in the Adamina Clans History.

Meka Prison - Located in the Ashen Land Territory. Where all countries send their unforgivable traitors, enemies, and prisoners.

Mira - The Goddess of Peace and Wonder. She is often depicted with a light side and a dark side, as oftentimes wonder can disrupt peace. She is considered the ruler of the Caelum, which is the Heavens of Vitaterrium.

Moonshifts - Equivalent to one hour during the night.

Rubrum Silva - The name of the Vermilion Forest before the reign of the Torrin Family.

Screamer - A position the Adamina Clan posts at all climbing posts, along with a Gatekeeper. This position is only at night since this is when most people are in their homes and not aware of their surroundings. They are to alert the Clan if something were to occur.

Sidereal Year - A full life cycle. Each Race has different lengths of life and rate of development. Ten sidereal years to a human is equivalent to 5 sidereal years to a Dwarf.

Sunshifts - Equivalent to one hour during the day.

Tempestas - The Goddess of weather. She is often worshiped in the southern countries and by sea folk. Ruler of the Water Vitaterrium.

The Slattern - A Tavern and Inn located in the city of Ko which is east of the Capitol in the Felguard Country.

The Snug Pillow - A quiet Inn located in the city of Jod, which is located on the northern end of the Felguard Country.

Vitaterrium - The World.

Vermilion Forest - The largest forest in the Realm of Limoria and possibly the whole world.

Games

Butcher - A card game where the goal is to have the highest total number by the end of the game. Depending on how many players, depends on how many piles there are. Each player has a respected pile they draw from, discarding any low numbered cards. There are generally four jesters in the game that can flip the game on its head. When a jester is pulled, all players must swap piles. Once all cards have been pulled, players count their hands. Tip is to move fast. You want to empty your pile of all its high numbered cards before a jester is pulled.

Witend- In simple terms, it is a game that challenges each player's intellect by requiring them to move pieces on a board with the goal to end with the most amount of pieces left on the board. There are many pitfalls and ways to attack your enemy, but be warned, every move a player makes could lead to either their victory or their demise.

Living Things

Eelger - An Eel that has tiger stripes across its body. Has razor-sharp teeth and can open its mouth as wide as it is long. Generally found in freshwater lakes like the Nymph Lake.

Feserpentline - A creature that is a mixture between a Snake and a Cat. Has four long legs, each with razor-sharp claws. A tail that acts like a snake's body. Through its matted fur, green and yellow scales are seen riddling its body like freckles, growing more obvious near its rear leading into its fully scaled tail.

Floaress - A small fluffy creature that, depending on its region, has a flower on the top of its head. It has butterfly-like wings, large holoptic eyes, and a wide mouth with small teeth. It lives mostly in meadows but sometimes wonders further away when mating season occurs. Their lives are spent tending to flowers and protecting them from harm. Generally very friendly creatures.

Passerinnet - a humanoid who shares many features with birds. Depending on their region in where their bloodline is from, depends on what type of bird they resemble.

Snapper - Giant rat/bear-like creature that wanders around the country scavenging. Fearsome beasts that adventurers should stray away from.

Werecreature - A creature that is born when a humanoid and creature conceive a child. The child is always born from the creature, and it can appear either more humanoid or more monstrous, but both are evil beings. They generally go mad from the impurity of their blood. It has never been seen that a Werecreature takes on more of the humanoid's morals and personality.

Phrases

Amare - Love.

Aperi ianuam ex hoc mundo ad, Awemother - Open the door to another world, Awemother.

Mame - Mother.

Etiem. Incunctanter - Yes. Without hesitation.

homo malus - Bad man.

Paulo puella - Little Girl.

Prohibere eum - Stop him.

Pulcherrima - Beautiful.

Tempus - Time.

Books

Fiends, Demons, Monsters, and Creatures alike - Generally seen as a children's book rather than a textbook. Is filled with every living and unliving thing that walks the Material Vitaterrium that is outside of a humanoid. Author Gema Vaun.

Languages of the Dead and Alive - Written by an anonymous author, showcases all languages that have been spoken, written, and read on the Material Vitaterrium. Speaks about origins, primary races, and the regions it was or is spoken. It does not teach the languages themselves.

Magicae Through Time - Written by Leana Varis, it

depicts the world's history in magicae as well as speaks to trends about magicae throughout the time.

Mystique in the Promise Land - A book by a prominent author in Limoria named Leana Varis. A famous researcher turned to writing as a creative outlet. She has both academic and fictional published works that are revered across the Realm.

Vitaterrium History - A book on the world's history which has been written by multiple historians, one of the most notable being J.T.N. He is known for his accurate retellings.

ITEMS

The Chalice - It is silver covered with symbols from the old world. There is a single garnet on the front in a pyramid shape. The tip comes to a sharp point. When a magicae user pricks their finger and drops it into the chalice, they are forced to submit to the chalice's owner, unable to utilize their magicae against them or their bloodline. If the magicae does not submit, they will face excruciating pain. Very few magicae users have been able to break the chalice's curse.

Xylia's Book - A children's story about family ties and a person's fate. Was written and illustrated by a famous Elvish author S.M Rose. This book was quite popular in the old world. There are only a handful of copies that have made it through the Ancestry War.

GROUPS

Adamina Clan - A group of 'misfits' that ostracized themselves from the Felguard Country.

Domi Nostrae - A large group that has been around since the Ancestry War. They believe that the doorways should have never been closed and that without the Magicae that comes from them, the Material Viaterrium will die. Mostly made of Non-Magicae users but still have a large number of Magicae users on their side.

M.G.A. - Magicae's Guided Assembly.

ACKNOWLEDGMENTS

This is all so crazy. I played a game, created a character, that character turned into a world, and that world turned into a novel. That novel is now something physical and not just ramblings inside my head.

None of this could have been possible without the help of some of the most amazing people in the world! I want to take a moment and thank them all here.

First, I want to thank YOU! Yes, you, reader. You are a part of this amazing journey I am on, and you have taken a chance on me by buying this book! I hope it inspires you, entertains you, makes you feel like you too can be the hero in your own story.

I want to also thank my friends and family who have had to put up with my craziness and often too imaginative mind. They have watched me pour myself into worlds of make-believe and wonder my entire life, thank you for never asking to change that part of me.

To my nephew, Bentley, who helps me come up with friendly creatures to fill my world with, and to my niece, Aria, who helps me maintain my childlike ability to play. You both allow me to continue to see the world as a magical place.

I really need to thank my wonderful editor and publisher, Chelsea, who has been an amazing resource and mentor through this process. I don't think I could have done it without you and walked away sane.